Creating Chaos

LACEY DAILEY

For Monique-
Our words are our asylum

ONE

A MUTATED BABY

GIDEON

THE COLOR WHITE is supposed to be calming. It's supposed to give people some overwhelming sense of peace. My parents are deeply into something called color psychology. They picked the colors of each room in our house carefully. According to them and the creators of color psychology, the color white opens the mind for the creation of anything one's brilliant mind can conceive. I guess maybe that's why whoever built this school a gazillion years ago wanted to paint every wall white—because they wanted to give the mind the option to conceive something brilliant.

The only thing the minds in this school have conceived is a truckload of ways on how to be a bunch of assholes.

It's sad, really. The moment my stark white Converse hit the stark white tile and I move to walk down the hall and begin my senior year, there's only one thing tumbling through my mind.

I hate high school.

I hate these white walls and the bullshit posters that cover them.

"The start of something new..."

"The beginning of the end..."

"Memories last a lifetime..."

"The rest of your life starts now..."

"You are braver than you believe and stronger than you seem..."

"Life begins where fear ends..."

I wonder if Lola and her minions knew that last quote came from Winnie The Pooh. Probably not. Combined, they have the IQ of a pigeon. She isn't exactly Senior Class President for her smarts. She's senior class president because she has tits the size of watermelons and her dad is the principal.

If you ask me—and nobody ever does —we shouldn't be spending time and money making posters filled with lies to stamp all over the washed-out brick walls.

These walls should actually be filled with warnings. Any upcoming freshman is going to see this horse shit and think the next four years are going to be the best of their life. High school is not a pleasant place.

It's even worse for people like me—an outcast.

I'm an easy target for insults and judgmental jabs. My parents are two men who were entirely too busy loving me and each other to raise me to fit high school's molds. I've never cared much about fitting in. In just nine months, we'll all be graduating and none of what happened within these walls will matter anymore.

Newsflash.

High school is only four years. The average American lives to be eighty years, so why are we so depressed it's ending?

A small elbow stabs me in the gut. "Do these posters make you nauseous? Or is it just me?"

Piper Dawson—my honorary cousin and best friend in

the entire world. If anybody understands what it's like to be an outcast, it's her.

A typical outfit for Piper is made of mismatched fabric pieces, neon lipstick, and bright pink hair. Around her eyes lies a different pair of tortoiseshell glasses every day. She doesn't actually need glasses. She just thinks they look cool.

Today, Piper is sporting a white, graphic tee with *"Ask me about my feminine agenda"* sprawled across her chest. She paired it with a denim skirt and Converse that lace up to her knees.

"It's not you." I confirm. "They are definitely nauseating."

"Why are you standing in the middle of the hallway?"

I point down the hall. "My locker is being overrun by Positive Polly and her friends." Lola and a gaggle of her girlfriends are huddled in front of my locker, stamping 'Keep Calm, Senior year is here' stickers all over it and the ones surrounding it.

"Those stickers should say 'Keep Calm, it's almost over.'"

"Nine months is a long time, Pipes."

"Nah." Linking her arm with mine, she drags me toward my locker. "It'll fly by."

"Thank you for your optimism, Yoda."

"Yoda was wise. Not optimistic." The wrinkle that appears on her forehead tells me she's thinking. "But I suppose the name fits because I'm also quite wise."

"You're a 17-year-old brooding, aspiring artist who hasn't traveled out of the country and is stuck in this high school every day." The corner of my lips twitch. "How are you wise?"

"I'm president of the art club."

"You're a self-proclaimed president. Besides, there are only four members."

"I am not self-proclaimed. There was a vote. It was unanimous. Not my fault I was the only one who showed up on voting day."

I chuckle, shoving my way through the crowd of seniors so I can get to my locker. "Can you take your stickers elsewhere, Lola? I need my locker."

"Well, well..." Lola flips her platinum blonde extensions behind her narrow shoulders. Her beady eyes scan me from head to toe as if she's waiting for me to shrink beneath her gaze. "If it isn't the incestuals. Did you have fun making mutated babies over the summer?"

Piper snaps her bubblegum. "Lola, come talk to me when you learn how to spell incestual."

"Why should I learn how to spell it? I'm not the sleeping with—"

"Move!" Using my shoulder and oversized backpack, I wedge my way between Lola and the bay of lockers. My hand shakes as I dial my combination, aggressively yanking open the flimsy metal door.

Less than ten minutes, and it's already started.

"Damn, dancer boy. What the hell is your problem?"

Stacey stumbles on a pair of heels, pushing her lips to her best friend's diamond covered ear. "I think it's because you brought up his mutant children."

"Can we please be done with this?" Piper knocks her head off the locker beside mine. "It's been going on for almost four years. It's getting old. If you want to be an asshole, find some new material. Gideon and I are not sleeping together. It's perfectly normal for a guy and girl to be best friends."

"It's funny that you think you know what normal is."

"It's funny that you think those extensions look real."

"Pipes, let it go. She isn't worth it."

Three years ago, my best friend and I scurried into this

building the same as every other eager freshman, wide-eyed with a soul full of goals we thought for sure we'd accomplish.

It took forty-eight hours for rumors to turn this building into one I associate with purgatory. Instantly, Piper and I made a pact we wouldn't stoop to the level that most everybody in this school resides on. Piper and I, we aren't assholes. We don't judge people based on rumors and hearsay.

"Yeah, Piper...." Lola sings, gathering her stickers. "Let it go." She pivots, the sound of her heels clanking on the tile growing softer the father away she gets. Her friends follow her, and I almost feel bad for them.

"Day one and it's already started." Piper runs her hand down her face. "Is it stupid I was sort of hoping everybody was going to come back mature?"

"No, it's not stupid. But it isn't realistic."

"Nine months, Gid. Then we are getting the hell out of this place." The shrill sound of the five-minute bell fills me with dread. "But first, you've got to get through chemistry." Reaching into my locker, Piper snags the textbook I'd pay any amount of money to be able to keep closed for the rest of the year. "Knock em' dead, G."

I press a kiss to her cheek and begrudgingly pull my textbook from her grasp. With my shoulders slumped, I turn away from my best friend and start towards chemistry.

I'm not sure what sort of hogwash my brain was cooking up when it decided scheduling chemistry as my first class of the day was a smart idea. Maybe it was thinking if I did it right away then I could get it over with.

School and I aren't friends.

Chemistry and I? We are *mortal enemies*.

I don't understand a lick of anything the teacher says, and I certainly don't understand why it's worth the migraine. The second I leave this place, I'm getting EMT certified and hauling ass to the Fire Academy. I don't need to memorize the periodic table in order to put out fires and save lives. But still, here I am, walking through the doorway of chemistry class, contemplating jabbing myself in the leg with a pencil so I can skip.

"Mr. Stryker." Mr. Grundy rubs his chalk covered hands down his trousers and smiles at me behind his handlebar mustache. "I trust you had a good summer."

My summer consisted of hanging out with my dads, a lot of swimming, wreaking havoc with my cousins, and a lot of time in the dance studio. "Sure, it was good. Thanks."

"Since it's the first day, I'm going to wait a few minutes to start class. Find a seat next to a partner. I see a few spots open."

When the word partner leaves his lips, I actually have to force myself not to grab the nearest pencil and start creating wounds in my flesh. Partner work is bullshit. Teachers think they are so clever partnering us up, forcing us to work with other people.

They claim it's a valuable life skill. I'm pretty sure they do it with malicious intent to torture us.

Scanning the room, I take in the tall lab tables and spot three empty stools. One is next to James Atcot, my ex-some-thing or another. We went out on one date last summer. I told him I thought we'd be better off friends and he hasn't uttered a word to me since. I flash him a small wave and mumble a hello. When he hurls a venomous scowl in return, I swivel on my feet and scan the spot next to Darcy Harwood.

Darcy's always been nice to me and doesn't participate in the rumors that get tossed around. Unfortunately, she's dumber than a box of rocks. Usually, I wouldn't judge some-body on their ability to do school work but when it comes to chemistry, I make her box of rocks look like a pile of geniuses. If I want to pass this class and graduate, I need somebody who knows what's going on.

That leaves one seat open in the very back—next to a guy I haven't seen before. He's wearing a green John Deere T-shirt that appears to be well loved, jeans, and thick brown boots. He has his head buried between the pages of his textbook. That's a good sign. Maybe he is a super genius of chemistry. I cross my fingers and slide into the seat next to him.

"Hey, man."

"Uhm, hi." I hold out my fist. "I'm Gideon Stryker."

"Elliott Oakley." He gives my fist a light bump. "Nice to meet you."

"I haven't seen you around here before."

"Yeah, I just moved here from Iowa."

"Whoa. You're a long way from home."

He lifts his broad shoulders in a shrug. "This is home now."

"Well, I hope you mean this town and not this high school." I lean close to him. "This high school sucks."

As if the universe timed it, a wrinkled wad of notebook paper smacks me in the center of the face. "Point proven."

Smoothing out the piece of paper, I forget I'm in a classroom with 17 and 18-year-olds instead of the 11-year-olds they act like. I peer down at the monstrosity that is a drawing of a baby with three arms, two unibrows, and three eyeballs.

ELLIOTT PEERS OVER MY SHOULDER, getting a good look at the cause of my internal humiliation. "What the hell is that supposed to be?"

"A mutated baby." I wad the piece of paper back up and toss it in the trashcan behind me.

"Do people give you pictures of mutated babies often?"

Stacey turns around in her seat. Her presence is almost enough to convince me to transfer out of this class. She smiles at Elliott. "Gideon has sex with his cousin. The drawing is a picture of their creepy, mutant child."

Any hope this dude was going to be my friend flies right out the window. "Thank you for that, Stacey."

She looks to Elliott as she's awaiting praise for warning him of my non-existent sex life. "I just want him to know what he's getting into agreeing to be your partner." Tossing her hair over her shoulder, she turns back around in her seat.

I let my book fall shut with a sigh and eye the spot next to Darcy. "Do you want me to move?"

"Is it true?"

"Is what true?"

"Do you really have a mutated baby with your cousin?"

"Uhm, no. I don't have a baby and I'm not sleeping with my cousin. People just like to make stuff up." Another piece of paper grazes my cheek. I nod solemnly. "I'll just move."

Long fingers wrap around my slender wrist, anchoring me to my seat. "Stay."

"Dude, you are going to get a lot of shit for being my partner."

Elliott smiles at me. He has perfectly straight teeth except for one. One little tooth on the bottom wants to be different. It wants to stand out, so it's crooked and corky. I love it immediately.

"I used to live on a farm, Gideon." He says, flashing me a wink inside warm, friendly eyes. "I'm pretty good at trudging through shit."

For both our sakes, this dude better be the shit trudging master.

TWO

TOTAL BESTIES

GIDEON

"YO! YO! YO! DINNER IS READY."

"Dad!" I pound down the stairs, using my sock covered feet and the hardwood floor to slide smoothly into the kitchen. "Nobody says yo anymore."

"Really?" My dad, Knox, turns around, placing a pot full of cooked noodles in the center of our dining room table. "I hear you kids say it at the dance studio all the time."

"Yeah, but we say one yo." Snagging a plastic cup from the cupboard above the sink, I start filling it with water. "We don't say them consecutively like that. It's lame. Trust me. I'm not cool by any means and I still know that."

"I think you're cool." He shoves some tongs in the pasta and drops a bowl of salad on the table.

"You're my dad. You're like obligated to say that." I plop down in a wooden chair at the long table that seats eight.

"Untrue. I could easily tell you how lame you are. But you aren't." He tilts his head to the side, attempting to peer into the living room. "BECKETT GREY! Get in here and eat."

Beck, my other dad, comes flying into the kitchen, sliding on his socks the same way I did. Sliding and dancing around is common in our house. The open concept makes it pretty easy.

Apparently, when my parents bought this place, it was an old farmhouse they fixed up. The kitchen and living room run directly into each other. My parents said they purposefully left it so open because they wanted to be able to see the whole house and anyone who came to visit at once. It felt more inviting to them that way.

Our living room holds sliding glass doors, leading out back to our patio and pool. Upstairs we have four bedrooms and two bathrooms. Even though it's only me and my parents, the extra space comes in handy when my family gets together.

Hence the table that seats eight.

Beck slides past Knox, planting a kiss on his cheek and falling into his chair in the kind of graceful way only a man who's been a professional dancer for decades could.

"Babe, do you think the word yo is lame?" Knox sits next to Beck while I sit across from them.

Beck helps himself to some noodles while shaking his head. "No way. The kids at the studio say it all the time." He shoves the tongs back in the bowl. "Yo, yo, yo! What up, what up, what up?"

"You guys!" I bark a laugh. "What is it with you saying everything in threes? Can't you just say it once? Like, yo what's up?"

"Doesn't sound as cool." Beck twirls his noodles with his fork.

"It sounds lame." I argue. "Like an old dude trying to fit in with the young crowd."

Knox snorts. "He is an old dude trying to fit in with the young crowd."

"I am not." Beck argues. "I'm young. Come at me when I'm eighty, Knox."

I roll my eyes. Beck's terrified of getting old. I'm sure that's totally normal for a parent whose kid is about to turn eighteen and graduate high school, but any stranger who sees my dad wouldn't think he's forty-four. Neither of my parents look their age.

Beck hasn't taken it easy on the dancing as he grows older. He dances just as hard as he did when he was my age. I know this because I've seen videos of him backflipping across his front yard in an attempt to impress Knox when they first got together. His refusal to lighten up is the reason he might be in better shape than I am and still has abs the girls I dance with fawn over.

Totally gross considering he's my dad, their coach, and his husband isn't ever too far away.

Knox has been a runner since he learned to walk. Like Beck, he hasn't lightened up since becoming an old fart. He's just as tone and fit as Beck is. Runs every morning and sometimes at night when he doesn't feel like cooking dinner.

Two years ago, People magazine named them Hottest Couple. As disgustingly adorable as the picture was of them with their foreheads pressed together while grinning widely at each other, I can't deny it. My parents make a good pair.

Not just looks wise—though they ain't lacking in that department. Knox's light brown hair has a hint of gray in it he refuses to color ever since Beck told him he looks like a hot, silver fox. The light scruff on his cheeks and chin hold the same salt and pepper look that has deemed him a DILF on the internet. There's no sign of wrinkles around his hazel eyes and no stress lines on his forehead.

Out of my parents, I resemble Beck the most. Aside from the dark brown eyes and the glasses he wears around them, I could actually pass for being biologically related to him. We have the same olive skin tone and dark brown curls. Major difference? His curls are loose and easy to style and maintain. Mine are a mass of ringlets that come from my biological mother's Greek descent. I'm not sure if I got my blue eyes from her too, or if I just got lucky. My eyes are one physical feature I haven't doubted or gotten insecure about over the years.

Beck's toe nudges my shin under the table. "Dude, you gonna eat that pasta or stare at it?"

"Sorry. Yeah." I shovel some carbs in my mouth.

"How was your first day of senior year?" Knox asks.

"It was alright." My thoughts can't help but drift toward my new chem partner—the one who didn't even blink when a mutated baby fell on our lab table. "We have a new kid from Iowa. He's my chem partner."

"Yeah?" Beck attempts to act casual. "He nice?"

Translation: Is he bullying you?

"Yeah. He's nice." I dip my chin, my lips pulling into a subtle smile while I consider the easy way he announced he had no problem dealing with haters for a complete stranger.

"Oh, shit." Knox points his fork at me. "You like him."

"What?! No, I don't." I've conversed with the guy for one class. "I barely know him."

"You're smiling." Beck smirks. "Totally smiling."

"He was funny." I shrug. "And nice to me. The second I sat next to him, I got hit with a drawing of Piper and I's creepy incest baby, cause that rumor is still a thing, and he still wanted to be my partner. I tried to warn him he'd get shit on over being my partner but he claims he has experience as a shit trudger."

Knox chokes on a sip of water. "What?"

"He used to live on a farm." It wasn't a conventional way to say he can handle a couple of bitchy bullies, but it made me smile all the same. Elliott Oakley is one less person in that school who doesn't look at me as a target. And if I'm lucky, one more friend to hang out with.

Beck looks amused. "What's the shit trudgers name?"

"Elliott Oakley."

"Hmm. Is he cute?"

I feel my face heat. "Why does that matter?"

"It doesn't." Beck quips. "Except that you've been smiling since you brought him up."

Ugh.

So, I have an itty-bitty crush on Elliott. Though my parents are my best friends, and I spend more time with them than what is considered cool, I was kind of hoping they wouldn't notice until I could get a grip and put myself into the friend zone before I do something dumb around Elliott.

I want a friend.

Just a friend.

Friends are cool.

"Gideon, are you over there mumbling to yourself about being friend zoned?" Beck chuckles.

"No."

"You lie, kid." Knox smirks. "You lie so hard."

So hard.

My parents attempt at using teen lingo will always crack me up. I don't blame their efforts considering they run a dance education studio where most of their students are teens. But still, *so hard?* What 40-year-old says that?

"So, is he cute?" Beck presses.

"Dad! Yes! He's cute." My cheeks heat. "He has a crooked tooth that makes his smile really unique and these boots that make him look all rugged and tough—so different from all the skinny jeans and boat shoes in our halls. I like different. We could be friends."

Knox clicks his tongue. "Friends, huh?"

"Yeah, dad. I barely know him. So what if I think he's cute? Lots of celebrities are cute and I'm not going after them."

"Alright, kid. You're right." Knox surrenders. "Just like seeing that smile on your face."

"Yeah." Beck nudges my shin again. "Just because you're almost an adult doesn't mean we don't worry about you getting picked on."

I poke at my noodles. "I love you guys, but having you worry about me being friendless aside from family, adds to my lame-o-meter percentage."

"But you aren't friendless." Beck winks. "You have Elliott. The shit trudger."

"Yeah." Knox nods. "I bet you guys will be total besties or whatever."

I'm not sure if one conversation makes Elliott and I friends but calling him an acquaintance feels weird.

Still, I can't help but consider that maybe not *everybody* in high school is a jackass.

Actually, Elliott Oakley seemed pretty okay.

THREE

A BUNCH OF WINNERS

GIDEON

"HI, GIDEON."

Elliott smiles at me as I slide into my seat and wait for Mr. Grundy to arrive. His crooked tooth has been making appearances since the first day of school—and the five days after when I kept getting hit with drawings of a mutant toddler we mutually named Helga.

I give him an easy smile back. "Hi, Elliott. How was your weekend?"

"It was great, actually. My grandpa got me a job working at Speed. You know it?"

"Oh, yeah." I nod my head, brushing away the curls that fall into my eyes. "That's the body shop that specializes in racecars, right?"

"Yeah. My grandpa used to be a racer. He worked in the shop up until about five years ago when the owner made him retire." His shoulders lift with his chuckle. "It pissed him off because my gramps isn't one to sit on his ass all day long."

"What's he do now?"

"Gramps? He builds model cars and chain smokes."

"You spend a lot of time with him?"

He nods, flipping open his textbook. "I live with him."

"Oh, cool. Does he live with you and your parents?"

His smile disappears, and I immediately regret asking that question. "It's just me and gramps."

I want to ask him to elaborate but I refrain when the expression on his face morphs into something that has me worried he's about to punch a hole in this desk or burst into tears.

Out of pure instinct and the need to provide him with some sort of comfort, I slide my arm across the table and wrap my hand around his wrist. His eyes dart to the spot we connect. His throat bobs thickly and he gives me a shaky smile.

"My gramps is pretty much my best friend. I used to want to be a racer just like him."

"Yeah? Do you race?"

"Not anymore." He shakes his head, eyes glued to where we're linked. "Life had other plans for me, I guess."

"Life's kind of a bitch."

His laugh is watery. "Yeah, it sure is."

I leave my hand on his wrist because it seems as though my attempt to give him comfort is actually working. Clearing my throat, I change the subject. "I know we went over this last week, but are you sure you aren't a super genius in chemistry?"

"Not a super genius at all, but I definitely know my way around the periodic table."

"That's fantastic news. I'll be useless."

"Don't worry, man. I can help you."

"Yeah?" Relief floods me. "That would be awesome. If I don't pass this class, I can't graduate. And I really want to get the hell out of here."

"I can imagine. I'm sorry about what those people were saying about you."

I brush it off because what else can I do? "People need someone to be an asshole to. I'm the easy target."

"Well, accusing someone of incest is total bullshit."

I laugh a laugh that has no trace of humor in it at all. "The funny thing is, Piper isn't even my actual cousin."

"Piper?"

"Yeah. The alleged mother of the nonexistent baby. Her parents and my parents are best friends. They went to high school together and kept in touch. They consider each other siblings, so when I was born they became my aunt and uncle and Piper became my cousin. My parents have a shit ton of friends, so I have a lot of aunts and uncles. Nathanial and Preston are seniors here too. They are two more of my non-cousins."

"So, technically, they aren't actually related to you?"

"No, but that isn't the point. Nate, Preston, Piper, and I are tight. We're family. We count on each other for every-thing. Pipes is my best friend. We hang out a lot and we're close. Somewhere along the line that morphed into incest."

"You guys get caught making out or something?"

I can actually feel my face twisting. "Dude, no. *Gross.* Piper and I are basically siblings. We aren't into each other like that at all. Somebody just got bored one day and started a rumor that hasn't gone away."

"Gideon, I'm sorry." It's the first time someone who isn't related to me has apologized to me for the rumors I've had to endure. "That sucks. If it's any consolation, at my old school, I got a lot of hateful opinions thrown my way. Of course, it wasn't as bad as sexing up my cousin but still."

I squeeze his wrist. "Being bullied isn't a competition. It sucks no matter how bad it is. I'm sorry you had to go through it." I drop my head, focusing on the blank piece of notebook paper in front of me. My stomach lurches. "And I'm sorry for anything that gets thrown your way for deciding to be my partner."

"Don't apologize for other people's actions, Gideon."

"I'm not." I argue. "I'm apologizing for dragging you into shit."

"Thought I already told you, I'm good at trudging through shit."

"Right. You lived on a farm."

"Yep. I mostly trudged through horse shit and cow shit, so I think I can handle some little girl shit."

I use the palm of my hand to muffle my sudden laughter. "You got boots for that?"

"Trudging through shit? Oh, yeah. They're called shit kickers."

"Shit kickers?!" I look down at his feet, finding his boots clean as a whistle.

"These aren't my shit kickers, Gideon. I don't wear shit kickers to school."

"Where does one get shit kickers?" Something flashes in his eyes. Amusement, maybe? "I think I should invest in a pair."

"Shit kickers are a dime a dozen in Iowa, my friend."

"So, I need to go to Iowa?"

"Nah, you could probably just order some off eBay."

I lean closer to him, the blood beneath my skin warming with the decrease in proximity. There's something about his presence that makes me comfortable.

In the week that I've sat beside him, he hasn't judged me or looked at me strangely. He hasn't called me a name or tried to make me feel bad about who I am. He just talks to me—like I'm a normal human being who likes to engage in a friendly conversation.

"My dad has the worst obsession with eBay."

"Gramps doesn't even know what eBay is. He doesn't even own a computer. I tried to teach him how to text and failed miserably."

I snort. "I wish my dads didn't know how to text sometimes. They're unreal."

"You have two dads?"

"Yeah. They adopted me when I was twelve hours old." I take my hand back and fiddle with the paper in front of me. My muscles tense, bracing for the insult as I ready myself to defend my parents.

"Oh, cool." Elliott lifts his pen and twirls it around his fingers. "Which one is obsessed with eBay?"

"His name is Beck." My joints loosen, the tips of my cheeks heating with the smidge of guilt I feel for assuming Elliott would judge my parents. I basically lumped him in with the rest of the people at this school when he's spent the last week showing me otherwise.

"My other dad's name is Knox. They own a dance studio here in Durham. It's called Art In Motion."

"Whoa." Elliott looks impressed. "The giant building downtown with all the windows?"

"Yeah. That's it."

"Nice. Do you spend a lot of time there hanging out?"

"I wouldn't say I'm hanging out." My lips quirk, and I swivel on my seat to face him. "I'm a Motionizer."

"Uh, is that North Carolina slang?" He laughs, but I can just tell it isn't because he's making fun of me. He's teasing me—in a playful and non-asshole like way.

"No. The Motionizers are Art In Motion's competitive dance team. We're kind of a big deal."

"Oh." His eyebrows lifts and he turns in his own seat, brushing his knees against mine. "Kind of a big deal, huh?"

"Basically." I swat my curls from my eyes. "I mean, you

could ask for my autograph, but nobody in this town gives a rip I'm a two-time national title winner."

"Two times? That's awesome. When I used to race, I was voted the National Hot Rod Association's Rookie of the Year twice."

"Well, damn. We're a bunch of winners back here. What the hell are we doing in the back row?"

"I have no idea." His chest heaves with his laugh. "Tomorrow we should probably bring our trophies and place them on our desks. Bitches better recognize."

He winks, and our eyes meet. His gaze is patient and kind, appearing as though he's waiting for me to tell him every last thing about myself. The attention makes me sort of loopy. It's the only excuse I have for blurting, "do you want to eat lunch with me?"

His eyes widen in surprise.

That totally sounded like I was asking him out. Didn't it? I shrink into my stool. "I mean, you probably have other people you met. So, whatever."

"Actually, I don't. I usually just sit on the front steps of the school."

"Alone?"

"Sure." He shrugs. "You're the only person who's actually had a real conversation with me." His expression falls stoic though there's something in the way his forehead wrinkles that tells me it affects him more than he's letting on.

"It's probably because they haven't seen your trophies yet." I offer him the biggest smile I'm capable of. "My cousins and I eat lunch in the art room. You should definitely join us."

"Okay." He nods, his hand tapping against his thigh. "Thanks. Where's the art room?"

"It's diagonal from the cafeteria. You can't miss it. Piper painted the door bright green."

"Are you in Art Club?"

"Nope. Piper is. The only art I make is with my body." My cheeks go up in flames. "With dancing!" *Kill me now.* "I make art with dancing."

His smile is back, and he's forced to turn in his seat when Mr. Grundy comes barreling through the doorway, a bagel in his mouth and piles of wrinkled papers in his grasp.

"I'll see you at lunch then, two-time national title winner."

"See you there, Rookie Of The Year."

"Twice." He whispers, giving Grundy his attention—but not before flashing me a wink that has my stomach doing a backflip.

FOUR

THE BRIGHT GREEN DOOR

ELLIOTT

WHEN I LEFT MOUNT VERNON, Iowa to live with my grandpa in Durham, North Carolina I thought maybe I'd have to learn the ropes of a new school. It took less than a day for me to uncover the truth.

This high school is exactly like the school I came from.

If I visited every public school in America, I'm certain they would all be the same. The rumors would be different, the people spreading them would be different, the bullies would be picking on a different kid, the popular girl would be humiliating somebody else, but they'd all be the same.

Regardless of what district you belong to, there are rumors and judgments in every high school. The only difference between this school and my old one is that I'm not the target of the rumors.

He is.

Gideon Stryker—my new chemistry partner and the guy ditching the cafeteria for whatever is behind this bright green door. A week ago, he tried to warn me. In an attempt to save me from the shit storm he's living in, he tried to move his place.

I respect that.

I respect he was going to slide out of his seat and let me start my venture into a new school judgment free. I respect it but I'm not sure I agree with it. If he isn't able to walk these halls feeling safe, nobody should be able to.

Using my fingers to push open the green door, I peer around the small art room. Each wall is filled with various paintings and drawings. Some colorful and filled with life. Others black and white and kind of depressing. Easels are set up in no organized fashion—open jars of paint still on the ledge and waiting to be used. The corner farthest from me holds a small sink. There's not a desk or a chalkboard in sight.

Maybe I should join Art Club.

I find Gideon sitting on the ledge of a purple windowsill. He's got fancy headphones slung over the top of the hot mess happening on his head. Dark little ringlets come from his scalp, pointing in all different directions and falling down to his chin. I approach him, though the music blasting from his speakers prevents him from hearing my steps.

I've been in the business of checking out dudes for years. I've seen some pretty gorgeous faces in that time, but Gideon? His face is *unreal*. It's probably half the reason so many girls insult him.

Because he's prettier than them.

He wears a face with bone structure so sharp, it looks like somebody actually chiseled it to perfection. His eyes are a bright blue, and in this moment, they're hazy. Like he's lost in thought or whatever place the music he's listening to took him.

Wrapping my fingers around a purple plastic chair, I drag it close to him and take a seat. His head turns slowly, and it's takes a moment for his eyes to meet mine. The grin he gives me takes up half his face and makes my stomach flip.

"Elliott." He beams, pulling off his headphones. "You came!"

"You invited me."

"Yeah." He turns his face away and swats at some of his curls. "I just wasn't sure if you'd come."

"Why wouldn't I? Isn't this where all the kids who win trophies hang out?"

A laugh falls from his lips. The sun coming from the window hits his smooth skin, making him light up. His eyes are sparkling so bright, I'm sure he's a star nobody has taken the time to appreciate.

My subtle gawking is interrupted when the door flies open, a pink haired girl with funky glasses stepping into the room. "What's so funny, Gideon?" She gives me a once over and then looks back to Gideon, wide-eyed. "And who is the hottie you allowed behind the green door?"

"This is Elliott." He announces. "He's my chemistry partner. He's excellent at trudging through shit."

"Pleased to meet you, Elliott. I'm Piper. What makes you an expert in all things shit?"

"He's a farmer from Iowa." Gideon answers for me, flashing me a small smile. "He also has two trophies."

"Two trophies?" She gasps, flailing her petite body into a blue bean bag next to my feet. "Holy shit. NATE! PRESTON! GET IN HERE! ELLIOTT HAS TWO TROPHIES!"

"Who the hell is Elliott?" Two dudes mosey through the door. One of them has shaggy sandy hair with a sandwich hanging from his mouth. The other has red hair long enough to be pulled into a knot on the top of his head. He stumbles over a roll of paper on the floor and falls into the bean bag next to the one Piper has claimed. He hasn't made eye contact with anybody because he's got his eyes focused on the camera hanging around his neck.

"Elliott is Gideon's chem partner. He's a former farmer from Iowa, and he has two trophies."

"Shit, dude." Sandwich dude shoves the rest in his mouth and thrusts his hand at me. "Nate Davis." Crumbs go flying when he says his name. "Two trophies? Nice."

I chuckle because what the hell is up with this family's obsession with trophies?

Man bun guy scooches forward in his bean bag. "Preston Shaw. Nice to meet you. I don't mean to be a jackass. I've just got some pictures to sort out."

"No problem, man. Do your thing."

He nods and falls back in the bean bag. Nate grunts and drops right on top of him. "Holy shit, you heavy bastard." Preston groans. "What the hell?"

"That's all muscle, my brother." Nate kisses his bicep.

"Sit in your own bean bag." Preston attempts to shove him away.

"He can't sit in his own. He and Gideon destroyed it." Piper peers up at me with annoyance beneath her glasses. "I bought four bean bags for me and my crew and what do they do? Pop the hell out of them!"

"It was for a good cause." Nate defends, wiggling his body and attempting to find a comfortable position while wedged between his two cousins.

"Offering Gideon ten dollars to back tuck off the window ledge and onto a cheap bean bag I got at Walmart was not a good cause."

"Yeah, but it sounded sweet when it popped and those little white bean things went everywhere."

"Hold up." My gaze transfers to Gideon. "A back tuck is a backflip, right? You can do a backflip?"

He shrugs, his face turning a warm red. "I told you I was kind of a big deal." ·

"Right." I grin, leaning closer to him. "I'm sorry for forgetting."

"I'll forgive you." He smiles. "Don't let it happen again."

"So, Elliott." Piper pulls a paintbrush from behind her ear and raises it in the air, twirling it around like some sort of magic wand. She's staring back and forth between Gideon and I with a twinkle in her eye. "Do you know how to milk cows?"

"Uhm, yes. I know how to milk cows."

"Pipes." Gideon pinches the bridge of his nose. "What the hell does that have to do with anything?"

She shrugs. "Just curious. Do you know to squeeze udders?"

"Oh my fucking god." Gideon mutters, covering his face with his hand. "Don't answer that, Elliott."

"Why can't I answer? Yes, Piper, I do know how to squeeze udders." I give her a wink. "I'm damn good at it too."

She cackles as Gideon's face turns the color of a ripe tomato. The expression can only be described as adorable. I'll say the word udder for the rest of the day if it never goes away.

"Excellent at trudging through shit and squeezing udders." Piper nods and turns to Gideon. "Nice choice in partner."

"Uhm, thank you." He mutters. "He wouldn't let me move after I got pelted with pictures of our mutated child."

Piper's face goes stricken. "Gid... I'm sorry. I wish they'd find someone else to torment."

"It's fine, Pipes. You and I both know I'm the easy target in more ways than one. Besides, I can take some torment if it means they'll leave others alone."

Something inside my chest goes milky with his words. This dude—who gets chewed up and spit out every day—is trying to make others feel better about something that may not even be happening to them? What is this dude made out of and why can't more people be like him?

"Gideon..."

"Piper..." His voice goes stern. "Drop it."

"Fine." She holds her hands up in surrender, and I watch as Gideon's face morphs. His smile melts away and is replaced with a blank, stricken look. Almost like he just put on a mask. A lifeless mask that blinks whenever the timer tells it to. A mask that's too afraid to do anything but stare.

He's still staring off into space when Piper chucks the paintbrush at him. He catches it easily between his fingers. "Knock it off, G. You're pissing me off. Quit letting catty bitches ruin your week."

"Don't worry." He smirks. "I'll be fun again at three o' clock."

"Better be." Nate grunts. "I hate grumpy Gideon."

"Fuck you, dude." Gideon cracks, chucking the paintbrush at him. It bounces off his shoulder and drops to his lap. "I'm not grumpy, Nate. I'm fucking cheerful."

I chuckle and Gideon flashes me a look. "What are you laughing at?"

"You. Most people don't use curse words to describe how cheerful they are."

"I'm not most people." He defends, shoving my shoulder playfully. "I'm fucking cheerful."

"Alright then." I grin, leaning into his touch when his hand lingers on my shoulder. "He has two trophies, and he's fucking cheerful."

"Would you like for me to write it down?"

"Only if your autograph is on it."

I watch his baby blues flash before his little chuckle fills the small room.

"So, Elliott." Piper steals my attention. "What are you doing this weekend?"

"Working."

"Where do you work?"

"Speed." Gideon blurts. "The racecar body shop."

"Yo!" Preston hollers. "That's sweet. You get to test drive the cars?"

"No. The bastards don't trust me because I'm not eighteen yet."

"Discrimination!" Piper thunders "I'll start a petition."

"Noooo." Nate groans. "Please, stop with the petitions."

"It's age discrimination."

"No, it's not, Pipes." Gideon laughs. "It's probably a law."

"It is." I confirm. "They can't let kids drive because if we crash insurance doesn't cover it."

"Are you saying you're a bad driver?"

"Hell no. I'm a great driver. I used to race, but it's still a law."

"So, if you work at Speed and used to race, do you drive a racecar?" Piper's bubble gum pops, muffling the word racecar.

"Actually, no. I drive a truck. It was easier for farming purposes back in Iowa."

"Laaaammmmeee." Nate bellows, poking Preston's cheek with the paintbrush. "You should sell it and buy a racecar."

That's not a bad idea. A truck wouldn't have been my first choice for a vehicle, but my father didn't give me a choice. He wanted to steer me away from racing as much as possible. On my sixteenth birthday, he gifted me with a Ford Ranger. I wasn't about to act bummed when I had just gotten a truck for my birthday. Despite the fact I knew deep down he was only doing it to keep me from the sport I loved, I wasn't about to show him how much he affected me. Not with my mama standing there with her big smile and camera pointed directly at me.

Now, I don't have parents. So I can buy whatever I want.

"They let kids with no licenses race cars?" Preston wonders, snapping pictures of Nate's feet.

"Well, no. I didn't race an actual car. I raced a dragster."

"Holy shit." Nate booms. "You were a drag racer? That's dope."

"And he has two trophies." Piper adds. "So, he must've been good."

"What is it with you guys and trophies?" I ask.

"Our family is crazy competitive." Gideon explains.

"Yo." Nate uses his foot to point at Gideon. "Wait until Uncle Beck hears our new crew member has two trophies for drag racing."

Gideon scoffs. "Don't get him started. He'll just ramble on about his People's Choice Awards."

"Whoa, your dad has won People's Choice Awards?"

"Yes, and he'll talk for years about it, so don't ask him."

"Noted." I smile at the way he tries to look exasperated at his dad's accomplishments, but it's a failed effort. His face beams, showing just how much he adores his parents.

"You should hang with us at Fritz sometime." Gideon throws out the suggestion and tilts his head away from me like he's afraid of my answer.

"I don't know what a Fritz is." I answer, forcing a smile from his flushed face.

"It's a club. It's the only one that allows minors."

"Three more months, G." Nate hoots. "Then we can get into the big boy clubs."

"You guys like clubbing?" I've never been to a club. Not once.

"We looooove it." Piper says. "We dance, meet new people, have a good time, and then return to this hell hole." She leans towards me and whispers loudly. "It's one of the few places Gideon doesn't have a huge guard up."

I assume she's referring to Gideon's mask. Right now, the mask is still intact, but it isn't hiding everything. I'd be interested to see what he looks like when he takes it off completely.

Gideon doesn't deny Piper's observation. He doesn't even comment. He just rolls his eyes.

"Sure." I mumble, wringing my hands together. Looks like my new friends are about to introduce me to my first clubbing experience. "I'd love to come sometime. If I don't have to work."

"Cool." Piper nods. "No cover fee night is coming up next month. Gideon will call you."

Gideon snorts. "I don't have his number."

"I can give it to you."

Shit.

I blurted that way too fast. Be cool, Elliott. He's not asking you out. "I mean, we'll need to meet up for our chem projects sometime anyway."

"Oh, yeah." Gideon nods, pulling his phone from his lap and removing his headphones cord. "Here." He hands me his phone and allows me to enter my number.

I hand it back and stand when the bell rings to signal the end of lunch. He cracks up laughing when he sees the name I entered.

ELLIOTT WITH TWO TROPHIES.

"Text me so I have your number too." I smile.

"I will." He smiles back and leads me out of the room

after we flash a few waves of goodbye to his cousins. "I'll see you tomorrow?"

"Definitely."

"And you should for sure hang with us every day." Gideon's cheeks turn red again. "If you want to."

"That'd be great. Thanks, man."

He nods nervously and swivels on his feet. "See you later, Elliott with two trophies."

"Later, Gideon."

He lifts his hand in a small wave and takes off down the hall. I watch him walk away for a second or two before I start towards my next class. I'm sliding into my seat when my phone buzzes with a text message from a new number. My smile splits my face in half when I see the message.

HEY, IT'S GIDEON. TWO-TIME NATIONAL TITLE WINNER.

FIVE

DIBS

GIDEON

"YA KNOW, I think you actually have to read the book to learn what's in it."

Piper's amused giggle fills my ears. I raise both arms and flash her my middle fingers, causing her laugh to deepen. My chemistry book comes off my head as I stare at her.

"I thought if I just laid it on my head all the words would seep into my brain and I wouldn't actually have to read it."

"Don't think it works like that." She kicks off her flip-flops and jumps into bed next to me.

Tonight is Friday night which means it's family dinner night. All my cousins and their parents come over so we can all have dinner together. Our parents have been doing it since they graduated high school like a hundred years ago. I'm betting Piper and I have about ten minutes before Nate and Preston bust in here.

"I thought Elliott was supposed to help you out?"

"He's my partner for projects. Not my tutor."

"What you're working on isn't a project?"

"Nope. I'm studying for the first exam."

She gapes at me. "You have an exam? We just started school."

I snort. "Pipes, we are three weeks in."

"Still. That's bullshit. We're seniors. We should get extra time to ease into things."

I couldn't agree with her more. I've been suffering through chemistry class for three weeks, and my head already feels like it's going to explode. That's an awful sign considering I've still got thirteen more weeks before the semester is over.

Fortunately, chemistry isn't complete torture. Sitting next to Elliott every day is certainly no hardship. Eating lunch with him isn't either. I like being around Elliott. If I go by the number of times I've seen his crooked tooth over the last three weeks, I'd say he likes being around me too.

"Are you thinking about Elliott?"

"What?" My head whips to Piper. "No. Why would I be thinking about Elliott?"

"Because you just smiled a little and your cheeks turned pink."

"No, they didn't."

"Yes, they did." She pokes my cheek. "They turn pink whenever he is around."

"They do not!"

"Gid, they do. You're totally crushing on him."

I swat her hand, tilting my chin so I can mask my heated cheeks. "So what if I am?"

"Don't get defensive. I'm crushing on him too. He's cute and he isn't an asshole."

"Dibs."

Her eyes bulge behind the lens of her glasses. "Did you just... call dibs?"

"Yes." My nod portrays confidence I'm not so sure I feel. "If it so happens he is into girls and guys, I get dibs."

"And if he is just into girls?"

"That's ten times more likely." I place my textbook back on my face. "All the hot ones are straight."

"That's not true. You're hot and you're hanging out on both sides of the track."

"Funny, isn't it? I'm into both genders and I still can't find anyone to buy me a pizza."

"I'll buy you a pizza."

"Maybe we should just be loners for life."

"I'm not entirely opposed to that but we are only seventeen." Piper carefully removes the textbook from my face before chucking it across the bed. "Maybe we should give it another ten years before we declare a life of solitude?"

"Deal."

"Besides, you and Sadie dated for months before she moved to college."

Sadie Watson was a senior last year and my girlfriend for a good portion of my junior year. We were friends first because she was a student at Art In Motion. We dated for almost six months before she moved to California to attend UCLA. She didn't go to Hillside, which was nice because she didn't have to hear firsthand all the shit people talked.

Sadie and I went to Fritz every chance we got and spent a lot of time with our lips locked. Even so, I wasn't super devastated when she moved. I liked her, and I was definitely attracted to her, but there was always something missing.

Pipes used to say we were friends with benefits because we never actually had meaningful conversations with each other. Sometimes, I wonder if she hadn't moved if we'd still be together or if we would've gotten bored.

"Maybe I should just go find someone from another school?"

"What about Jamie?"

Ah, James Atcot. Last summer after Sadie moved, he

started working at the cafe in the dance studio. He didn't keep it a secret that he liked me, so when he asked me out I figured *what the hell?*

I've known for years I'm bisexual but Jamie was the first guy I'd ever actually gone out with. It was clear he was super into me, so I felt like an ass when I didn't hold the same feelings and was forced to tell him that. He acted cool about it in the moment but after that glare he gave me the first day in chem class, I'm pretty sure he hates me now.

"Jamie and I would've never worked out. I didn't have any feelings for him."

"And you have feelings for Elliott?"

I shrug and try to act nonchalant. "I don't know."

"You're such a liar."

"Ok, fine!" I flail against my mattress. "I like him. You were right. He's cute and he isn't an asshole. He doesn't listen to the rumors and he talks *to* me instead of *at* me. Not to mention, he is funny as hell and hot as fuck. Who knew clunky brown boots and jeans with permanent dirt stains could be so hot?" I fan myself. "And did you see the T-shirt he was wearing yesterday? It was the same one he wore on the first day of school. It stretches across his chest showing off all his dips and ridges. Good God, Pipes, when he wears that shirt to class, it's basically like I'm not there because I don't listen to Grundy. Not when Elliott is sitting next to me with his pecs on display."

I exhale, staring at the ceiling, refusing to meet Piper's eyes while I wait for her to comment on my confession.

A beat of silence takes over room before she rolls over and starts cackling into one of my pillows.

"Holy hell, Gideon Stryker. You've got it way worse than I thought."

"He's nice to me, Pipes. It sounds stupid, but I like talking to somebody who doesn't look at me like I'm from a different planet all because I'm bisexual and best friends with my cousin."

"It's not stupid at all." Her hand slides across my comforter, linking with mine. "By the way, I'm not actually crushing on him. I just said that to get you to admit your feelings. I could see the first day we ate lunch together you liked him."

"Is that why you were saying stuff about udders? Because you were feeling him out? Seriously, Pipes? You knew him for like sixty seconds."

"So? He was making you smile. I barely knew his name and I could already see you weren't being super guarded around him."

I squeeze her hand. "That's because I feel like I don't have to be."

"That's a good thing, Gideon. Maybe you should try to feel him out. See if he's into you. I'm betting he is."

"Doubt it."

"Are you blind?"

I sit up. "Excuse me?"

"Gideon, he looks at you the same way you look at him."

"How do I look at him?"

"Like..." She sits up, rubbing at her forehead. "Oh hell, I don't know! I'm not a romance expert. You guys are just playful and happy."

My eyebrow lifts. "Playful and happy?"

"Yeah, like you remember when we were in that tots dance class?"

"When we were like two?"

"Yeah, and we wouldn't dance at all? We would run around and scream. When it was partner time, we would just make eye contact with somebody, smile, and that was it. All it took was a smile and we were holding their hands and creating chaos for the rest of class. Just like that. That's what

I think happened with Elliott. You gave him a smile and now the two of you are running in circles, screaming and laughing."

"Uhm, okay." I force out a wobbly breath, shoving my hand in my hair.

I consider her analogy, and though it was the wierdest thing I've ever heard, it kind of makes sense. I can be myself around Elliott. I don't get that privilege a lot.

"He makes you laugh, Gid. He makes you smile and isn't that what a relationship is supposed to be? Complete maddening chaos that is fun as hell?"

"Actually, Pipes, I don't think I've heard someone say that. But I understand your point."

"So... you'll pursue it?"

"If he's not into me?"

"Feel him out first. Call him cute or brush his arm or something."

"What if he rejects me?"

She smiles, resting her head on my shoulder. "You'll find someone else to make maddening chaos with."

I don't want to.

Though I've only known Elliott Oakley for a short amount of time, I'm certain when I say I don't want to make chaos with anybody but him.

SIX

I THINK YOU'RE CUTE

ELLIOTT

GIDEON STRYKER—HIS name should be right next to trouble in the dictionary.

I was supposed to come to Hillside High, lie low, and graduate. Gideon shoved a wedge in my plan to breeze through senior year. He fucked everything up, and he doesn't even know it.

I *like* Gideon. I'm attracted to him in ways some people think is a sin. I've imagined his Piper proclaimed washboard abs at least a hundred times in the last month, and I often find myself drowning in the smile that's becoming a more frequent thing.

Half of me wants to know if Gideon likes me back. Sometimes I think he does, and other times I think he is straighter than a board. The other half of me doesn't want to know because if he does like me back, I'll struggle with whether or not I should do something about it.

In Mount Vernon, I was the only openly gay kid. There were a few kids who were gay that didn't feel comfortable coming out. There were also a couple of straight guys who claimed they weren't gay then proceeded to play "I'll touch you if you touch me" in my room at night. I've fooled around with a lot of guys but I've never actually been in a relationship.

Nobody ever liked me enough to grant me that sort of title. Not one of the guys from my old town wanted to say, "Hey! That's Elliott Oakley and he's my boyfriend."

Those guys were users. They hid me, used my body to their advantage, and then sent me on my way. It hurt like hell, and I decided trying to have a relationship at seventeen was pointless.

Then I met Gideon Stryker, and I can't remember anything anymore. Not my plan to lie low, and not the many reasons I swore off teenage relationships.

Trouble.

The guy makes me the kind of nervous that turns the tips of my ears red and forces a coat of sweat on my palms. Even so, I can't stop staring at the side of his chiseled face. I'm becoming infatuated in a way I used to swear was utterly disgusting.

"Elli..." Gideon whispers from the side of his mouth. "Pay attention."

"Did you just call me Elli?"

"Yeah."

"Why?"

His lips pull into a smile. "Because it sounded cute."

I'm smacked across the face with a surge of unfamiliar feelings and the strange urge to hold his hand. I struggle to ignore it.

I'm not sure I want to fall into a relationship with him. It'd hurt like hell if he tried to hide me away like the others did. What would happen to the goo in my chest if I discovered that the curly haired boy who despises chemistry, has two trophies, and is the sugary, sweet guy I let eat my fries doesn't want to be seen with me?

His knee knocks against mine. "You're still staring, Elli."

"You're still calling me Elli."

"It's still cute."

"So are you."

His eyes sag from his face. I contemplate banging my head off the table.

"You think I'm cute?" His stunned eyes are focused on Mr. Grundy but I know I've stolen all of his attention.

"Will you two homos shut up?" Stacey sneers over her shoulder. "Go plan your sexcapades somewhere else. Some of us are trying to learn."

Gideon's mask snaps in place, and he sinks into his seat like he's trying to disappear. I open my mouth to give this bitch a piece of my mind but quickly decide against it. I don't want to give someone the ammo to fire more shots at Gideon. What if he isn't gay? I just started another rumor that isn't true all because I called him cute.

Way to go, Elliott.

I spend the last twenty minutes of class bobbing my knee up and down and shaking the stool I'm perched on. It does nothing to calm my nerves or quell the anger I feel at Stacey for forcing his mask to snap all the way on. I can only hope I didn't just screw up our entire friendship when I called him cute and vomited my feelings all over him.

When the bell rings, I fly out of my seat and rush him out the door like a crazy person.

"I'm so sorry." I blurt the apology the second we are in the hall and away from other's.

He looks taken back, his mask faltering. "Why are you sorry?"

"Because that chick was just a major bitch because of me."

"That was my fault, Elli. Not yours." His smile is sad. "I told you I had a target on my back."

I shake my head aggressively. I'm not letting his mind convince him he did something wrong. "Gideon, no. This is my fault. I just got you called a homo because I said you were cute."

He hugs his books to his chest. "It's no big deal. Happens all the time."

"People calling you cute?" Why do I suddenly feel like I need to put a dent in somebody's locker?

"No. Not that. I meant people call me a homo a lot."

My heart sinks. Is there any derogatory term he hasn't been hit with? "Why would people say that?"

"I guess because it's true? Because people decided the bisexual kid needs to be tormented? I don't know. One day I'm a faggot and the next I'm sleeping with my cousin." His mask snaps right back into place though I'm not sure anything could shield the sadness in his normally vibrant eyes.

"I'm so sorry, Gideon."

He dips his head, his curls dropping into his eyes. "Most of the kids here are straight. People are afraid of what they don't know." He kicks his toe into the ground. "That's what my parents say to make me feel better anyway. Whatever."

"Not whatever. It's bullshit. People used to say that same shit to me at my old school."

Any sign you're driving down a different side of the racetrack in Iowa is a big hell no. And I'm not just talking sexual orientation. I'm talking anything—clothing choice, career aspirations, after school activities, music choice.

Even a little swerve to a different track and you're lit up with red flags and forced to remove yourself from the race. With so many people betting against you, you'll lose anyway. I took my seat on the loser's bench with the rest of the freaks and dealt with it. I wasn't about to sacrifice who I was for a bunch of dicks in high school.

But damn it, Gideon doesn't belong on the loser's bench. I'm starting to think maybe I don't either. The two of us combined have four trophies for shit's sake.

"You're bisexual too?" I think something in his eyes flashes with the question. I wish I could tell, but it's a lost cause with all the curls in the way.

"Well, no." I smile. "I just like to hang out on the dude side of the racetrack but I'm still a proud marcher in the rainbow pride parade."

He chuckles, brushing away his curls. "My dads joke they are going to bring one to Durham."

"They should. They might win a trophy."

"Oh God. They don't need any more trophies."

"Then we should start it. We can have joint custody of the trophy."

We both laugh. I picture us making a schedule for who would take care of our trophy on which days. His mask finally starts to crack, his lips turning up as though they are on the brink of gracing me with a megawatt smile.

The moment is almost perfect. In a blink, it's ruined by some beefcake shoving my shoulder unexpectedly and forcing me to stumble. "Better watch out, new kid. He might try to unzip your pants."

"Do you have a sister?" The guy next to him cracks. "Because he might go after her too."

Gideon's almost smile vanishes as he looks around the hallway. Likely for a place to disappear. Me? I'm ready to smash some heads.

"Hey, man. You like bullying other people because of who they are?"

The beefcake stops and cocks an eyebrow. He grins like he's excited and pops his neck. "You got a problem with that?"

Oh, hot damn.

I let my books hits the floor, a loud thud echoing off the bay of lockers. "Yeah, I do. Fuck you and your pretentious friends. You think you're better than him? You think just because he's different you get to beat him down?" I hold out my arms. "Screw you, dude."

His face burns. "I don't like wasting my energy fighting low life losers so I'll give you a chance to apologize."

"Apologize to Gideon for being a homophobic prick."

He takes a heavy step forward, fists clenched. "What the fuck did you just call me?"

"A homophobic prick." I say it slow and steady just to make sure he understands.

He looks back and forth between Gideon and I several times, eyes shifting. He takes maybe two breaths before he's doubled over, laughing hysterically. "Oh, I get it. You're sticking up for him because the two of you are sucking each other's—*pop!*

The blood that gushes from his nostrils his dark and thick. My ears ring as I stare at him clutching his nose, blood seeping between the cracks of his fingers. I blink, checking my hands for bruises.

There aren't any. It wasn't my fist.

Gideon's chest pumps harshly beneath his T-shirt—his bright blue eyes now impossibly dark. He takes one step forward, violent eyes locked on the bloody beefcake. "Talk to him like that again and I will rip your fucking limbs off."

Gideon doesn't shout. He doesn't even raise his voice. He keeps it even and steady, not wavering once. There's no quiver or sign that he's scared or regrets what he just did.

"You're a psycho." Beefcake barrels down the hallway, his friends lifting their middle fingers as they race to follow their leader.

My eyes track the drips of blood on the tile and the

nosey audience that surrounds it. The second the bell rings, feet shuffle and the hallway clears as quickly as it filled.

It's almost like it never happened.

"I'm so sorry." Gideon bends over, picks up the textbook he let hit the floor, and takes off down the hall.

"Gideon, wait! Stop."

He doesn't stop. He moves fasters like he wants nothing more than to get away. I yank my own book off the floor and chase after him, terrified that if he gets away, he won't be coming back.

"Gideon..." I grab his shoulder and turn him around, causing his book to crash to the floor again. "*Please*, wait."

I slide my arm down his shoulder and clutch his hand so he can't run away. Then I squat down and lift his book off the floor, keeping my eyes locked on his feet so I can see if they start to take off.

"I'm so sorry." His voice comes out filled with air. "I'm so sorry they said that to you."

"I don't care what they said." I stand up and squeeze his hand, causing a violent flinch to wrack his body. My heart stops for a beat or two when I lift his hand and discover it swollen and the beginnings of a bruise forming. "Gideon..."

"It's fine." As quickly as he snatches it away, I snatch it right back.

His breathing hitches when I lift it to my lips and press a kiss to each one of his purple knuckles. I'm playing with fire, putting my lips against his skin. But damn it, I can't stand to see these marks on him. I can't stand that he's in pain at my expense. Even if it's just a small amount.

"Elli..."

"You asked me a question earlier." I whisper against his skin. "I didn't get a chance to answer."

"I did?"

"You asked me if I thought you were cute. The answer is yes, I do."

"Oh." He blows out breath big enough to sway his body. "Thank you."

"You're welcome." I keep hold of his hand. His skin on mine is warming my insides. "Should we get some ice for your hand?"

"Nah. It's fine."

"Gideon..."

"It's fine, Elli. I promise." Have I mentioned how much I love when he calls me Elli? If anybody else called me that, I'd knock them on their ass, but him? He's special. "I actually have a history test to go fail."

"I'm sure you won't fail."

He flashes me a crooked smile. "School and I aren't friends. I thought we covered this."

"Actually, you told me you and chemistry weren't friends."

"I downplayed that relationship. We hate each other. Mortal enemies."

"Mortal enemies, huh?"

He nods and goes silent, eyes glazing over as if he's lost in some other world. I study him carefully, getting almost no time to appreciate him before he blurts, "you want to come over tonight?" He chokes on the breath he takes. "For chemistry, I mean. Ya know because we have that project and we should probably get started on it. I'm gonna need all the time I can get just to figure out my half of it. I have dance practice until six so maybe you could come afterward? If tonight doesn't work then maybe tomorrow? Or if you don't wanna meet at my house, we could meet somewhere in town. Or if you..."

I pinch his cheeks together to get him to stop rambling. I'd meet him in the center of a landfill. "Tonight works great.

Text me your address." I release his cheeks. "Also, maybe text me a time you'll be home from practice?"

"I can do that." He nods and gestures down the hall with his head. "I'm, uh, gonna go fail that test now."

His hand starts to slide from mine. I squeeze lightly, stopping him. "I'll walk with you." Twisting my hand, I entwine our fingers. He stares at our linked hands now dangling between our bodies, a look of shock on his face.

I'm shocked too.

I'm shocked I'm not terrified, and I'm shocked I'm finding myself hoping he never lets go.

"You don't have to do that." He whispers.

"I want to."

"Are you sure?"

The answer is easy. "Positive."

He nods softly and leads me down the hall to the history classroom. Stopping beside the old door, he's forced to pull his hand from mine. "Thank you for sticking up for me."

"Thank *you* for sticking up for *me*."

He turns to step inside before he stops, his swollen hand frozen on the handle. He peers over his shoulder, eyes hitting me like a freight train. "Hey, Elli?"

"Yeah?"

"I think you're cute too."

SEVEN

SOME REALLY AWESOME STUFF

GIDEON

"SO, we got an interesting call from your school today."

I stare at my dads across the counter. I'm perched on a stool, attempting to decipher the expressions on their faces. The lines in each of their foreheads tell me they're irritated.

"Was it a call from Principal Donahue telling you that I may or may not have punched Blake Hamilton in the face?"

"Is it true?"

I lift my hand off the counter and show them my bruised knuckles. The knuckles that are up in flames not because they hurt, but because Elliott had his lips on them.

"Christ." Knox spits. "Dude, what the hell?"

"He pissed me off."

"Obviously." Beck rolls his eyes and moves to the freezer. Grabbing an icepack, he slides it across the counter-top. "Ice it."

"It's fine, dad."

"Don't argue with him." Knox stares at me pointedly until I place the ice pack on my hand. He nods approvingly and brings his arm around Beck's waist, pulling him close.

He does this because he's concerned about me and he

knows Beck is too. My parents handle everything life gives them together.

Knox and Beckett Stryker are the poster children for young love lasting a lifetime. They met at sixteen, got married three months after they graduated high school, and have been inseparable ever since. You'd think after being married for so long, they'd bitch at each other and the PDAs would have disappeared.

You'd be wrong.

I've witnessed my parents making out more times than I can count. I've never heard them raise their voice at each other or get into anything more than a tiny disagreement. Their marriage is rock solid. It's like something out of a Disney movie minus the singing animals.

"Gideon." My dads force my attention. "Talk to us."

"He was talking shit about Elli and I lost my cool." I lift one shoulder in a shrug and shove my uninjured hand through my curls.

It's not a big deal to me.

It's a huge deal to them. Not just the fact that I punched someone but that I lost my cool in the first place. I'm not one to get into fights at school, or anywhere really. I'm not somebody who goes around punching people and telling them I'm gonna rip their limbs off.

It's just not me.

But today was different.

Any degree of chill I had melted when Blake turned his torment from me to Elli. I'm not proud of it, but I'd do it again if it means Elli doesn't have to hear that shit ever again.

Knox nods his head, tapping his knuckles against the counter. "Elliott's coming over tonight to work on your project, right?"

"Yep."

"And what exactly did Blake say that caused you to punch him in the face?"

"He announced to the senior hallway that Elli and I are sucking each other off." I have no problem being upfront and honest with my parents.

"And are you?" Beck asks easily.

"No, but even if we were it's none of his damn business."

Beck smiles, pleased with my answer. "Very good point."

"Beck, really?" Knox's jaw hits the granite countertop. "You're smiling right now? Our son almost got suspended."

Beck nudges him with his shoulder. "Baby, please, if somebody would have said that about us when we were in high school, you would've ripped them apart."

Knox considers this for less than a second before allowing his lips to pull into a small smile. "That's true."

There is no doubt in my mind Knox would've destroyed anyone who spewed any sort of hate to Beck and vice versa. My parents are each other's heroes. They'd cover each other no matter the line of fire. A little suspension wouldn't stop them. Kind of like a little suspen—

Wait.

"Hold up, did you say I almost got suspended?" I was sitting in history class, trying to fail my test, when Principal Donahue walked in and called me into the hallway.

Apparently, somebody saw Blake in the bathroom cleaning up his bloody nose and ratted him out. Blake wouldn't say what happened because he's smart. He knew the second he snitched on me, I'd snitch on him.

An eye for an eye.

If Blake gets suspended or detention for any reason, he'll get kicked off the football team. Principal Donahue must've learned from somebody in the hallway I was the one who hit Blake. I kept my mouth shut. I figured he'd be calling my parents. I didn't think there was gonna be a threat of suspension involved.

"Your ass is lucky." Knox points at me. "If Blake decides to say what happened, you're gonna be suspended for a week."

"Which really can't happen, Gideon." Beck scrubs his face with his palm. "You need to be at school so you can learn and graduate. If you've got a problem, walk away or talk it out."

"And what if neither is an option?"

Knox sighs roughly. "Look, kiddo..."

My impending lecture is cut short by a knock on our front door. "Elli's here." Sliding from my stool, I leave the ice pack behind.

He knocks once more, and my hand shakes as it reaches for the doorknob.

I'm nervous.

Less than six hours ago, Elli kissed my hand, and I melted into a puddle on the tile floor. I tried to pull my hand away—give him an easy way to take back what he did.

He didn't take it back. He took more. Linking our fingers together, he held on tight.

With confidence I'm not sure I feel, I pull open the heavy door and offer him a friendly smile. "Hey, Elliott."

"Hi."

I gesture with my head. "Come on in."

Elli steps inside, his eyes wandering. "You have an awesome house."

"Thanks." Beck strides into the entryway with our fat cat hanging over his shoulder. "I bought it myself."

I roll my eyes. "Elliott, this is my dad."

Elliott shoves his hand at his chest. "Hi, Mr. Stryker. Nice to meet you."

Dad returns his handshake, laughing. "You can call me Beck, Elliott."

"Beck." He nods. "Got it."

"So, you're here to save my son from eternal damnation?"

"Oh my God, dad." I snort. "Chemistry isn't *that* bad."

He eyes me behind his glasses. "It was when I was in school."

"Which was like what? Fifty years ago?"

He points his finger at me, trying but failing to hide his smirk. "You're a little shit."

"You love me anyway."

He winks at Elli. "He's right. He's my most prized possession. I'm counting on you to get him through chemistry without jabbing a pencil in his cornucopia."

"Cornea, babe." Knox comes around the corner and extends his hand. "Hi, Elliott. I'm Knox. Gideon's other dad."

Elliott shakes Knox's hand and looks between my parents. "So, which one of you has the People's Choice Awards?"

Beck's face erupts into a shit eating grin. "That'd be me. I'm glad to hear my son has been bragging about me."

"I have not been bragging about you!" I shove his shoulder. "I'm way cooler anyway."

"It's because you have my genes, kid."

"I do not have your genes, you goon."

Elli clears his throat. "Gideon told me he was adopted."

"We trained him to lie." Beck says. "It was a miracle, really. When Knox found out he was pregnant, we made sure to keep it a secret. He's writing a book about it."

"It's true." Knox throws his arm around Beck's waist, dropping his head to the shoulder that doesn't hold the cat. "We tried to make it happen again but some miracles only happen once."

"You won't tell our secret?" Beck narrows his eyes. "Will you?"

"Of course not." Elliott laughs, turning towards me. "Dude, your dads are awesome."

"Come on, Elli." I fake an annoyed groan. "Don't tell them that. Their egos will explode."

"Well, you're awesome too." I'm suddenly desperate to link our fingers and attempt a repeat of this afternoon.

As if he can read my eager mind, Elli stretches his arm outward and grabs my injured hand, raising it to his lips. Right in front of my parents, he locks his warm gaze on my stunned one and presses a kiss to each of my knuckles.

My knees wobble.

"You should get some ice for this."

"Ice is for wimps." I manage, turning my hand and linking it with his. "Come on, you can save me from eternal damnation."

I lead him up the stairs and push open the door to my bedroom, gesturing for him to go inside. He peers around, taking in the queen-sized bed with balled up red blankets, my metal desk, a few dressers, and a suede loveseat resting beneath a large window.

I pull him to the loveseat and sit down, patting the spot next to me in invitation. He drops his backpack and plops down, keeping my hand in his.

"So, where are your trophies?" He teases. "I don't see a glass case."

"They're in my closet."

"Closet? Why? You need to display them so you can brag to everyone that comes in here."

"Ah, nobody really comes in here except my parents and my cousins. They don't give a damn."

"I'm in here." He argues "And I give a damn."

"Are you planning to visit me often?"

The silence between my question his answer feels like it lasts forever. The air compacts in my lungs and escapes in a whoosh when he says, "I'll race right here the second you call."

The intensity lingering within his eyes tells me how much he means it.

An uncountable number of feelings overcome my body. It's a lot to process, so I dip my chin and use my curls as a shield to mask my warm face.

After a beat, he squeezes my hand. "So, where should we start?"

"You tell me, man." I shrug, blowing curls from my face when I'm confident I've successfully gotten a grip. "I haven't even read the assignment."

"For real?" He laughs. "Are you gonna make me do all the work?"

"Of course not. I just need you to tell me what to do."

"You're about to be a real pain in my ass, aren't you?" The smirk on his face tells me he wouldn't care at all.

"Probably. I get called that all the time."

He chuckles lowly and grabs the sheet of paper with our assignment on it. We sit here, our hands linked like it's the most normal thing in the world, and I watch his dark brown eyes scan the instructions.

My eyes scan him.

His thick hair is long. Not as long as the mop I've got on my head, but it's long enough that the ends keep falling into his eyes. The sides are shaved a bit shorter, and he's got scruff lining his cheeks and chin. He isn't blonde but I don't think I would classify him as a redhead either. The strange color falls somewhere in between.

The skin covering his body is impossibly tan. I assume that has something to do with the fact that he used to be a farmer and spent a lot of time outside. On his chin lies a moon shaped scar, and he has two dimples that appear in his cheeks when he smirks at me.

They're on full display.

"Are you staring at me?"

"What color is your hair?"

"No idea." He runs his hand through it. "My mom used to say it's strawberry blonde."

"I like it."

"Thanks. I like your hair too. It's wild."

That's an understatement. "These curls are untamable. I cut them down every summer and I swear to you they grow back more out of control every year."

"Out of control, huh? I like that." My heart quickens when he pulls his hand from mine and his fingers find a misbehaving curl falling into my eyes. "You're different here than you are at school. You're more relaxed—more outgoing and wild like your hair. You don't wear a mask here. You're just... you."

"Well, that's because..."

"I know why." He whispers, his finger still wrapped around my curl. "It's because of what people say to you. You hide who you are to stop some of the hate. I get it. But, Gideon, you don't have to hide who you are from me, okay?"

"I know." It was clear the moment I met Elli I didn't have to hide any pieces of myself. He isn't judgmental or rude. He doesn't find joy in bringing other's misery. He knows what it's like to be different.

I sit silently, my breath coming out in shallow pants as he takes his time twirling my curl around his finger. Almost as though he's committing the feeling to memory.

I have this overwhelming urge to ask him to kiss me. I'm not sure I possess what it takes to purse my lips and do it myself. Clearing my throat, I open my mouth to form the words of my absurd question when he pulls away quickly, leaving me startled.

"So, should we do this thing? I'm going to take my job as eternal damnation saver very seriously." He pulls his MacBook out of his backpack, setting it on his lap. "This actually doesn't sound too bad."

I make the sign of the cross over my chest and clasp my hands together. He smirks at me, giving me a glimpse of his quirky tooth before it's gone.

"Do you have a computer? Or do you wanna share mine?"

"Uh, yeah. I do. One sec." I jump up and snag my computer from my desk, trying to get my brain to switch to chemistry mode.

It's a lost cause.

When I sit back down, he slides closer, forcing my mind to the spot our thighs are touching. I lift the lid of my computer, positioning my shaky fingers so I can type in the password.

Once I'm logged in, I look up to find him staring at me. "How'd you get a black one?"

"A black what?"

"MacBook."

"It's a skin, dude."

"A what?"

"A skin." I laugh, peeling the corner and showing him that it comes off. "It's like a giant sticker to make it all fancy."

"Oh, that's pretty cool. Do they come in red?"

"Yeah, man. They come in all colors. Why? You like red?"

He nods. "Red's my favorite color."

"Mine too."

"Oh. Why is your computer black?"

"It's understated." I reposition the skin, smoothing out the wrinkles. "Doesn't draw so much attention."

He studies me with hazy eyes for a moment and opens his mouth like he is going say something. He must decide against it because he shakes his head, erasing his thoughts, and hands me the sheet of paper with our assignment outlined on it. "There are two parts. A paper and a presentation. Which do you wanna prepare?"

"I'll write the paper."

He looks at me skeptically. "Seriously?"

"Sure. Just as long as you tell me what to write it about."

He shakes his head, amused. "Pain in the ass."

"Dude, come on. Remember that time you said I'm really awesome?"

"Okay, really awesome." He laughs, slamming his computer shut and abandoning the work we haven't even started. "Tell me more really awesome things about yourself then."

This sounds way better than chemistry. "Okay. Like what?"

"Anything. You've been my best friend for a month and I feel like I know nothing about you. I know you're a dancer. I know you like to steal my fries. You appreciate your parents in a way most teenagers don't and you'd sell your kidney if it meant it'd get you out of chemistry class."

I ignore the jerk in my heart when he says I'm his best friend. I resist telling him I'd keep my kidney and gladly suffer through chemistry as long as he keeps showing up every day. "You forgot to mention my trophies."

"Ah, yes. Your trophies." He winks. "I still don't see them."

"I'll have to get them out and polish them."

"You should hire someone for that."

"Do you know anyone?"

"We'll find someone together. Mine got dusty in the move." We share a grin. "Now, tell me some really awesome stuff."

"Okay. Well, my middle name is Mason after my dad Knox. I listen to a lot of different types of music, and I love to swim. I grew up in this house and this town. My dads like to travel so I've been all over the world. I have a small obsession with fire." I chuckle at myself like a total goober. "Okay, I lied. I have a big obsession with fire."

He smiles at me like those few facts just gave him everything he needed. "Why?"

"I have no idea. I've been obsessed with firetrucks and fireworks since I can remember. My favorite pastime is lighting them up and watching them blow. It doesn't happen often because my dads don't like to buy them for me."

"Why not? They seem like pretty laid back guys."

"They usually are, but after four trips to the ER because I lit myself up, I think they're a little scared."

His eyes pop from his face. "Four trips to the ER? Dude, what'd you do? Set yourself on fire?"

I roll my eyes. "No, the flame like barely touched me."

"Barely touched you, huh?" He doesn't look convinced. "Then why'd you have to go to the ER?"

"So, maybe it was a little bad. On the bright side, I have some sweet scars."

His eyebrow reaches his hairline. "So, what you're saying is, I should never buy you fireworks?"

"Please." I scoff. "I'll be eighteen in like six weeks. I'll buy my own damn fireworks." I bust out laughing at the horrified expression on his face. "Okay, Elli. Your turn."

He shakes his head like he's trying to get his wits in order. "Okey dokey. My middle name is Dean because my mom liked the way it sounded. I like anything with a set of wheels and taking shit apart so I can put it back together again. I would eat a cheeseburger for every meal if I wouldn't die of congestive heart failure, and I hate chocolate." He takes a breath. "I also have two trophies."

I gasp dramatically. "You hate chocolate? Oh, the horror!"

"There are a lot of other ways to eat unhealthy besides chocolate."

"But chocolate is the best."

"I prefer peanut butter."

"Dude." I stare at him. "Chocolate and peanut butter is like the best combination ever created."

"Maybe I'll try it sometime. Just for you."

I throw my hand over my heart. "You're so good to me, Elli."

He chuckles. It's such a sweet sound. Everything about Elli screams gruff—his boots, the scruff lining his chin, the permanent stains on his jeans. But his laugh? It's not tough at all. It's playful and it's light and it affects the beats that fill my chest. "So, why did you and your grandpa relocate to Durham?"

His smile disappears, and I regret my questions. "I, uhm, I moved here to live with my grandpa after my mom died."

My heart drops directly into the pits of my stomach. "Elli... I'm so sorry. I didn't know."

"It's okay. It was last August. I still have trouble talking about it."

"Of course, you do. I'm so sorry for asking." I wish I could rewind time and stop myself from asking. I hate I just reminded him he lost his mother.

"Gideon, hey, it's okay. You didn't know." I attempt to turn my head away. He uses his hand to grip my chin and stop me. "Don't turn away."

"I feel like an ass."

"You didn't know, baby." He whispers. "It's okay."

For a moment, I forget how to use words. He just called me baby. It was clear as day and I'm 100% sure I didn't imagine it. He drops his hand from my chin and rests it on top of mine, rubbing lightly. "Besides, my gramps and I are doing great."

He hasn't mentioned a dad, so I don't ask. "What's your grandpa like?"

"He's crotchety." He smirks. "His name is Thatcher, but he tells everybody to call him Spanky."

I imagine a grumpy old man shouting at everybody to call him Spanky. "What the hell? Why?"

"That was the name he used back when he was a racer. He's seventy-four now and hasn't raced in thirty years but he likes to be reminded of his glory days."

"That's pretty awesome."

"These days, he just smokes cigars and pushes my buttons. My grandma died over ten years ago. I keep telling him to get off his old ass and find a girlfriend but he won't listen."

I snort. "How does a 74-year-old find a girlfriend?"

"The grocery store? Bingo hall? The chick with the walker sitting at a slot machine? I don't know but he's lonely."

"He has you."

"Yeah." He grins like he's never been prouder to be a grandson. "He does but I'm at school a lot and I'm always at the shop. I spend way too much time there."

"Maybe we could get him a dog? Or a cat?"

"We?" The look on his face tells me I said the right thing.

"Yeah. I could help find one."

"I like that idea."

I smile. Somehow suggesting buying his Grandpa

Spanky a cat is making me feel like I just won the lottery. "Sometimes I have good ideas."

"I think you probably have good ideas all the time but nobody takes the time to listen to them."

Well, he just hit the nail in the coffin there. But I'm not about to jump into that hole. After the mention of his mom, I refuse to let this conversation go back to a dark place. "At school that's true but on the dance floor it isn't. I'm pretty darn good if I do say so myself. I probably spend just as much time at the dance studio as you do at Speed. I'm a student, but my dad also lets me teach two baby jazz classes."

"How do you teach a baby how to dance? Babies can't even walk."

"Elliott." I nudge his knee. "They aren't actually babies. The youngest is four, but we call them the baby classes."

"Got it." He nods. "That makes more sense. You like teaching?"

"I love it. The kids are awesome."

He grins and squeezes my hand. "I'd love to see the studio sometime."

"Yeah?"

"Yeah. Definitely. I'd love to watch you dance." His shoulder nudges mine. "Something tells me you don't wear your mask."

My face heats. He's right again. I don't wear my mask when I dance because it isn't necessary. On the dance floor, I do everything right. Nobody judges me.

"You still want to come to Fritz?" I blurt. "You could watch there."

"That club you and Piper were talking about a while ago?"

"Yeah. Next weekend they're having their no cover fee

night. We always go. You could come with us. I mean... if you wanted to."

"Okay." He agrees instantly, surprising me. "I'll come."

"I'd like that a lot."

"So would I." He smiles again before letting go of my hand and opening back up his MacBook. "Now, let's save you from eternal damnation."

EIGHT

IT'S A GIFT

ELLIOTT

CONQUERING ETERNAL DAMNATION? Check!

Gideon and I spent every night for a week working on our project. I'm pretty sure he still has no idea what paper chromatography is but I'm confident he bullshitted the essay enough to get us at least a B. It isn't an A but he says it's a step up from the C+ he's usually idling at.

All week he apologized profusely for not understanding, and all week I'd have to keep reminding him I didn't mind explaining things to him. I actually looked forward to him having questions because it was an excuse for him to text me. After I answered his questions, we kept texting about random stuff, neither one of us wanting to be the one who ended the conversation.

Last night we had a conversation about whether it was SpongeBob or Patrick who was the real Dirty Dan. After an hour of shooting the shit, we agreed it was Sandy.

Our conversations about nothing happen frequently. To my delight, it's slowly turned into very unsubtle flirting. I went from being cynical about love to one of those disgusting teens who uses emojis on a daily basis.

The number of selfies I have of him making silly faces saved on my phone is un-flippin'-real. You'd think I'd get sick of staring at him with his eyes bugged out and lips pursed.

I don't.

He's so damn adorable—a total goof. I love that he doesn't feel the need to hide how kooky he is for me. I love that when I'm around, there's almost no sign of his mask.

Did I mention I also love when he calls me Elli? My mom used to call me that. It was our special thing, and I swore I'd never let anybody else have it. Then he peered up at me behind a mass of curls in the middle of a chemistry lecture and I couldn't do anything but smile when the nick-name fell from his lips.

He hasn't mentioned the way I kissed his knuckles or the way I keep calling him baby. He hasn't mentioned the two times we were studying on the patio in his backyard and I slid my hand down his arm and entwined our fingers.

Part of me thinks he's just holding his breath—like he thinks one day I'm gonna stop talking to him and all this will be over. Little does he know, I'm holding my breath too.

"Hi, Elli."

"Holy shit!" I jump and slam the door to my truck shut, willing my heart to slow down so I don't have a heart attack in the school parking lot. "Dude, you just scared the hell out of me."

"Sorry." He smiles one of the mega smiles he saves specifically for the special people in his life. How lucky am I that I get to be one of them? "I just wanted to give you something before we headed into the school."

"Oh." I look down and find a flat something or another wrapped up in red paper, clutched in his tight grasp. "What is it?"

"Uhm..." His face becomes a tomato. "It's a gift. For you.. Elli... From me... Gideon."

I stare into his nervous face, my heart melting in my chest. "You got me a gift?"

"Uhm, yeah. I just wanted to say thank you. You know, for helping me out and being so patient. I know you probably felt like you did all the work on that project, so I just wanted you to know I appreciate you and what you did to help me."

If there was any doubt in my mind at how incredible Gideon is, it'd be gone. "You didn't have to do this."

"I wanted to." His nervous expression robs me of his sweet smile. "If you think it's weird, I can just take it back. It's no big deal."

I pry it out of his tight grip with a smile. "No. It's mine." Slowly, I peel back the red paper only to be met with more red.

"It's a skin." He blurts. "For your computer. You don't have to use it if you don't want to. I just remember how you liked mine and how your favorite is red, so I just thought that maybe you would like it."

Over the last month, I've learned when Gideon gets nervous, he turns his face away. Like he's afraid of what reaction he'll be met with.

When I'm met with his profile, I grab his chin and pull it so I can see his face again. His eyes are focused downward, refusing to meet mine. I find a curl and twirl it around my finger. "Thank you, baby. I love it."

"Yeah?" I don't know if it was the declaration of love for the gift or the fact that I called him baby. Either way, I'm rewarded with his grin.

"Yeah. It's awesome." I tear off the rest of the paper and throw the wad in my truck, sliding the skin in my backpack. "I'll stick it on when we get to chemistry."

He scoffs, starting into school with me by his side. "Ah, you mean the torture chamber?"

"Hey, we're starting a new unit today. Maybe it will be something simple."

"It's cancer."

My feet stutter against the pavement. "What did you just say?"

"Uh, cancer. That's what our new unit is on. We're gonna study it. I think like how the cells form and why it spreads so fast or something."

Painful memories I've worked so hard to stuff down, snap to the surface in an instant. I feel a very familiar burn in my eyes and ache in my chest the moment visions of my mama start playing in front of me.

It's all my eyes will see—her small body getting swallowed by the oversized blankets on her big bed. I stare at her pale hand and bony fingers, remembering the way it shook when it was trembling in mine. An unrecognizable growl rips from my throat the moment I remember the day she died and what that sick son of a bit—

"Elli!" Gideon's startled voice rips me from the visions of my past, forcing me to concentrate on his baby blues and the feel of his hand in mine. "Are you okay?"

My first instinct is to lie to him, tell him I'm fine and walk away. I don't know why I don't. Maybe it's his hand in mine or the way he's staring at me with big, worried eyes. Maybe it's because he steps closer and grabs my other hand, not giving a shit we've attracted an audience. I'm not sure but lying to him just doesn't seem like an option.

"No."

Nodding, Gideon lets go of one hand, keeping a hold of the other. He drags me down the hall, not stopping for anything. He moves past our lockers and right past chemistry class, pulling me behind him the whole way. I let him lead me until he comes to the bright green door and throws it open.

"What's wrong, Elli?"

He looks at me with patient eyes but the way he gnaws at his bottom lip tells me he's confused by my actions. "I'm sorry I just lost it for a minute back there."

"It's no big deal. I'm just worried about you."

"You are?" When my mom died and I left Iowa, I was convinced the only person who'd ever give a damn about me ever again was gramps. Flurries of warmth spread through my body at the thought of him caring enough about me to be worried.

"Of course I am." He hesitates before stepping close and putting his hands on my hips. "You looked...." He pauses like he's searching for the right word. He's silent for a long moment before he goes with, "haunted."

Disturbed. Tormented. Troubled. Anguished—a list forms in my head as I watch a red pen place a giant check mark next to each and every one. Slowly, I watch the word haunted get written in bold letters. I can almost hear the sound of the pen swiping the paper, marking one more thing that's wrong with me. I'm haunted by the memory of my mom's death every single time I allow myself to think about it.

"Your mom had cancer." He whispers, shifting so his arms wrap around my waist in the most comforting way. "That's how she died? Isn't it?"

"Ovarian." I focus on my words and not the memories that come with them. "They say it's the one that's hardest to detect. By the time we caught it, hers had already spread." He squeezes me tighter, prompting me to lift my arms and wrap them around his back, seeking his comfort. "She fought it for a year before she died. I left Iowa the day after her funeral. I guess... I'm, uh, still struggling."

This isn't surprising considering I haven't given myself more than a day to mourn. I haven't cried since the day I left, and I haven't allowed myself to feel any sadness. Sometimes, I pretend I'm just hanging out at grandpa's house. When I have to face the fact that she's never coming to pick me up, I start to lose it. I hate dropping my guard long enough to lose it. I'd rather just pretend.

"It's okay to struggle with it, Elli. She was your mom and now she's gone."

"Yeah because cancer killed her. I have no desire to sit inside a classroom every morning and be reminded that cancer kills people. I already know and it's bullshit, Gideon. It's bullshit that some people get to live and my mom had to die." I slam my eyes shut the moment they start burning, forcing the moisture to stay put. "She was a good person. She was a special education teacher at my school. She volunteered at daycare at our church after school every day. She was one of the good ones and now she's gone. I just don't understand why it was her. Why did she die when other people get to live? And now I have to go into that classroom and listen to a bunch of bullshit instead of getting the answer I really want."

"Elli..." He inches closer and rests his head on my chest. "I don't think anyone will ever be able to give you that answer. That's life. It's unfair, and I'm so sorry."

He's a couple of inches shorter than me, so I rest my head on top of his. Looking at him, you'd think his curls would be scratchy or itchy. They aren't. They're soft against my cheek and they smell like peaches.

I hold him tighter, feeling the burning behind my eyes lighten. "Her name was Lucille. Everybody called her Lucy. I just called her mama."

"She was wonderful."

I chuckle at his quick reply. "How would you know?"

"Because she made you."

Just like that. A woman he's never met is wonderful all because she made me. "Baby..."

The five-minute warning bell sounds. He presses a quick kiss to my chest. Before I can analyze the action or the way the leftover moisture in my eyes suddenly disappears, he lifts his head and his baby blues hit me full force. "Can you do this?"

"Yes." I'm not actually sure if I can but I have no other choice.

He nods and backs away, pulling open the door. "Let's go then."

I take a breath so I can get my wits back in order before following him out the door and down the hall. We both slide into our seats just as the final bell sounds. Mr. Grundy wastes no time diving right into the topic that makes my eyes sting and my chest ache. When he brings up the different types of cancers and mentions ovarian, I'm positive I'm gonna lose my shit right here in chemistry class. Then Gideon's hand is in mine and the burning in my eyes is easier to manage.

For the rest of the class, he keeps his hand underneath our desk with his fingers wrapped around mine and his thumb moving across the top of my hand. When the bell rings, he doesn't let go. He keeps a hold of my hand and walks me all the way to my next class. He doesn't say anything, but he doesn't have to. I understand.

He's with me.

NINE

KISS ME

ELLIOTT

I WALK INTO THE CLUB, feeling like I just stepped into a parallel universe. This isn't me. I'm not the club kind of guy. I don't dance. I don't drink. I don't smoke whatever the hell I smell in here and I sure as shit haven't seen this many half naked girls in one place. Mount Vernon's idea of a fun Friday night was fishing on the dock and sneaking a couple of beers.

"Dude, in or out?" The bouncer is staring at me, waiting for me to make my choice. I'm just about to bolt and hope Gideon will understand when a small hand with purple nails wraps around my wrist like a shackle.

"Elliott! You made it."

Piper drags me inside, my feet moving quicker to keep up with hers. When I get a good look at the size of heels she's wearing, I walk faster so she doesn't trip over my clumsy feet and break an ankle. She stops abruptly at a high table with no chairs and rests her elbows on top. "HEY! You want something to drink?" Her shouting really isn't necessary because even with the ear-splitting volume, I'm still right in front of her.

"No, thanks." I semi-shout back. "I'm good."

She tosses her pink ponytail over her shoulder and flashes a friendly grin at me. Today, her tortoiseshell glasses are neon pink. Her plunging shirt isn't leaving very much to the imagination, and I wonder how the hell her jeans aren't cutting off her circulation. She smiles knowingly at me. "The club scene isn't really your thing, huh?"

"This is the first time I've ever been to one."

"What do you think so far?"

"Uhm." I glance around the building. It's packed full of all sorts of people. There are waiters balancing trays filled with shots and drinks on their shoulders while they weave in and out of clumps of people. Random high tables like the one Piper and I claimed are strategically placed throughout the space. The dance floor looks like a mosh pit from a rock concert, and there's a purple velvet rope blocking off anyone from going up the wide staircase. "It's, uh, pretty loud in here."

She laughs. "Honestly, Elliott. You look like I just forced you into purgatory. Relax a little."

"Relax." I nod. "I can do that. Is Gideon here yet?" I scan the area though I'm not sure how the hell I'll find him in the middle of the storm that's brewing in this building.

"He's dancing." She points her finger towards the center of the dance floor.

I follow her finger and scan the mosh pit, looking for his curls. It takes me a while to spot him in the center of flailing bodies, but when I do, my jaw unhinges. My eyes roam— memorizing each move his body makes.

Holy hell.

He wasn't kidding when he said he could dance. His chest is pumping wildly, his hips grinding slowly, and his feet are flying effortlessly. His jeans are almost as tight as his cousins and the T-shirt he's wearing is pulled tight across his chest, showing off every little indent in his skin.

My throat dries.

Piper laughs. I pick my jaw off the floor and and push my eyeballs back in my head so I can give her a small amount of attention. "You gonna ask him out? Or are you gonna let someone snatch him up?"

My ears redden. "Uhm..."

"Nevermind!" She shouts. "Don't answer that. He's coming over here."

"Elli." Gideon's hand grips my shoulder, warming the skin beneath my shirt. It's there for only a second before slipping down my arm, leaving behind a heat spot I'm positive will remain for the rest of tonight. "You came."

He's beaming and I smile back at him, unable to do anything else. "Yeah. You invited me."

"Yeah, but I wasn't sure if you'd show up. I'm glad you did."

I wasn't so glad I showed up until this very moment. His smile is taking up his entire face, his bright baby blues sparkling. His face is glossy with sweat, droplets dripping down his neck. Still, he smells good enough to eat—which is incredibly tempting.

I back one step away, wringing my hands together. "You're, uhhh, really good at dancing."

Piper snorts causing Gideon to give her a look before giving his attention back to me. "Thanks. You wanna join me?"

My stomach rolls. "Absolutely not." His face falls, and I feel like a dick. "It's not that I don't want to hang out with you but I don't dance. Not like that at least. The last dance I danced was at Junior Prom, and I'm pretty sure it was the cha cha slide."

He smiles and offers me his hand. "I'll teach you."

I must feel like being humiliated because I place my shaky hand in his steady one. How could I not? He's offering it to me and I already know how perfectly it fits with mine.

He squeezes tightly and pushes his way through the crowd, dragging me directly into the storm. As soon as we're immersed, his hands hit my hips and he starts to move. Me? I stand there terrified and wishing I could go home and milk a cow or something.

"Stop thinking, Elli." He demands. "Just dance with me."

"Ya know." I smirk, attempting to deflect from my impending dance debut. "My mom used to call me Elli. I swore I'd let never let anybody else call me that."

His body stills like somebody just turned off the music. "I didn't..." He shakes his head, his eyes becoming wide. "Why didn't you tell me to stop?"

"Because you're special." The words leave my mouth before it dawns on me that I maybe shouldn't have said them. Then again, I've called him cute and baby, kissed his knuckles, and held his hand. Clearly, I have zero self-control around him. Looking at him now, eyes wide and full of possibility, I'm starting to think that isn't such a bad thing.

"How special?" He inches closer, his hands sliding from my hips and up around my neck. "How special?"

"Gideon..." My throat runs dry at the feel of his chest against mine.

"Elli...."

"I can't dance like that."

"Just follow my lead."

"I'm usually the one in charge."

"Not tonight." His fingers find the ends of my hair. "Please, Elli? Dance with me?"

"Okay." He smiles his megawatt smile, and I no longer care about embarrassing myself. He wants me to dance with him, so I will. At this point, I'd give him anything he asks for and all he has to do is stare at me with his big blue eyes and smile.

His hands settle back on my hips as his start to grind again. I do my best to mimic his movements. I lose my footing a couple of times but he doesn't seem to mind. He keeps moving and I go wherever he pulls me.

Tonight, he pulls me right into the heart of a tumultuous storm, my heart in my throat and my stomach in knots as I try to keep up with the demand to keep moving. Pure joy mixes with the makings of indisputable terror. Gideon Stryker is taking a hammer to all the concrete walls I built after my mama died and he's cracking the hell out of them, one by one.

"Told you this was easy." He shouts, moving faster and forcing me to move with him.

"I wouldn't call it easy."

"Elli, you're killing it."

"And you're a liar." I laugh. "But I appreciate it."

He winks at me, moving closer as the song morphs into something slower. He turns around, bringing my arms around his waist while his hands find a home in my hair. Slowly, Gideon's hips start to sway back and forth, turning me into a puddle of testosterone. In less than one beat of the music, we're grinding on each other, moving in sync like we've done this a million times before.

Maybe it's because I've never actually danced like this before, or maybe it's the way my brain can't focus on any detail of this moment except the way his body seems to melt right into mine, but I decide immediately this moment is single handily the hottest of my entire life.

When a new song starts, Gideon surprises me by twisting his body and clutching my hand, dragging me out of the storm with undeniable purpose in each of his quick steps. He could be pulling me into a back alley to beat me up and steal my wallet. I wouldn't care at all.

I just wanna be where he is.

He weaves through a bunch of tables and hundreds of people, down a flight of concrete stairs. He pushes me into a dimly lit hallway I'm positive we're not supposed to be in, drops my hand, and stares at me with parted lips and wide eyes.

I don't dare move when he steps closer to me, sliding his hands up my arms and around my neck. The blood beneath the skin he just caressed starts to bubble as his fingers find the ends of my hair.

"I like this spot." He sounds winded. "It's rough and soft at the same time. Kind of like you."

"Like me?"

"Yeah. Around other people, you come across closed off and gruff. You don't speak or smile much. Around me though, your smile is all I see. You make me laugh and talk to me about nothing. So yeah, rough and soft. Rough with others. Soft with me. Why is that?"

"Pretty sure I already answered that question, Gideon."

He tilts his head and brings his bottom lip between his teeth. "You did?"

"You're special." Now that I've said it, I want to make sure he knows it. Gideon's special. The assholes at school don't recognize it. I do.

A strangled sound comes from his chest. "Why me?"

I ignore his question because I'm not sure I know how to put that answer into words. I just *know*. I can feel it in the way my blood warms whenever he's around. Or the way he's managed to put giant cracks in the wall I swore would stay rock solid. Or the overuse of those damn emojis. "You brought me down a creepy stairwell to play with my hair?"

He shakes his head, curls swaying with the movement. "I brought you here because I need to ask you something."

"Okay." The tremors in his hands tell me the words about to come from his mouth are making him nervous. The thought alone makes me nervous too.

"Do you like me?" He blurts. "I know we're best friends and we get along great. You call me baby but maybe that's just a thing people do in Iowa. Like they call all their friends baby? I don't know but surely you don't hold hands with all your friends, right? I guess what I'm trying to ask is, are you attracted to me? You called me cute but a puppy or a little hamster is cute. Do you think I'm hot? Would you wanna date me? Maybe make out? Grind a little more on the dance floor? I could buy you a cheeseburger. Maybe one day you could be my boyfriend."

It's becoming abundantly clear that Gideon Stryker rambles when he's nervous.

"Of course, I've never actually had a boyfriend. Have you? Maybe we should have talked about that before I dragged you down here. Maybe you don't want a boyfriend. Or maybe I really am special."

"Gideon..." I rasp his name, feeling some sort of surge spread throughout every inch of my body. "You wanted to ask me if I liked you?"

I thought I'd made the answer pretty obvious with the hand holding and the way I can't keep my hands off his curls. Then again, I'd never actually said the words. I'm not great with words.

"No." His answer confuses me until his hooded gaze somehow finds my eyes beneath a mass of curls and he whispers, "I wanted to ask you to kiss me." Those eight words yank all the air from my lungs. "I've only ever kissed one dude before and it wasn't that great. I mean, I wasn't sure what we were expecting. We didn't have great chemistry. I haven't wanted to kiss anybody since. Then I met you. You and I... we uh... we have chemistry. Not the class but like the feeling. At least, I think we do. Unless you can't feel it like I can. If that's the case could we possibly forget this conversation ever happened?"

I don't let my brain overthink this moment. I grab his shoulders and slam him against the concrete wall, forcing a rough tremor to escape his petite body.

Kissing him has been on my mind since the second I sat next to him on a small couch and wrapped a curl around my finger. I was close enough to feel his low breaths whispering across my lips. It took gallons of willpower and a harsh memory to get me to retreat.

He pulls his bottom lip into his teeth. I shake my head slowly, using my thumb to pull it right back out. When I kiss him, I want all his lips. I want to feel every inch of them —just in case it never happens again.

"You want me to kiss you, Gideon?" I ask slowly, giving him a chance to change his mind.

"Yes." He breathes the answer effortlessly, closing his eyes and tilting his head like my kiss is what he's been waiting for all night.

No pressure, Elliott.

I shuffle closer, the tips of my boots rubbing the tips of his sneakers. Our chests knock together as he allows me to invade his personal space.

I dip my head and press my nose into his neck, inhaling him and attempting to commit this exact moment to my memory forever. I memorize the way his curls are sticking to his forehead with a sheen of sweat, the way his lips are parted in anticipation for what's about to be the best kiss of my life, how his nervous fingers feel when they grip my hips. I even memorize the odd scent of sweat and peaches that seems to be floating off him. I memorize all the elements that most seem to take for granted. When I look back on this, I don't want to just remember the kiss. I want to remember the whole damn moment.

"Where, Gideon?" My lips whisper against his glossy skin. "Where do you want me to kiss you? Here?" I press a kiss to the bottom of his neck, smiling softly when I hear his little gasp. "Or here?" I run my nose up his neck and press a kiss to the underside of his chin. "Maybe here?" His cheek gets a kiss next before I move to his lips. "Or would you like it here?" I speak so softly, I barely hear my own words.

"There." He pants, my chest rocking from an intense spasm when his lips brush against mine softly. "Right there."

I grab his shaky arms with my shaky hands and carefully bring them around my neck. "Find that spot you love, baby." He grips hard on my hair, holding on tight so he doesn't fall off whatever ride we're about to go on.

"What the hell are you waiting for?"

I chuckle softly and grab his hips, lifting. He gets it immediately and wraps his strong legs around my waist. I back him further into the wall and press as close to him as I possibly can.

"You weren't close enough yet."

I slam my lips to his. A noise I had no idea I was capable of making comes from my throat and descends into his mouth. He tastes *good*—so much better than I ever thought possible. Like a cross between the best decision I've ever made and the worst one.

I wish immediately I could kiss him every moment for the rest of my life.

I kiss him like I'm never gonna kiss him again. I nibble on his bottom lip until his chest is knocking against mine roughly and his hips are moving back and forth. When my body heats up to the point of igniting, I pull away and press my sweaty forehead to his. It takes a while for our breathing to go back to normal. When it finally does, he sucks in a breath and lets out, "Holy hot hell almighty."

I manage a chuckle.

"There really are two sides of you. Christ, Elli. You walked into this place looking terrified. I practically had to beg you to dance with me. Then I drag you into a creepy stairwell and rough Elli slams me against a wall and kisses me brainless." He fans himself, sagging against the wall. "Wow. I was really expecting to have to convince you."

My tingling lips quirk. Even with my plan to end high school a teenage loner, trying to avoid him or the feelings that have hit me like a MAC truck over the last two months would've been like trying to avoid the rain in a downpour. Damn near impossible.

Now that I know how it feels to kiss him, I won't be trying to ignore my feelings. Screw my original plan and screw the reason for it. Plans change, and I like the way my new plan's eyes are a bit hazy and his lips are a lot swollen. "Listen, baby, you don't have to convince me to kiss you. You want a kiss? Just ask."

He raises his eyebrows. "Just ask, huh? How many dudes does that work for?"

"Excuse me?"

"How many guys get to ask you for a kiss? How many guys do you call baby? How many guys get to see your soft side and then get mauled by the rough side?"

"Gideon." I shake my head, letting my lips whisper across his flushed cheek. "I swear on Grundy's mustache and pictures of a mutated child that nobody but you gets that offer. Nobody but you gets to see my soft side."

If only he understood how true that statement is. The last person who saw my soft side was my mama. The day she died is the sole reason I swore off significant others. But I can't ignore Gideon any more than I can ignore my mind screaming warning signs at me. Gideon just trumps the warnings.

His body spasms beneath my touch. "Because I'm special?"

"Yeah, baby, because you're special."

I'm rewarded with his megawatt smile. "So, does that offer stand anywhere? Or just in creepy stairwells?"

I throw my head back laughing. "Come on, we should go before we get caught and this turns out to be the place where the thugs sell their drugs."

He drops to his feet and rolls his eyes. "Elli, please. The thugs don't sell drugs in this club. They do it in the one across the street." He grabs my hand starts back up the stairs.

"How do you know that?"

He looks over his shoulder and smirks at me. "I don't. I was just screwing with ya."

I shake my head and let him lead me back into the heart of sweaty bodies, twisting my hand so our fingers entwine. I spend the next three hours dancing, kissing his neck, and memorizing more details.

By the time we leave, I'm satisfied my lips have been permanently seared into his skin and he has been seared into my soul.

TEN

HE CALLED ME HIS

ELLIOTT

"BOY, stop pacing before you put a hole in my damn floor."

"I need help."

Gramps drags his attention away from the kitchen table and the model car it holds. The house my grandpa lives in is basically a cottage with only one bedroom. The living room is the size of my palm, holding only an old couch covered in an awful plaid print and a deep red recliner that creaks every time he sits down in it.

The kitchen isn't much bigger. There's an island in the center and a round dining room table butted up next to it, leaving almost no room to move around. The hole I'm pacing into the old tile is about the size of a paper plate.

There's a den in the back of the house where he used to play cards when his racing buddies came over. When I moved in, it became my bedroom. I sleep on the pull-out and keep all my clothes in the suitcases I brought them in because I didn't want gramps to have to buy me a dresser. He did me a favor by taking me in. I can't ask him for anything else.

Except, maybe some advice.

"Aren't you a little old to be getting stuck in the zipper?"

"Gramps, this is serious! I need help."

"Did you get somebody pregnant?" His chubby face twists. "Wait, don't you like guys? You can't get a guy pregnant these days, can you? Hell, I don't know. Times are changing and I can't keep up. The lady at the superstore asked me if I knew my PIN number and I didn't know what the hell she was rambling about."

"Your debit card, gramps. She was asking for the PIN on your debit card."

"I don't have a debit card."

"Yeah, you do."

"That's my credit card."

"It's a debit card."

"Well, what the hell is the difference?" He scans me, hikes up his belt, and shifts in his seat. The wrinkles in his face deepen. "Never mind. We can talk about that later. Tell me why you're ruining my kitchen floor."

"There's a guy." Normally, I wouldn't be sharing all my secrets with my grandpa, but I have no friends here except Gideon. I sure as shit can't talk about Gideon to Gideon.

"A guy? The person you were with last night? Somebody you didn't impregnate?"

"No, gramps." Good grief. I mentally add my brain deteriorating to the list of reasons why I'm not looking forward to getting old. "I didn't impregnate him. It doesn't matter what year it is, a dude can't make a baby with another dude. Gideon doesn't have ovaries."

"Gideon? That's his name?"

"Yes, his name is Gideon Stryker. He's beautiful, gramps." Maybe I shouldn't be spilling my guts like this, but who is gramps going to tell? The cashier at the superstore? "I met him on the first day of school because he chose to sit next to me in chemistry class. We were supposed to just be friends but... we got more chemistry than we bargained for."

He nods and scratches his hairless head. "I'm, uh, not seeing the problem here, kiddo."

"I kissed him!"

"Uh, okay."

"It was amazing. Seriously, I've never felt that way before and I've kissed a lot of dudes."

"Whoa, Elliott." He grunts. "I don't need all the details, kid. Just tell me what you need help with."

I take a deep breath and shake out my nerves. "I need to ask him out."

"*And?*"

"And I need you to tell me how to do it."

He stares at me for a beat before he cracks up laughing. He pounds the table with his fist and runs his hands along his hairless head, cackling his ass off. His round body shakes with laughter. I'm not sure if he's actually crying or if he pulls the handkerchief out of his breast pocket and wipes his eyes for show. When he sees how serious I am, his laughter dies. "Elliott, I'm pretty sure you just ask. There is no science to it."

"Ah, well that's good. He sucks at science."

"You want to take him on a date?"

"Yes. I have take him so I can tell him he's my boyfriend."

His gray eyebrows raise. "You're gonna tell him, huh?"

"I can't take no for an answer, gramps. He's special."

"What do you need my help for?"

I groan. How is he not getting this? "I need your help because I don't know the proper protocol of first dates. Do I bring him something? Take him somewhere fancy? Wear a tie?"

"Look, kid, the only woman I went on a date with was

your grandmother. Our first date, I bought her a lemonade and we sat in the park."

"Damn, gramps. That is corny as hell."

"Oh, piss off, boy. At least I wasn't scared."

"Well, excuse me for wanting to do this right so he doesn't argue when I tell him he's mine."

"I can't really help ya, Elliott. Times were different back then." Gramps turns his attention back to the model car he is building. "Is this date happening tonight?"

"Yep."

"Well, you better go shower. You can't show up on his doorstep looking scrubby. Christ almighty! It's almost four in the afternoon and you're still in your pajamas."

"That's because I've been thinking."

"Go think in the shower or else he's gonna be thinking about slamming the door in your scrubby ass face."

"Really?" I tug at my hair. "That's the only advice you can offer me? Go shower?"

"Look, kid, you know Gideon. Not me. You shouldn't need my advice. You're declaring yourself as his boyfriend so you should know what makes him happy."

"Anything will make him happy." That's the easiest question I've ever had to answer. "Gideon's thankful. Kindness drips off of him. I could show up on his doorstep with a rotten banana and two left shoes and he'd be happy just because I was thinking about him. He isn't fancy either. He's simple. He'd be happy with jeans and pizza."

"There ya go." Gramps smirks at me and brushes his hands off. "You're welcome."

"What the hell? You didn't do anything."

"I sure as shit did. Your ass would still be pacing holes in my floor if it wasn't for me. Good lord, he's just a guy."

I point my finger right in his chubby, wrinkled face. "No, he's not. He's more than that. He's an incredible person and he's mine. I want to make him happy, gramps. I want to do right by him."

"The fact that we are even having this conversation tells me you already are."

"It's not enough."

"Twenty bucks says you fall in love with him."

What the hell? My heart flips twice in my chest and my jaw hits the old white tile. I haven't even told him he's my boyfriend yet. "What?"

"Twenty bucks, Elliott." He winks, turning back to his model car. "You're about to get wrung through the ringer."

I want to argue. I don't. I just turn and head down the hall to the shower. Falling in love with Gideon Stryker? That sounds like a bet I wouldn't mind losing.

———

THE WOODEN DOOR creaks as it opens and a pair of eyes meet mine. They aren't the blue ones I was hoping to see. "Elliott, hi."

"Hi, Mr. Stryker."

"Beck."

"Right, Beck. I was just wondering if Gideon's here?" After I showered and made myself less scrubby looking, I gave myself a pep talk. It didn't really work but nervous is good, right?

"Well, he lives here. So I assume so." Beck turns around in the doorway and tilts his head. "GIDEON! ARE YOU HERE?!"

"DAD! I LIVE HERE."

Beck nods and gives me his attention. "He's here."

"Awesome." I chuckle, shoving my hands in my front pockets. "Could I talk to him?"

"That depends." He looks me over slowly, scanning me

from head to toe. He doesn't have a glare or the stereotypical "dad look" on his face, so I'm not entirely sure if he's trying to intimidate me or if he's looking for something. "Are you the reason my son has a hickey the size of a grapefruit on his neck?"

Ah, shit.

"Uhm, yes. I hope so." Even though I'm about to sweat through my T-shirt, something is telling me that honesty is the best policy when it comes to Gid's parents.

His eyebrows raise. "You hope so?"

"Yeah, because if it wasn't me then it was somebody else and that would mean I'd have to run that person down for putting their lips on my boyfriend."

Beck blinks. "You and Gideon are together? He didn't tell us that."

"Well, that's because he doesn't know it yet. If you'd let me in, I could tell him and he could tell you."

Beck's face full of amusement tells me he is pleased with my honesty. He pulls open the door and gestures with his arm for me to step into their long entryway. "GIDEON! GET DOWN HERE!"

"WHY?!"

Beck's eyes roll behind his glasses as he leads me down the hall. "BECAUSE I SAID SO AND I BIRTHED YOU!"

"LIAR! A YOUNG WOMAN WITH WONDERFUL GENES BIRTHED ME!"

"GIDEON!"

"DAD! I'M COMFORTABLE!"

"YOU'RE LAZY!"

"THE LAST TIME YOU MADE ME MOVE IT WAS TO SCRATCH YOUR BACK!"

"DUDE! IF YOU DON'T COME DOWN HERE, YOU'LL REGRET IT!"

"DOUBT IT!"

Beck sighs deeply and points up the staircase. "Go for it. I need to rest my vocal cords." With that, he turns and heads into the kitchen, leaving me to walk up the stairs in search of my almost boyfriend.

When I reach his bedroom, I prepare myself to knock. Instead, I find his door cracked open. Using my finger, I slowly push it open the rest of the way. I find Gideon lying in his bed on his stomach, facing away from me. I can just make out his profile. His curls are covering his eyes, but his soft smile and fingers tapping at his phone screen are still visible. I hold back my chuckle when I feel my phone go off against my leg and dig into my pocket to pull it free.

GIDEON: HEY, YOU.

ME: HEY, BABY.

I'm so happy his curls don't mask his cheeks flushing.

GIDEON: WHATCHA DOING?

ME: AT THIS VERY MOMENT?

GIDEON: YES. LOL. IS IT SOMETHING WEIRD?

ME: WELL, I DO SORT OF FEEL LIKE A CREEPER. I'VE BEEN STARING AT THIS GUY FOR A WHILE.

GIDEON: OH... LIKE A PICTURE?

ME: NOPE, IN PERSON.

His smile flips. I'd feel like a jackass if he wasn't about to find out it's him I'm staring at and likely won't stop staring at.

GIDEON: WHY ARE YOU STARING AT THEM?

ME: BECAUSE I LIKE LOOKING AT HIM. I'M TRYING TO FIGURE OUT HOW I'M GONNA ASK HIM OUT.

Gid's face falls into his pillow as he lets out a loud groan, kicking his feet like he's throwing a mini tantrum. I stifle my chuckle and ignore the caveman in me that's excited he's pissed I'm checking someone else out. His face stays in his pillow long enough to give me the opportunity to walk over and sit on the edge of his bed. He jerks when he feels the weight change but doesn't move.

He growls. "What do you want?"

"To take you out for pizza."

His body goes stark still, almost like he's arguing with his ears and trying to figure out if he imagined my voice or not.

I make sure there's no doubt. "I'd also like to kiss you again. Actually, if you took your face out of your pillow, I'd do it right now."

His body jerks and flips over. Once his eyes find mine, they widen and his lips form an O when he lets out a little gasp. "Elli..." He sits up quickly.

"Put some shoes on, baby. I'm taking you out for pizza."

"You are?"

"What? You think I just came here to make out or something?"

"Uhm, yes?"

"No. I'm taking you out for pizza. I'm driving, I'm paying, then I'm gonna bring you back here."

His megawatt smile hits me square in the chest. "Is my Elli taking me out on a date?"

He called me his.

"Yes."

He shivers once before his forehead drops to my shoulder and he presses a light kiss there. "Can we get double pepperoni?"

I chuckle. "We can get whatever you want."

"Cool." He slides off the bed and grabs some shoes off the floor. I spot his hickey immediately. It's peeking out of the collar of his shirt and isn't nearly the size of a grapefruit. I know just looking at it that it came from me. That's the soft spot I couldn't keep my lips away from last night.

Slowly, I stand up and wrap my arms around him from behind. He stills when I run my nose along his neck and press a kiss to the soft spot I marked. Eventually, it'll fade and the world won't be able to see it. But it won't matter because I'll make sure the world still knows he's... "Mine."

ELEVEN

SCREAM YOUR HEAD OFF

GIDEON

MINE.

One word. Four letters. So much promise. He barely said the word. It was just a puff of breath across my neck but I heard it like he was standing right next to me with a blow horn.

Mine.

One word sent shivers of anticipation down my spine and kickstarted my heart like I just got done running around the world.

Mine.

My new favorite word. A word I don't think I was supposed to hear because he hasn't said it since.

"Gideon..."

"Yeah?" I snap my head upwards, meeting his questioning eyes. He pushes away his empty plate and reaches for my hand. "What's on your mind?"

"Nothing." I mumble, casting my eyes down at my plate and the pizza sauce smeared all over it. He squeezes my hand and grunts. I think that means I'm supposed to stop bullshitting him. I don't. Because what if he said it but didn't mean it?

"Gideon..."

"Hmm?"

"What's on your mind?" He asks again. This time, it's in a tone that says he wants an actual answer.

So, I give him one. Not because he's being bossy, and I think it's hotter than hell, but because I want an answer too. "I heard you."

He lets go of my hand and uses his thumb to push my chin upwards. "You heard me?"

"In my room. I heard what you said."

"Yeah?" He drops his hand and grins. "Good. You were supposed to hear it."

Shivers run down my spine again. "I was?"

He snorts. "Duh."

"Duh?" I laugh. "I didn't know I was supposed to hear it. You barely whispered it."

"I was right next to your ear."

"So, you meant it? You want me to be yours?"

"You already are mine."

My eyebrows raise in amusement, my eyes staring into the pursed lips that tell me bossy Elliott is out to play. "I am?"

"Uh, yeah. I called you mine. You heard it." He claps his hands together. "Done deal."

I bust out laughing. "Do I get a say in this? Or are you just gonna tell me I'm yours?"

He sits back in the booth, folding his arms over his chest. "I already did tell you. I didn't hear ya objecting to it."

"Well, that's because I wasn't sure if you meant to say it."

"I did." I stare at him, feeling my cheeks heat. He grins

so big, I fear his smile is about to slide right off his face. "You're so damn cute when your face turns into a tomato."

"Dude, stop." I throw my hands over the cheeks that never give me any privacy.

"Aw. Come on, baby." He tugs at my wrists. "I love your tomato face."

"Screw my tomato face." I groan, dropping my wrists.

He spits out the water he just sipped, laughing hysterically. "I'm still not hearing any objections."

"Oh." I try to think of one reason why I should object. Not even a hint of a reason comes to mind. "Would you be mine?"

"Duh, baby. What did you think? I'm yours. You're mine. That's how it works."

"So... we're in a relationship then?" Elli isn't the best talker in the world. The only time he's willingly opened up to me without me having to decode his grunts and breath-filled mumbles was when he told me about his mom. Normally, I don't mind decoding him. But this isn't a topic fit for playing the guessing game.

"Yes."

I chuckle when that's the only answer he provides me with. "So, I can call you my boyfriend then?"

He grunts. "You better."

"We're exclusive. Right?" The thought of sharing Elli makes me want to flip over the booth were in. The look on his face tells me it makes him want to flip this whole damn restaurant.

"I'd like to meet the ballsy son of a gun who tries to swipe my baby away from me."

"I don't want to be swiped, Elli. I like being yours."

He smiles, leaning back in the booth. "You ever been somebody's?"

"Is this you trying to ask me if I've been in a relationship before?"

He nods.

"You first." I challenge.

"No."

"No you don't want to go first? Or no you haven't been in a relationship before?"

"No, I haven't been in a relationship before."

"Really? No ex-boyfriends back home missing you?" I tease.

He snorts. "I have a lot of ex-lovers. I highly doubt any of them miss me."

"Ex-lovers?"

"Uh, yeah." Grabbing his napkin, he starts tearing it to pieces. "Back home, I fooled around a lot. I was the only openly gay kid. Some of the guys in my town thought that was an invitation to use me as their experiment. It was the same thing every time. I've never been in a relationship before because nobody wanted to claim me." The remains of his napkin sprinkle the table. "They were ashamed, I guess."

My heart cracks as I stare into his wide, fearful eyes. I'm starting to understand why he's reluctant to share his past. It's like he thinks I'm going to change my mind about him right here and now. As if I'm suddenly going to find him repulsive or shameful. I grip his hands fiercely. "I will never be ashamed of you, Elliott Oakley."

"I know." He smiles, bringing each of my hands to his lips. "You punched some guy in the face for me."

"I'd do it again."

"I don't doubt it."

I was hoping his eyes would start to sparkle again. They don't. They cast downward to the table littered with dirty silverware. "When I moved here, I told myself I was gonna lay low. No relationships, no hook ups, no nothing. I wasn't about to give someone ammo to mess me up even more than I already was. Then I met you." His eyes hit me like a punch in the gut. "Mess me up, baby. Do your absolute worst. I want you to be mine. Even if it ends in disaster."

"But... why would we end in disaster? Why are you even thinking about that already?"

He's silent for a long time. So long that I think he's reached his maximum capacity of sharing thoughts for the day when he finally speaks. "When my mom died, it was like I got hit by a bus I didn't know was coming towards me. Even though I knew she was sick, it still felt like it came out of nowhere. It fucked me up and ever since she died, it's like my brain is constantly searching for the worst possible outcome of everything."

"So you'll be ready." I whisper, understanding entirely. "Your brain is trying to make sure you don't get hurt again. It's trying to warn you."

He nods miserably. "I'm sorry, Gideon. We're barely together and my brain is already coming up with ways to break us up."

"What would break us up?"

"The paranoia I'm about to have over the ex-someone you're about to tell me about."

My eyebrows lift in shock. "How'd you know I have an ex?"

"Baby, please. You're incredible. Somebody must've noticed."

"Elli, you can lick my washboard abs. You don't have to suck up."

His smile sends a crack right down his solemn face. "I'm looking forward to it. But first, I need to know who to watch for."

"She doesn't live in the state anymore. Her name is

Sadie. We danced together. Dated for a while. We broke up when she left for college. That's pretty much it."

"Do you still talk to her?"

"Sometimes. We text every once in a while. She comes to visit the dance studio whenever she's back in town."

"You gonna tell her about me?"

"Duh." I scoff and shove his shoulder playfully, hoping to lighten the mood. "I'm going to show her a picture and make her all jealous that I have a hot boyfriend."

"What if she tries to get you back?"

"I'll tell her I'm taken."

"Are there any other ex-girlfriends or boyfriends?"

"Uhm, sort of. You know James? From chemistry class?"

"James Appleweed? You dated him?"

"Atcot." I chuckle. "And sorta. He was the one I told you about last night at Fritz. The one guy I kissed but didn't have chemistry with. We went out once and it's not like it was awful or anything, we just didn't click in that way. I told him I thought we'd be better off friends."

"And are you? Better off friends?"

"Not sure. He hasn't spoken to me since."

He flashes me a playful wink. "Maybe he just wanted to steal your trophies."

"Maybe." I laugh, brushing curls from my face.

"So... is that it then? No other girlfriends or trophy thieves?"

"Nope. Just them."

"You promise?" The sudden vulnerability clogged in his throat kills me.

"I promise, Elli. We've been official for all of two minutes—"

"We've been official since you jumped me in a stairwell. You just didn't know."

"Perhaps, you could start informing me of things." I smirk. "Communication is key, ya know?"

"Communication, huh? I'm not great at that."

"Eh. You're doing pretty good right now."

"Really? Talking about my past non-relationships kind of makes me feel like I'm stuck in some chaotic tornado I can't get out of."

"I'll help you through it. I love chaos."

"You love chaos?" He stares at me like I just confessed to having a third arm hidden beneath my shirt.

"Yeah." Reaching for his shaky hands, I give them a squeeze, hoping to steady them. "When you were a kid, did you ever just run around in circles, screaming your head off just because it was the best goddamn thing ever? People would watch you in confusion because they had no idea why you were doing it? But you kept going because for some reason, it was the most fun you'd ever had?"

He smiles, lost in a memory. "It drove my mama nuts. I loved it."

"So, let's do that now. You and me. Let's make some chaos. The kind you don't want to escape from. Let's just run around in circles, laughing and smiling at each other. Enjoy life with me, Elli. Trust that I'm not gonna do anything to hurt you. Just jump into the chaos with me and scream your head off."

That was absolutely one of the most outrageous things I've ever said. It made complete sense in my head. I'm staring at him, wondering if it's making sense in his too.

His face is expressionless—not so much as a twitch. He drops my hands, grabs my face, and practically jumps across the booth to fold his lips over mine. I groan deeply, meeting him halfway. When my fingers find my favorite spot, I melt right all over the dirty table.

"Uh, excuse me?"

Elli rips his lips from mine with a sigh. "Yeah?" He wipes his mouth and stares up at the waitress poised at the end of our table.

"Here's your change." She thrusts some cash at his chest. "Maybe you should use it to buy a room."

"Thanks for the idea." He flashes me a wink. "Come on, baby. Let's go make some chaos."

TWELVE

A REALLY FAST BIKE

ELLIOTT

"OAKLEY! CATCH!" My head snaps upward just in time to see a rag flying at my head. "Wipe up, kid. Shift's over."

"Yeah, one sec." I tuck the rag into my back pocket and dive back towards the junior dragster I've been helping to restore. Speed is a unique auto shop because it specializes in motored vehicles used for racing—which is why I'm double checking engine work on a dragster instead of changing tires on somebody's Lexus.

Thatcher 'Spanky' Scott is apparently a racing legend here at Speed. It's both cool and frustrating I'm constantly being compared to gramps. I used to be a drag racer when I was a kid. I started at the age of five, but my father made me quit when I was thirteen and got into a crash that resulted in a hospital visit. I never had my chance to roll with the big dogs. That's the frustrating part of being compared to gramps—I never got a chance to keep training. If I would've, I know I could've made him eat dirt.

"Dude!" Dan, the owner of this place and the man who can have an orgasm just by looking at a sweet car, whacks my back. "I know you love this job, but you're seventeen. I'll get my ass in trouble if you exceed your hours. Child labor laws."

"So, I'll clock out and keep working. Nobody will know."

The cigarette in his mouth bounces when he laughs. "So I can get in trouble for paying you under the table?"

"You don't need to pay me. Call it volunteering."

"The dragster will still be here next week, Elliott. Go enjoy your weekend."

We have a stare down for a moment, his eyebrows raising above his amused dark eyes. He blows out a long drag of his cigarette and stares at me pointedly until I pull the rag free and start wiping the oil from my fingers. It's still early enough that I can make an appearance at Gideon's family dinner.

He's been begging me to attend for the duration of the three weeks we've been officially dating. Despite the fact that it physically pains me telling him no, I didn't want to ask to leave work early when they'd just brought in a dragster that looks like it's been sitting in a barn for ten years. I made it my life's mission to restore it.

Of course, Gideon wasn't upset in the slightest when I explained this to him. He told me he is happy I have a job I'm so excited about. Despite his astonishing support, I know he wants me to meet the rest of his family. He's just putting my needs first. Because he's incredible.

I throw in the towel. Literally. "Fine. The dragster is almost done anyway, and I'm not ready to let it go yet."

Dan chuckles through a puff of smoke. "Like the car, do ya?"

"It's a dragster, Dan. Not a car. And are you shitting me? It's amazing. A classic. If this was mine, I'd build a huge garage solely for keeping it in."

"You want it?"

"Yeah, right." I laugh. "Maybe one day though."

"It's yours if you want it. One condition though."

"What? I don't get arrested for grand theft auto?"

"Nope." He pulls another drag of his cigarette and lets it out on a sigh. "You have to race it."

My stomach does a backflip. "What?"

"Look, kid. We all knew who you were when you got hired in."

"The legend's grandson?"

"You're a legend in your own right." He throws his cigarette butt on the concrete floor and stomps on it. "Could've been something big."

"What? With drag racing? Dan, I haven't raced in over four years. Not to mention I was a *junior* drag racer."

"You were a sponsored racer who won five titles in a row. You got voted Rookie of the year twice. That's a big deal."

That's where he's wrong. It *was* a big deal. It isn't so much anymore. As soon as I thumped my head hard enough to need hospital time, my dad forced me out of it. I cried for weeks. Racing was what I had. After a while, my dad sold my dragster and life went on. It wasn't what I had anymore. It was just a piece.

"Look, Elliott, I'm not here to pressure you but Spanky tells me you still follow racing."

"Of course I do. I'll always love it. I just don't do it."

"You could."

I blow out a heavy breath. "I'm sorry?"

"Elliott, you recognize this dragster?"

I peer down at the long body and worn seat. "Should I?"

"Considering it's yours. Yes."

My body jerks roughly. *I'm sorry... what?*

"Uhm, no. My dad sold it."

"To an anonymous buyer who happened to be your

grandfather."

"Excuse me?" My jaw joins his cigarette butt on the concrete.

"Elliott." He laughs, running his hand over the dragster. "This dragster has been parked in our garage for four years. We took the body off when you got hired. We thought maybe you'd like to be the one to get it ready to race again."

"Where is it?" I look frantically around the room as if the body of my dragster is going to fall from the sky. "Where's the body? Is it protected? Are there dents?"

"No. But it needs a paint job. Badly. You up for it?"

"Up for it?" I'm not sure my mind is fully registering this conversation. "Restoring my dragster and racing again?"

"Races start in April, kid. We've got time to get you back where you used to be. Speed is gonna sponsor. All you have to do is say yes."

"Okay. So, what? You and gramps just planned this behind my back? Oh hey, the best junior racer in the nation doesn't have a dad anymore so let's push him back into racing? What the hell? I've been working on my own dragster for three weeks and nobody told me? That's total bullshit, Dan. What do you expect to happen? I'm not the best anymore. I haven't been inside a dragster in four years."

He gestures towards the dragster. "So get in. You said it was almost done, right? Engine looks good?"

"Uh, yeah. Just needs new tires. But that doesn't mean..."

"Get in, kid. I'll start it up for ya. It's just like riding a bike."

"Actually, this is way fucking faster than a bike."

"You scared?"

I scoff. "Hell, no. I was devastated when I couldn't race anymore."

"Which is why I bought your dragster."

I snap my head towards the sound of gramps' voice. He's leaning against a toolbox, arms crossed over his chest. "You called me bawling the night your daddy took away your helmet. I called him and told him what a prick he was. I bought your dragster just in case you ever wanted to give it a go again."

"Oh, really? 'Cause it looks like you're forcing me into it."

"Oh shut your trap, boy. I'm doing no such thing. I'm giving you a choice. You can restore it and keep it in my garage until I die or you can race it. I'll help coach you, get you ready for the season. You won't be eighteen until May which means you have one more season to take back your title before we decide to roll with the big dogs."

"Alright." I link my fingers behind my head. "Can we just slow down for a second?"

I've never given myself an opportunity to think about whether or not I'd want to race again. If my father said no, that was that. I didn't figure I'd get the chance before I turned eighteen. Sure, I could've started up again once I graduated but if you aren't a recent junior title holder, you'll almost never get a sponsor to help you 'roll with the big dogs.'

"Elliott." Gramps' rough hands grip my shoulders. "If you don't want this, I'm fine with that. But I wanted you to have the choice. You loved racing with every ounce of your soul. I can't count the number of times your mama called me to tell me you snuck out to go practice. The damn police picked you up four times for driving that dragster on the open road."

I chuckle, remembering the way mama wanted to punish me but never did. She thought being passionate about something was necessary. She thought ambition and drive were what made great people.

Mama fought with my father about taking away racing. I heard them at night shouting at each other. In the end, he won—because he always does. Even when she refused to fight anymore, he still fucking won.

"Here's the thing, boy. You loved this sport. You used to tell me when you got your own car you were gonna find an air freshener that smelt like—"

"Burnt rubber." I grin. "My favorite smell."

"You don't have to do this if you don't want to, Elliott. But after everything you've been through, I'm goddamn sick of watching things you love get ripped away from you. I can't bring back everything. What I can bring back is this. It's yours if you want it."

For the first time in four years, I give myself a moment to think about being back on the track. The memories I'm hit with feel euphoric. Strapped in so tight I can barely move. My heart stalling with nerves until I see the green light and it kickstarts with my car. I remember the challenge of holding the wheel straight when the speed forces you to shake. I can even remember the way it felt the second I crossed the finish line and scored my second winning title. My mama was jumping up and down, gramps was grinning, and everybody up in the stands was screaming.

I jump into my dragster carefully, gripping the wheel and placing my feet on the pedals. Despite the way my legs have grown in four years, I still feel like the inside of this dragster was made especially for me.

Dan was right—it's just like riding a really fast bike. He starts the engine I just spent almost a month restoring. Gramps' wrinkled face sparkles, his eyes wide and hopeful. Anticipation and excitement explode inside of me, and I match his knowing smirk with my own.

"When do we start training?"

THIRTEEN

WET JEANS

ELLIOTT

I RAP my knuckles against the large wooden door for the third time, resisting the urge to put my ear to the wood and listen for any sounds of life. The number of cars parked in the driveway tell me there are people inside. Unless everybody got abducted by aliens and is currently trapped inside a spaceship on their way to meet Starlord and the rest of the Guardians.

Which is pretty unlikely.

I knock again because I'm not sure if Gideon and I are at the stage in our relationship where it's acceptable to just mosey my way inside his house. Despite that I've been here more than a dozen times since we've been dating, I don't know what the protocol is or if there's some sort of moment that defines when I'm allowed to barge in without formally being invited.

I'm severely overthinking this. Everybody is probably out back on the patio, swimming or something. I repress the urge to call him and ask for help. I reach for the handle like an adult.

The door swings open before I have a chance to prove to myself I'm not a total chicken.

"Who are you?"

I blink, scanning the man who just pulled open the front door, very suspiciously wondering how he didn't rip the door off the hinges. The dude is *huge*. At least a foot taller than me with shoulders as wide as my dragster and biceps comparable to the size of a bowling bowl. Since he isn't already intimidating enough, he's got a tattoo sleeve running from his wrist up to the edge of his short sleeve.

"Hi." I clear my throat. "I'm Elliott."

"Ah. Gideon's boyfriend." He lifts his arm and waves me in. "Come on in, kid."

"Thanks."

"I'm Ryder." He says, shutting the door behind me and extending his hand. "Piper's dad."

Of course, the big scary dude helped create Piper. She may be little but she sure as shit is intimidating when she wants to be.

"Nice to meet you." I return his handshake, tightening my grip on his so he doesn't rip my arm off.

"You too. Everybody is out back. Food's on the picnic table. Help yourself."

"Thank you, Mr. Dawson."

"Ryder." He grunts, slapping me on the back and pounding back towards the living room and through the patio doors.

What a head trip. These people are allowed to walk around and help themselves in a home that isn't theirs and they don't care about formality. My father would've had my tongue if I didn't address Ryder as Mr. Dawson.

Toto, we ain't in Kansas anymore.

I slide off my boots, abandoning them in the entryway and shuffling towards their patio. The outdoor adventure land is probably the size of gramps' whole house. It's a two-tiered concrete patio complete with a table and chairs set and a few fancy couches surrounding a small fire pit. There's a special place on the patio for a grill and a built in cooler. They've got a speaker system set up, playing softly while they splash around in the pool.

Their pool is in the center of it all, spanning the length of half the house. Gideon's sitting on Preston's shoulders, attempting to take down Piper and Nate in a game of chicken. I use all my willpower not to oogle his shirtless, wet body.

I tell myself only a pervert would oogle the way water is dripping down the ridges in his chest around his entire family.

And then I do it anyway.

Just for a second.

"Elli!"

Piper uses Gideon's distracted gaze as an opportunity to whack him in the side and throw him into the pool. Gideon's shout mixes with the sound of his body smacking the surface. Droplets of water fly upward and splash the edges of the patio surrounding the pool.

When his head emerges, he's halfway across the pool, swimming towards me with the makings of a grin forming on his face.

"Elli. You came." He presses his palms to the edge of the pool, lifting himself out of the water with ease. Water drips down his body as he approaches me, his hands swatting at his hair. It's the first time I'm seeing it wet. It looks so much longer without his dry, springy curls intact.

"Hey, baby." I reach outward to pull him in for a hug. "Sorry I'm kind of late."

"That's okay, Elli. I'm happy you're here." He swats at my hands. "Don't hug me. I'll get your clothes soaking wet."

"I don't care." I really, really don't. "They'll dry."

His cheeks warm. "Let me get a towel first."

I drop my hands and watch him jog to the other side of the patio, yanking a towel from a wooden chest and drying off at the speed of the light. He abandons it on top of the chest and jogs back over to me, throwing his body into mine.

"I'm really happy you came." He pushes his face into my neck. I probably smell like nitromethane and grease. He clearly doesn't give a shit. "How was work?"

"It was really great. I actually have something to tell you."

"Yeah?" He kisses my cheek, bouncing on his toes with excitement. "What is it?"

"I'll tell you later." I link our hands, his still damp from the pool water and mine still stained with grease. "Introduce me to your family."

I'm idling with anticipation over Gideon's reaction when I tell him I'm getting back into racing. But tonight isn't all about me. It's about him and finally giving him the chance to introduce me to his family. His eyes lighting up like sparks on the cement after I spin a burnout tell me just how much this means to him.

"Okay." He squeezes my hand. "Everybody is probably staring at us anyway."

I risk a glance over his shoulder, finding his assumption correct. His family is sitting around the patio, not even attempting to hide that they're all staring directly at us. His cousins in the pool are smirking, and Nate's making some obscene hand gesture.

"Nate is ridiculous."

"I'd be worried if he wasn't." Gideon tugs my hand, dragging me towards the waiting adults. "Don't worry. My family is nice. And you can call them by their first names."

Ah, my boyfriend knows me well.

"I met Ryder already. He answered the door when I knocked."

"You don't have to knock, Elli. Just walk in."

Apparently, the moment that said I'm allowed to bust in had already happened and I missed it.

"This is Elliott." Gideon announces, thrusting his hand at me like I'm a prize on the Wheel of Fortune. "He has two trophies."

I fight a laugh. "Uh, hi. Nice to meet you guys."

Gideon's grip on mine tightens as he uses his other hand to start pointing. "This is Uncle Jude and Aunt Brenna, Nate's parents."

I extend my hand and mumble a hello, gawking at Jude's facial features. Nate is a carbon copy of his father. If it weren't for the stubble on Jude's face, I'd say those two could easily swap lives for a day.

I shake more hands, mumbling a polite greeting to Sebastian, Mimi, Quinn, Ryder, Marisa, and Jack. After that, I'm dragged to the edge of the pool and introduced to Preston's brother, Nate's sister, and Piper's sister.

I flash a wave, my mind working double time to remember everybody's names. Back in Iowa, it was me and my parents. I was an only child and so were they. I had no direct aunts and uncles. The only cousins I had were technically my parent's cousins and would never play a single thing with me when I was younger.

When gramps used to come to Iowa to visit us, I'd be out of this world excited because he'd always make time just for me. We'd spend time at the racetrack, go to the park, go for ice cream. He was really the only one who made an effort, and it sucked he lived five states away.

I didn't have Friday night family dinners growing up. No big pool to play chicken in or have competitions on who can make the biggest splash. There were no stories around a bonfire or fights over a bag of chips. It was just me, sneaking out alone to drive my dragster and spending the rest of the weekend in my room grounded.

"Do you feel overwhelmed?"

"Yeah." I nod, tilting my head and flashing him a shaky smile. "But only because I didn't grow up with a family this big."

"Well, you can have this one now."

Simple as that. I just met them, probably already forgot which kid belongs to which set of parents, but he'll share his family with me anyway. That overwhelms me so much more than all the people still gawking at us.

"I'm sorry it took me so long to get myself here."

"That's okay, Elli. Next time, you can bring your suit and we'll school Nate in a game of chicken."

Spending Friday nights hanging with my boyfriend and my new friends will be a lot different from spending them alone in my room with Netflix and junk food, tuning out my father's rambling. Leaving Iowa kind of feels like I got out of jail or something—like I was living life but missing out on all the things that actually made it fun. Or as Preston says "Polaroid worthy." Ain't nobody wants to see a picture of me with my hand in a Doritos bag.

"That sounds like a lot of fun."

"It will be." Gideon squeezes my hand. "Especially when Nate cries."

I throw my head back, cackling with laughter. "Will we get a trophy?"

"We better." He scoffs, bringing my hand to his lips and kissing my knuckles softly. "Do you have your phone and wallet in your pocket?"

"No." I tilt my head. "My phone is in my car with my wallet. Why? Wanna rob me?"

He shakes his head, stepping closer. My body heats when his arms come around my waist, his nose brushing against mine. My eyes flutter closed, waiting for the moment his lips make contact with mine.

And then we're tipping. His grip on me tightens, and I realize what he's doing too late.

We smack the water, our bodies separating from the force of the hit. The cool water feels fantastic on the hot, sticky skin that's a prerequisite for restoring racecars for hours.

What doesn't feel fantastic is the chaffing in my jeans and the sudden wedgie I can't seem to remove.

"Gideon Mason!" I shout, spitting water from my mouth the second my head hits the surface.

"Oh, shit!" Nate bellows. "He just middle named you, bro."

Gideon slaps his hand over his mouth, holding back a burst of laughter.

"You little sneak. What if I couldn't swim?"

He drops his hand, flashing me a lopsided grin. "I would've saved you."

"Oh, really?" I swim towards him, our bodies linking together like two magnets that don't like to be apart. His legs lock around my waist, my arms secured around his back. "You would've saved me?"

"Yeah. I would've pulled you out like a hero and given you mouth to mouth."

"You goober. You don't have to drown me to give me mouth to mouth."

His fingers dig into the place he can't ever seem to keep himself from touching. I'm starting to think he doesn't even realize he's doing it—just plays with the ends of my hair as an afterthought. "Are you mad at me?"

It seems physically impossible for me to be mad at him.

Not when there's a twinkle in his eye that tells me all he wants is to include me in all aspects of his chaotic life.

"Yes." I lie. "Because I have a wedgie that's gonna take me a day to remove."

I swallow his laughter with my lips. A sweet sigh flows from his mouth to mine while we sink deeper into this pool and all the feelings buzzing between us. I'm not going to overanalyze him or the feelings or why it feels so natural to have him in my arms.

I'm just going to enjoy it.

It's been so long since I truly enjoyed anything for myself.

"Wait." He drags his lips from mine. "What happened at work? You said you had to tell me something great."

"Oh, yeah." I guess between wishing his family had name tags and attempting to sew our lips together, I forgot. "Do you remember how I've been fixing up that dragster?"

"Yeah. Did you get it done?"

"Almost. But that's not the great part. The great part is that it's mine."

He blinks. "Wait... what?"

"When I was thirteen, some anonymous buyer bought my dragster. Turns out, the buyer was gramps. The dragster I've been fixing is mine, G."

His face morphs into a cross between disbelief and excitement. Exactly what I was feeling when I was attempting to wrap my mind around it.

"Are you gonna start racing again?"

"Yeah. Gramps is gonna coach and Speed is gonna sponsor. I'll start training as soon as it's restored."

"No way. Elli, that's awesome. When's your first race?"

"The season starts in April."

He hoots, planting a kiss on my lips. "I can't wait to watch you win another trophy."

My smile tears my face in half. Not because he's excited for me, or even because he mentioned a trophy. *Nope.* My smile is for us and the way he casually told me he still pictures us together in April.

"You can watch me practice sometime if you want to."

"If I want to?" He looks at me like I just asked if he wanted to cut his own leg off. "Are you crazy? Of course I do. Elli, this awesome. I'm so excited for you."

"Thanks, babe."

"Tell me when you're gonna start practicing. I'll be there."

"Have you ever been to a drag race before?"

"No." He kisses my cheek. "But this will be extra cool because it's you racing."

"You don't have to suck up. I'll give you my autograph."

"Nice. I can't wait to sell it and make millions."

I chuckle, holding him close until he starts to shiver. "We should get out before we turn blue."

He reluctantly pulls away and hoists himself from the pool, fetching two towels and tossing me one. What seems like a gallon of water pools at my feet while I attempt to sop up the water coming from my jeans. I peel off my damp shirt and set it aside with the towel.

"You wanna stay for a while? Make S'mores?"

If I wouldn't have already been planning to stay, the hopeful look in his eyes would've done me in.

"Sure. I'd love that."

Ignoring how uncomfortable my wet jeans are, I sit next to him, hoping the fire will dry me off quickly.

My face heats when Gideon starts talking a mile a minute about my racing and my trophies and how really fucking awesome I am.

He turns his head, his curls reappearing from the heat of the fire. The glow from the flames warms his face. I cup his cheek and kiss him softly, giving no cares about the hoots from his family.

"What... what was that for?"

"I don't know." I lie, linking my hand with his and avoiding telling him the truth.

That kiss was full of gratitude. For him and the way he's so effortlessly proud of me and my accomplishments without knowing at all how much it affects me.

My mama used to be the only one that'd come to my races—my only fan unless gramps was able to travel to us.

Now I have Gideon. Something strange erupting in my stomach, and the sight of him cackling with chocolate smeared across his lips is telling me he isn't going anywhere.

FOURTEEN

THE EXCEPTION

ELLIOTT

THE RICHTER SCALE was developed eons ago with the sole purpose of measuring the magnitude of an earthquake. People say that when stuck in the worst part of an earthquake, it starts with an overwhelming jolt to your body followed by a few seconds of violent shaking, causing difficulty to hold your limbs still or walk in a straight line. There's really no way to escape it. You can't close your eyes, turn your head away, or cover your ears. Nothing. It's the kind of thing that rocks your body—something you feel deep down into your bones. Even if you know it's coming, you're still going to flinch.

Wally Parks started drag racing and created the NHRA almost twenty years after Charles Richter named an earthquake scale after himself. There was no way Richter could have known that the scale he created to measure the incredible strength of the earth cracking in two could also be used to describe the unique feeling of being behind the wheel of a dragster. It starts the same as an earthquake would. Except it's all intentional and nobody wants to escape it.

From the second the light turns green on the Christmas

tree countdown, every racer in the history of ever prays for the violent jolt, followed by seconds of incessant shaking. We pray for our limbs to turn to jello and love the struggle that comes with attempting to hold the steering wheel straight. Most people try to run from an earthquake—pack up their family and get away from it before it comes.

Drag racers willing walk right into it, strapping themselves in arm restraints that tie directly into our seatbelts. We want no way out. And the bigger the jolt, the better.

People who don't follow racing take one look at a drag race and claim it's easy. I mean, all we have to do is drive in a straight line, right? *Wrong.* Try driving in a straight line in the middle of an earthquake with an engine behind your head, roaring so loud, you can't hear anything else. Sound easy? It's not. But damn is it exhilarating. I wouldn't trade the inability to walk straight afterward, the permanent smell of burnt rubber, or the sound of the engine blowing my eardrums out for anything.

Drag racing is so much more than obnoxiously loud cars. It's a sport, a passion, a way of life, and a feeling so powerful you fall into sensory overload and get rocked with a sensation it takes an earthquake scale to measure.

I took a four year hiatus and thought maybe I'd grown out of my love for drag racing. I worried the spell had been recast on someone else and I'd have to find my passion somewhere else.

I finished my dragster alongside Dan, airbrushing new paint on the body, all while praying I was wrong about the spell being recast.

The second I slipped into a brand new fire suit and a pair of ugly racing shoes, Spanky strapped me in. I knew instantly how terribly I craved for the light to turn green so I could drive straight into an earthquake.

"Elli!"

My memories leave me so I can chuckle at my boyfriend, barreling down the track, arms flailing as I maneuver my helmet off my sweaty head.

"Holy shit. That was amazing. You were so fast!"

"He wasn't fast enough."

Gramps is one tough coach. I love his grumpy old ass for it. If I'm gonna win back my title, I can't pussyfoot around.

I peel off my gloves and peer into his wrinkled forehead. "How much faster?"

"At least a second."

"I can do it."

"I know you can, boy. So quit driving like a sissy and step on the damn gas."

"Driving like a sissy?!" Gideon gapes at gramps, looking shocked this old geezer has the audacity to call me a sissy. "That was so fast. HE'S GONNA WIN SO MANY TROPHIES!"

"Baby." I chuckle, squeezing his shoulder. "Why are you yelling?"

"Oh." His tomato face starts to appear. "I guess I got overly excited."

Gramps whistles and starts hobbling off the track. I leave my dragster where it's at and grab Gideon's hand with the one that isn't holding my helmet so I can lead him off the track. It's unnecessary. There's only one possible building we could be going into but I can't help myself. Gramps says I'm a fool for love.

I think he needs to lay off the oldies music.

"Boy, your boyfriend is almost as bad as your mama." Gramps winks at Gideon over his shoulder. "His mama had a T-shirt with his face on it."

Gideon's eyes light up like he just witnessed a unicorn fall from the sky. "Where do I get one of those?"

"G." I squeeze his hand. "You don't have to wear a shirt with my face on it."

"I want to." He argues. "I'm supporting my racer boyfriend. Do you have foam fingers?"

"We can get you one." Gramps calls over his shoulder. "Boy, you better stick around. You'll fit in nicely with the top fuel fans."

"What's a top fuel fan?"

Gramps pushes open the door to the track's locker room. I hold the door from behind him and let Gideon go first before I answer.

"Top fuel dragsters are the big dogs. Professional racers drive them. The fan base is insane."

"Hold up!" Gideon cocks his head, gaping at me. "There are dragsters bigger than the one you just drove?"

Gramps snorts and eases down on a wooden bench. "Boy, that's a junior racer."

"Baby, top fuels are way bigger and way more powerful. They can complete a quarter mile in under four seconds. One dragster is more powerful than the first four lines of the Daytona 500. Them suckers burn through twelve gallons of nitromethane in one run."

He blinks. "I don't know what language you're speaking, but I'm loving it."

My lips pull into a smile. "They're really fast. Basically."

"Basically." He muses. "You're gonna be some sweet ass drag racer one day, flying down a racetrack at the speed of light."

"Basically, yeah."

He whoops. "My crush on you just escalated."

"Your crush?" I feign hurt. "That's all?"

"Maybe I'll let you take me on a date once you get that top fuel thingy."

Gramps' raspy cackle fills the small room. "Boy, you kill me."

Gideon just smiles his megawatt smile, swaying back and forth on his feet, not giving a damn in the world about the strange smell of sweat and burnt rubber likely permeating his nostrils.

I unzip my fire suit, revealing my sweaty T-shirt underneath. Gideon eyes me. I might be getting excited he's checking me out if that's actually what he's doing. It's not. He's been my best friend for months, my boyfriend for a month and a half. I'm very familiar with his pursed lips and narrowed eyes.

"Listen, fire lord." I chuckle. "The suit is fire safe."

"Are you sure? It doesn't look thick enough."

"Thick enough? Gideon, I'm driving a dragster not fighting fires."

His eyes narrow like he's some overcautious fireman who hasn't lit himself up four times. "What if the engine blows up and you turn into a human fireball?"

"I won't turn into a human fireball if the engine blows up."

He puts his hands on his slender waist and cocks his hips. "How do you know?"

I slip off my fire suit the rest of the way and shake my jean-clad legs out. "Because when I was thirteen, my engine exploded. As you can see, I'm very much alive and didn't turn into a human fireball."

He looks stunned. "Well, the fire suit must've worked then."

Gramps cackles again. "Boy, I've been in the racing scene a long time. Nobody has turned into a fireball."

Gideon's narrowed gaze focuses on Spanky. They have what seems to be a staring contest before Gideon's face relaxes. "Alright. I'll trust you."

"What?" I scoff. "You trust him and not me?"

"Sorry, babe. He's a legend, you're not."

Gramps doubles over laughing. "I knew I liked you for more than just your respect of a good model car."

Gideon winks at him and focuses his gaze back on me. "Babe, I gotta go to the studio. Are you sure you can come tonight?"

I roll my eyes. "Gideon, it's your birthday dinner. I'm not gonna miss that."

"Today is only Sunday. My real birthday isn't even until Tuesday. You should practice."

"I'm not practicing during your birthday dinner, you goober." I grip his waist and yank him into my body. "We're having a party tonight and I'll be there."

"It's the second week of December." He argues. "It's going to start snowing soon. You have to practice."

"Gideon." I kiss his nose. Of course, he's more concerned about me practicing than being in attendance for his eighteenth birthday celebration. Since the first time he watched me drive weeks ago, he's been incredibly support-ive. Gramps says it's because he saw the happy beams coming off my face and loves to see me all cheery. I think he needs to get his eyes checked if he's seeing happy beams coming off my face. "I'm coming."

"He better go." Gramps grunts when he heaves himself off the bench. "He's been stressing about what to get you for weeks. I thought he was going to faint. Pacing around my damn kitchen like a lunatic."

Thatcher Scott, everybody. 74-year-old embarrassment with no filter.

"You got me a present?" Gideon's eyes sparkle, his smile lighting me up in a way no exploding engine ever could. "You didn't have to get me anything."

I've learned over the years through observation and a lot

of movies that when your significant other says you don't have to get them anything, you better get them something really damn good. Gideon is the exception to that rule. When he says you don't have to get him anything, he means it. Gideon would just be happy with a phone call or a telegram from 1842.

Gideon Stryker is turning out to be the exception to a lot of rules.

"Which is exactly why I got you something, babe."

"Well, thank you." His cheeks redden as he presses a kiss to the underside of my chin. "I'll love it."

Since the moment it showed up on my doorstep, I've been going back and forth with my decision. After he met gramps a few days after we sealed the deal, he started in with the model cars. At first, I thought Gideon was faking his interest just to be polite to my gramps. After a few visits, it dawned on me he was actually really intrigued. Gramps helped me find an old model fire engine on eBay. I have high hopes he's going to go nuts.

After I got a long lecture about the important difference between a firetruck and a fire engine, I was pretty sure I ordered the right thing.

"I gotta go, Elli."

"Okay." I cup his face. "Gimme a kiss."

His voice drops. "Spanky is watching."

"No, he's not."

"Yeah, I am." Gramps laughs hard enough to rattle his gut.

"Then close your eyes, old man."

"Two seconds."

I yank Gideon's face to mine and give him a kiss that lasts a lot longer than two seconds.

FIFTEEN

CAKE WAR

ELLIOTT

THERE ARE a lot of reasons why I loved my mama with all the pieces of me. The way she seemed to sweep in and shield me even during the moments I never asked for it was only one of them. She felt a lot like a force of nature.

Unstoppable.

Unchallengeable.

Unforgettable.

But she was also an enigma. A mystery in her own way because while she felt forceful and displayed undeniable strength in her weakest moments, there was always something unquestionably calm about her. She was gentle in a way that still radiated strength. She was nurturing and soft —kind in every way a person could be. When the one who was supposed to love her fiercely ripped her apart during her weakest hours, there was still nothing but the odd combination of tender strength inside her body as she held my hand.

She was caring in an almost unthinkable way—a way that everyone expects mothers to be but aren't always. Maybe I'm biased—because I'm her son and was conditioned to love her the moment I was born and laid on her chest. I don't think that's the case. There are a lot of reasons why children start off loving their parents with every bone in their tiny little bodies but grow up to lose mass respect. Unlike my father, my mama had captured my respect and held it until her fragile body couldn't hold on anymore. After her last few breaths, her generous and caring spirit seemingly stayed behind and hovered around me like a shield until I was able to pack my things and drive across country to live with an old man who calls himself Spanky.

I think maybe that's why I'm so drawn to Gideon—he exudes the same type of tender force my mama did. Even when he was slamming his clenched fist into another person's face, there was still a sense of tranquility in the air. Even when he's being beat down, he still finds it inside himself to be kind.

I've overanalyzed the fact that I'm falling for a guy who reminds me of my mama way more times than I can count. It sounds freakishly strange. When I mentioned it to gramps the day I ordered Gideon's present, he looked at me like I'd just told him racing was a waste of time. I proceeded to ramble for a while, trying to explain it wasn't Gideon's looks that reminded me of my mama. It was his aroma. The sort of vibes someone got about his personality when they first met him. My mama and Gideon are the same that way. One conversation with them and you know they're good people.

If I'd only explained that to gramps a little better, he'd stop cracking inappropriate jokes.

But I didn't know how to explain it then. I might have never known how to explain it if it weren't for a few hours ago when I showed up at the studio and watched as he crouched down low and placed stickers on the hands of eager children calling him "Mr. Giieeeoon." Even as the kids slapped his face excitedly and tugged on his shirt, begging for attention, he didn't push them away or act weirded out that their chubby fingers were poking him in the face over and over. He actually seemed to revel in hugging the same kid three times because they apparently forgot they already hugged him and giving out double stickers to the kids who ripped it off their hand to oogle the design and then proceeded to let it fall on the floor.

"Dude, you're being so obvious."

I blink away my thoughts and look to my left, finding Nate sitting beside me at the picnic table, scarfing down his third piece of Gideon's chocolate cake. "Huh?"

He points his fork across the patio. "You. Staring. It's gross. Knock it off."

I flick a chunk of cake off his fork and stare happily at Gideon sitting in a lounge chair, talking excitedly with my gramps about his fire engine. He flipped his lid when he opened it. Said thank you more times than was necessary, and I was overcome with the strange urge to poke him. I thought maybe my finger will go right through him and I'll discover he isn't actually real. If he was anybody else, I'd say the kindness and enthusiasm for giving kids adhesive objects on the afternoon of his birthday party, or overdoing the thanks after receiving a gift was a punk act to make himself look better. But nope. Not Gideon. He's sitting next to my gramps, emitting happiness in a way I used to find utterly annoying on anybody but my mama.

Add another rule Gideon is the exception of.

"Did you just flick my cake?"

"Yup."

My smirk fades the second I'm whacked in the side of the face with a pile of frosting. I gape at Nate like he's lost his ever-loving mind. "Dude. You did not just do that."

"Don't ever flick a man's cake, Elliott." He points his

fork at me, his eyes narrowing like he just uttered a prophet and is trying to sew the idea into my brain.

"Ooooo! Frosting." I have no time to blink before my boyfriend comes from nowhere, grips my head, and licks the side of my face. "Yum."

This family is so weird.

I run my hand down my cheek, doing nothing but smearing saliva and leftover frosting into my scruffy face. I peer into his guilty eyes. "Aren't you supposed to be talking to gramps?"

He plops down next to me, licking frosting off his lip. "I'm attempting to give him a break from my excessive fire engine rambling."

Nate groans. "Great. Now you get to torture us."

Gideon tries to act pissed. "Gimme my cake back, assmunch!"

Assmunch? That's interesting. I'll have to use that one.

Nate raises his fork in the air and bellows loudly. "Neverrrrrrrr!"

For the third time in less than three minutes, I'm caught entirely off guard as Gideon's slender body flies across the top of the wooden table and slams Nate's cake filled plate into his smug face.

"Dude." Nate gapes at Gideon, chunks of cake dropping off his stunned face. "Did you just initiate a cake war?"

There's a long stretch of silence as they stare at each other. Gideon is working hard not to erupt into a fit of laughter at Nate attempting to get his tongue to reach the frosting on his forehead. After a second, Nate stands up and scoops a handful of cake off his face.

"Elli, run." Gideon blurts.

What the hell? "Run where?"

"Just run." He commands, rolling off the picnic table like Jackie Chan in that one karate movie and running full speed at the folding table next to the sliding doors that holds the cake.

His warning dawns on me a second too late.

"CAKE WAR!" Nate's scream rattles my brain the same moment he plops what's left over of his cake on the top of my head.

After that, the green light goes off and cake starts flying. Massive pieces of spongy batter and sugary frosting are pelting my body, coming from all different directions. I sit there like a loser, gaping at the swarm of people dodging hits and scooping the ammo off the patio to reuse. My eyes land on Knox and Beck stepping out of the house and onto their sticky patio. I hold my breath as Knox gets wailed in the face with a pile of dirty frosting. Beck doubles over in laughter, pointing at Knox's covered face as he loses his shit. It lasts barely a second before Knox scoops it off his face, pulls the waistband of Beck's pants outward, and drops the cake inside.

"Elli!" Gideon's chocolate hands grip my shoulders. I chuckle at his appearance. The whole left side of his face is covered in frosting. It's matted into his eyebrows and stuck in his eyelashes. "What are you doing just sitting here? You are awful at cake wars."

"I've never been in a cake war before." If this was my house, my father would've shut this shit down the second even a crumb hit his patio. He despised anything fun. He was a total grinch and the exact opposite of my mama.

Gideon grabs my hand and plops a wad of cake into it. "Fire!" He shouts, squatting down and giving me clear access to toss the cake over his head and hit a number of people. There are grown adults cackling loudly and tossing dessert in his backyard. As I look for my target, I can't help but think of ants. This cake is gonna attract a lot of ants. I don't know what it says about me that while everybody else can take part in the cake war that's happening in this massive backyard, I have an urge to clean it all up. I can practically hear my father's voice barking at me to get the hose and clean up the mess I made.

But I don't have a father anymore. And he doesn't care what I do.

"Elli! Throw the cake. You fail at this."

I close my fist around the cake, grinning at the way it sticks to my fingers when I peel it back open. "I already threw it."

"Oh." He pops back up, studying my face. "You did?"

"Nope." I slam the cake directly into his face and take off running, laughing as he chases me around the yard. I run rampant, scooping up piles of cake mixed with grass and chucking them at the first body that flies past me. Laughter is bubbling out of me in waves, I can barely breathe.

I don't stop.

I keep tossing and laughing and running and dodging. It's not even my birthday—not my party or my celebration. But I've never had so much fun.

"This is total chaos!" Nate screams, his whole head a ball of frosting.

Gideon and I lock eyes from across the yard, grinning at each other as we take in the mayhem happening around us. This *is* total chaos. And as my chest warms with laughter and the strange effect of his smile, I'm hit with the bizarre realization that I've never been happier.

"Make some more, Elli!" Gideon hollers, dodging Piper's throw.

I yank some cake covered grass out of the ground and join Nate and Preston in some weird battle howl as I chuck more grass than cake and make a shit ton of chaos. I keep creating it, laughing hysterically at gramps' grumpy, caked filled face and digging frosting out of my ear. I'm sure it's only been ten or so minutes, but I'm so caught up in the chaos, it feels like it's been going on forever.

I'd be okay if it never ended. But it does. It ends abruptly the moment I watch Gideon barrel across the patio as his toe makes contact with a slab of frosting. His arms go wild as he tries to right himself. A shout rips out of his mouth, frantic hands attempting to grab the table next to him before he hits the concrete with a thud.

GIDEON

"Gideon!"

A loud grunt barrels out of me the second my limbs decide to body slam the concrete in the midst of a cake war.

In case there was any question, the concrete won.

"Gideon!"

The corners of my mouth pull into a smile as I spot him barreling towards me, chunks of cake stuck on every surface of his body. "Are you okay? Babe, holy shit! That was such a hard hit."

He dives towards me, gripping my face and tilting my head back and forth, inspecting it from all angles.

"I didn't hit my head, Elli. I'm fine."

"Uh, yeah. If having a bruise the size of Daytona Speedway on your back is fine."

"Totally fine." I grunt obnoxiously in my attempt to sit up. I'm not sure how big the Daytona Speedway is, but I'm betting whatever is forming on my back right now is gonna give it a run for its money.

"Nope." He blurts, wrapping his arm around my shoulders and tugging. "No sitting up. Laying down is cool."

"There is a cake war in session. I can't forfeit!"

"You aren't. You're taking a timeout."

I don't know who made him the king of cake wars, but

I'm liking his rules. So, I relax as much as one can on a slab of concrete covered in birthday dessert. He lays down next to me, our sticky fingers entwining. I lift our enclosed fists to my mouth and lick a glob of frosting off the back of his hand.

"There is a large chance you just ate some grass."

"Yum. Grass."

"You're such a goober." He chuckles lowly, sliding his body so close, my curls brush against his forehead when we turn our heads and our eyes meet. "And really beautiful."

The smile that erupts on my face would be painful if I wasn't so happy.

And he thinks he's bad at words.

"Thank you. So are you."

His lips quirk and he shakes his head, our lips touching as we lay on our sides in a pile of sugary goodness. "Not just those crazy curls and big baby blues. Your soul is beautiful."

I'm not sure where souls come from, or who made mine. But I'll be forever grateful that I'm in possession of the one he finds beautiful.

"Ya know, for claiming to be bad at this relationship stuff, you're pretty damn romantic."

He chuckles, squeezing my hand. "Before my mama died, I promised her I would say the things that sounded scary in my head because those were usually the best things to say."

"Your mama was pretty wonderful."

His smile goes shaky. "She really was, babe. I wish she could've met you."

"She knows who I am." I whisper. "Wherever she is, she's seen us together."

"Well, I hope she's not watching all the time. That'd be awkward considering the number of times we've made out in your car."

"Elli!" I push my head into his sticky chest. "You're awful." I say, trying to hide my smile.

"Cake for everyone!"

Our chests knock together at the force of the laughs induced by Nate jumping over the top of us, his T-shirt tied around his neck as a makeshift cape.

"I think we're actually in the center of chaos." I laugh, inspecting my family still running and dodging like they haven't lost any energy.

"Yeah, me too." He kisses my nose as I melt into the pile of frosting. "And I think I really like it here."

I'm beginning to think I was wrong about Elli—and he was wrong about himself. He is good with words. Even the scary ones. Maybe he just has to trust someone before he rewards them with the beautiful, endearing words that fall from his mouth.

I don't know what I did in another life to be gifted with a boyfriend that will lay on a slab concrete in the middle of a war and hold me as if we're laying in a bed made of feathers in the center of paradise. But the longer I lay here, in the heart of chaos, I find myself desperate to create as much as possible.

"There are no stars tonight." He observes, rolling to his back and patting his chest.

I rest my head on it eagerly and peer into the clear sky. "When I was a kid, I used to think that stars were people when they die."

"Not me. My mama isn't a star. She's a cloud."

"A cloud?" I tilt my head, giving my eyes open access to study his. Since the day he told me about his mama's cancer, he talks about her more and more, giving me bits and pieces of sweet memories and loving moments.

"A rainbow one." His lips pull into a sad smile. "I used to think all angels lived in the clouds. That each cloud was a little town and where we died determined what cloud we got sent to. When my mama died, I decided she lived in a rainbow cloud."

"Like the kinds of clouds you see when the sun rises or sets?"

"Exactly. There's something so powerful about the moment the sun decides to move. But also something extremely calming. My mama was both those things."

"Powerful and calming?"

"Yeah. She made me feel unstoppable without letting me get ahead of myself. I always felt like I was walking on water around her but still felt impossibly grounded. I haven't seen a cloud like that since I moved here."

"You'll see her, Elli. I'm sure of it. You're still the man she inspired you to be. She's still helping you be a calming force of power."

"I'm not so sure it's her helping me anymore, Gideon."

"No?"

His eyes finally make contact with mine. The intensity lingering within them forces all the air from my lungs as I'm pulled directly inside his milky eyes. His cheeks warm beneath the frosting as his finger captures a misbehaving curl. He lifts his body upward, sending electricity down my spine when our lips connect.

"No, baby." He whispers, his grip on me tightening. "I'm pretty sure it's just you."

SIXTEEN

DISGUSTINGLY ADORABLE

ELLIOTT

I WAS NEVER a fan of snow. Snow meant I couldn't race, the farm was harder to take care of, and the house was always cold because my dad was a fucking drill sergeant when it came to the furnace.

I was always wet—my boots, my head, my hands, my coat. Snow sucked, and I did what I could to wager with Mother Nature and trade some extra rain or sweltering hot days for the least amount of snow possible.

But that was then.

And this is now.

Now? I like snow a whole lot. I like the way it falls lazily and makes a cushion on the ground. I like flopping next to Gideon and making snow angels before attempting to carefully maneuver out of them. I like sitting behind him on a sled, my arms and legs wrapped around him tightly. I like when it gets cold and wet, giving us an excuse to make giant blanket forts to drink hot cocoa in like a couple of middle schoolers.

I like the way his cheeks get red and little snowflakes fall onto the tip of his nose. I like the way I kiss away the moisture and he lights up like the Christmas tree I helped gramps set up.

I barely scowl at gramps these days when he calls me a sap and makes obscene kissing noises every time Gideon is around.

My eyes barely roll when he tells me I'm still a fool for love.

Slowly but surely, I've made peace with the idea that I'm turning into someone who's totally fucking cheery. Honestly, if I wasn't me, I'd find myself disgusting.

"I swear to God, if you two don't stop eye-fucking across the room, I will vomit."

I've reached the point where I make high school seniors vomit. Not a hard task to complete, but still, if Nate Davis can't stomach his sandwich then pigs are probably flying somewhere.

I lift two middle fingers, watching Gideon's smile creep up his lips.

"I have to agree with Nate." Preston blurts, shoving his hand in a bag of Pretzels. "You guys are acting like you didn't spend the entirety of Christmas break together."

"Didn't you spend like the actual Christmas day together, cuddling and comparing what Santa brought you?" Nate shudders like the idea of spending a holiday with a significant other is blasphemy.

"As far as I'm concerned, Elli is what Santa brought me."

Oh.

God.

We are disgusting. *Seriously.* Disgustingly adorable. I want to vomit and kiss his face off at the same time.

"I just died." Piper flails in her beanbag. "That was it. I'm dead from that comment."

Gideon howls in laughter, his chest rumbling. He

laughs so hard I'm afraid he's about to fall out of the windowsill he's claimed his spot during our lunchtime.

"We'll tone it down." I say. "Probably."

"Probably fucking not." Nate belches loudly. "You two dudes spent Christmas together. That's serious."

The truth is, I woke up Christmas morning with a knot in my chest so tight, I could barely breathe. I had absolutely no desire to get out of my sofa bed. It didn't take long for my jackass brain to remind me that was the first Christmas without my mama. I couldn't summon the will to move.

Then gramps called in the troops. Knox, Beck, and Gideon showed up like the cavalry without any horses. I stared at the wall until Gideon laid next to me and forced his hand in mine. I let him pull me out of bed. My first smile of the day came when I got a good look at what he was wearing.

Footsie pajamas.

I shit you not.

My boyfriend was wearing Christmas themed footsie pajamas.

And I thought it was cute.

What universe is North Carolina in?

"Maybe you're just jealous." I quip, popping a chip in my mouth.

"Jealous of what?" Nate gawks. "Dopey eyes?"

"That I got to see Gideon in his footsie pajamas and you didn't." I flip him off again and mow down on my chips.

I'm thankful Gideon showed up but I feel queasy that it took *him* to pull me from my bed. I've confided in him enough he knows how unbearably painful that morning was for me. And he likes me enough to drop his plans and spend hours sitting on gramps' old carpet, eating waffles from a paper plate.

Don't get me wrong, I'm excited about the adorable part

of vomity. But the other part of vomity comes from the uneasiness at how quickly all this could come crashing down. I've witnessed the crash firsthand—been part of the wreckage. I'll be damned if I let anyone force me into a crash.

But Gideon wouldn't do that.

Right?

"Maybe you're just jealous that I've seen Gideon naked and you haven't."

I choke on my chip.

Gideon's face morphs into a tomato. "Nate, we were kids."

"You have no chill, Nathaniel. None." Piper shakes her head.

Preston snaps a picture of the wall. "How do you know he hasn't? Maybe they just don't want to share all their details with your obnoxious self."

"Sure they do. That's what the group chat is for."

Ah, the infamous group chat. It's been ongoing since the second Gideon and his cousins were in possession of cell phones. Two days after Gideon was mine, I was added to the chat. I turned it on mute once. They all threatened to eat my future babies. So I turned it back on for the sake of my future children.

"This conversation sucks." Gideon blurts.

I couldn't agree more. I haven't seen Gideon naked but I sure as shit won't be posting it to the group chat when I do.

This family has no boundary lines.

"I'm picking a new one." I tip back in my chair, wadding up my empty chip bag. "How're the new classes going?"

"That is the lamest conversation change ever." Piper frowns. "There's so much to talk about. NASA hiding time travel from us. The extinction of the Whooping Crane.

Harambe. But no. You want to know about the coffee stain on Ms. Row's shirt in history class this morning."

I'm tempted to ask what a Whooping Crane is but the wish to avoid one of Piper's rants is too strong.

I'll google it.

"Coffee stains are cool." I shrug.

"So is not having chemistry!" I laugh at the way Gideon's eyes light up.

Our new semester started the day we returned from break. Gideon passed with a B. We celebrated with a lot of kissing and some other things I won't be putting in the group chat.

"Yeah but like aren't you soooo devastated you and Elliott don't have a class together anymore?" Nate teases.

Gideon rolls his eyes. "It might be hard for you to believe, but I can function when Elliott's not around."

"Well, you probably have to function alone if he hasn't seen you naked."

Preston chokes on air.

"Alright." I stand from my chair. "I'm leaving this conversation."

"No worries. We'll keep ya updated in the group chat, man."

Shaking my head, I shuffle from the room and towards my locker. The bell is going to ring for class soon anyway. Opening my locker, I snag my notebook and pop a piece of gum in my mouth.

His arms sneak around my waist from behind.

"We are pretty disgusting, huh?" He mumbles into my back. "Good lord, I can't even stand here without wanting to touch you."

I chuckle and close my locker. "You should put that in the group chat."

"Oh God. Can you imagine if we put every aspect of our relationship into that group chat?"

I spin in his hold. "Should I forward them the shirtless picture I sent you last night?"

He frowns. "Absolutely not."

"Baby, I was kidding."

"I know. But I just got strangely jealous for some reason."

"What do you have to be jealous of?" I grab his hand. We start the short walk to his locker.

My boyfriend's mind must be lost. In less than five months, he's turned me into a lovedrunk sicko who talks about his mama and engages in public hand holding. As far as I'm concerned, he's got superpowers.

"I don't know. You met me on the first day of school. It's not like you had a chance to scope out other options."

"Babe, come on. No way." I squeeze his hand. "I came to this school with the intention of scowling at couples and the idea that relationships were a waste of time. You changed that."

"I guess I'm pretty awesome or something."

"*Or something.*" I muse. "You are the one who grew up in this school. It's filled with people you could've fallen into a relationship with."

He rolls his eyes and starts to turn the dial on his locker. "I've dated nobody in this school that seriously. Except you."

"Probably because I'm pretty awesome or something."

"*Or something.*"

The warning bell rings and I slide my hand back in his. "I'm gonna walk you to forensics."

He looks to his left, chuckling when he finds the classroom door a whole two steps away. "How chivalrous of you."

"Put *that* in the group chat. Nate won't believe it."

He chuckles and checks the hallway for teachers before kissing my cheek and heading into the forensics classroom. I spin on my heels, walking down the hall and sliding into the woodshop just as the final bell rings.

Woodshop is my new favorite class. We didn't have this sort of fancy class in Mount Vernon. This is only the second day, but I learned yesterday all the stuff I'll get to build.

I'm basically getting furniture for free. Who funds this school?

I relax into a stool at the very back and twiddle my thumbs. Literally.

James Appleweed slides into the stool in front of me, patting the seat next to him and gesturing for the girl scampering through the room to sit in it.

I don't remember them from the introductions we were forced to do yesterday. Must've just transferred in.

"Really, J?" The girl huffs and brushes her long dark hair behind her shoulder. "Woodshop? Really?"

"I didn't want to take poetry."

"I'm going to be awful at this." She says it like it's a warning.

He just laughs and slouches. "So, Gideon's like in love with the new kid or whatever. I heard they spent Christmas together."

God.

I swear there are like little, invasive cameras in the walls of high school. How is it that everybody literally knows everything? How is my Christmas morning any of this kid's business?

"Doesn't mean it actually happened. You gotta stop listening to everything you hear."

My eyes roll to the back of my head. That sounds like the kind of advice you give a friend to get them to shut up so you don't have to listen to their problems anymore. I bet this girl listens and believes every damn thing that gets spewed about Gideon.

"Probably not. I'd be surprised if they lasted until Spring. Gideon's good at overlooking the existence of the people he's dated."

The twiddling of my thumbs stops abruptly.

"They like hold hands everywhere, J. Stop being salty."

"I'm not being salty. There are other hot dudes. Just saying Gideon probably hasn't gotten what he wants yet."

A harsh scoff rocks my body, my stool shifting against the cement floor. Appleweed turns in his seat, his eyes scanning me quickly. There is not a hint of guilt or remorse on his face despite that he was just caught talking shit about my boyfriend while less than six inches away from me.

"Oh hey, Elliott."

Elliott.

Guess he is aware my name isn't actually 'new kid'.

I fold my arms across my chest, tipping back in my stool. "If you have something to say about my relationship, I'm right here to listen."

"I don't have anything to say. But if you want my advice—"

"I don't."

"Fine." He holds up his hands like he's gonna surrender but not before he hurls a sentence that punches me straight in the gut. "But you should know the real reason Gideon rejected me is because I wouldn't let him put his hand in my pants. So if you aren't putting out, you better soon."

This kid is lying through his smirk. Gideon has never pressured me to do a damn thing. Every time we've fooled around, it's been mutual. No way would he dump me over something so shallow.

"That's bullshit."

"Fine. Don't believe me. But the second you stop touching his dick, you'll be out the door like I was."

"Jamie." The girl beside him fakes a gag. "What the hell? TMI!"

"Listen, Appleweed." I lean forward in my stool, resting my elbows on my knees and looking straight into his beady eyes. "Stop spreading rumors about my boyfriend, or I will make you stop."

"Honey, they aren't rumors." He slides his stool away from me, picking at his hair. "Just ask Sadie why he broke up with her."

A truckload of doubt floods my body and I become really, really angry.

Angry at Jamie for making me doubt my boyfriend's intentions.

Angry at myself for not being more careful and getting disgustingly adorable with him.

Angry at Gideon for downplaying whatever the hell happened with Appleweed.

Most of all, I'm angry at the world. And I don't even know why. Maybe it's because I let my guard down and trusted a guy I'm falling deeply for and the world decided to thrust all these doubts and complications into it.

It made it all messy—and that's why relationships are bullshit.

Because people lie. People betray others, and everything comes crashing down in the time it takes for a jealous kid to cover me in his word vomit.

I'll be damned if I let Gideon force me into the crash I worked so damn hard to avoid.

SEVENTEEN

SMITTEN

GIDEON

HI. **I'M WAITING BY MY CAR FOR YA.**

I study my text and add three heart emojis before I send it. Yes, three. I'm a nerdy romantic. Sue me.

It's both hysterical and endearing Elli keeps pretending he can't decide whether he's repulsed by us or completely smitten. He's totally smitten—and would definitely make fun of me for using the word smitten before his cheeks got warm and he found an excuse to hold my hand.

I'm not completely sure what type of relationships Elli witnessed growing up, but I know the type of marriage I grew up watching. It's entirely my parent's fault I'm a total cheeseball when it comes to my relationship with Elli. Anything sappy or cheesy or teetering on the edge of just plain overboard, I'm a goner for. Like so far gone I jumped on a plane and flew across country gone.

Every touch, every smile, every dopey eyed look, and ridiculous comment has my heart pumping overtime. I'm positive it's because I grew up watching my parents so open with their affection and love for each other that I have no issues being a sappy dork twenty-four seven.

Things at lunch today made it pretty clear my sappiness is infecting Elli.

He totally loves it.

I pocket my phone when I see him barrel out the front doors, moving towards me quickly.

"Hey, you." I start as soon as he's in earshot. "I was starting to think you left without saying goodbye."

"Did you lie to me about James Appleweed?"

"Lie about what?"

"You tell me, Gideon!" He barks, forcing a rough flinch to erupt from my stunned body. "What's the real reason behind you ditching him?"

"I told you. We kissed twice and there was nothing there. I ended it. He said okay. I reached out to still be friends and he ignored me."

"Bullshit." He spits.

I jerk. "Are you calling me a liar?"

"I wanna know why he warned me in woodshop that you'd dump me the second I stop unzipping your pants just like you did with Sadie."

"Elli...." His features are stone, eyes blazing in a way I'm unfamiliar with. My heart plummets to the bottom of my stomach.

He's supposed to be different.

He's not supposed to listen to the rumors people must spend hours creating about me. "I don't... that's not true, Elli. He was the one who initiated the kiss, not me."

"What about Sadie? Didn't get pissed when she didn't put out for you?"

I blink roughly, trying to decide if I heard that sentence correctly. "What?"

"James seems to think I'm gonna get dumped when you get your fill of me."

Un-fucking-believable. "Oh, *James* seems to think, huh?"

"Yep."

"And what do you think? You think I'm some sleazy horndog who goes around using people for sex and ditching them when they don't give it to me? You think after spending all these months with you I've just been thinking about the perfect time to seduce you and dump you when it doesn't work?"

"I..."

"All these months you didn't even blink at the rumors that were spread about me or us or Piper or a stupid ugly baby but the second some dude I dated for a half a second makes me out to be an asshole you believe it?"

He blinks a few times, absorbing what I said before his stone face starts to soften. "Gideon..."

"Save it!" I yank open my car door and climb inside. Before I can slam it shut, he shoves his boot in the bottom to stop it from latching.

"Wait... Gideon..."

"Back off." My eyes burn. "We've had an amazing couple of months together. I've never done anything that would give you a reason to believe I'm that type of person, and now your opinion of me changed based on some shit talk? Awesome, Elliott."

"What was I supposed to do, Gideon? He just came at me with some suspicious warning about you. I got confused!"

"Then you could've come to me and we could've talked about it. Do you honestly believe him?"

He doesn't speak. A beat of silence goes by and he opens his mouth. A faint sound passes through his lips.

"Awesome. You believe him. Move out of my way, Elliott."

"Gideon, please, stop..."

"Knock it off!" My voice cracks, and I struggle to hide it. "I don't have time for this."

His face pales. "You don't have time for me?"

"I don't have time for this untrustworthiness bullshit." I kick his boot off my car, determined to get away from him so I can be alone when I lose my shit. "Why don't you go find James and be his boyfriend? At least you can say you trust him."

Slamming my door, I step on the gas and drive out of the parking lot at a speed that would earn me a hefty speeding ticket if a cop was around to see it.

Cranking up the volume, I put the pedal to the floor and I drive.

I drive until the ache in my chest starts to let up and the sting behind my eyes goes away. By the time that happens, my favorite playlist has run its course three times and I find myself in the parking lot of the dance studio, idling next to my parent's Range Rover.

I flip off the ignition and drag myself out of my car, shuffling towards the studio rooms. I'm determined to find an empty one so I can dance until I forget that high school has poisoned my boyfriend.

At the last minute, my body shifts and I'm walking up the wide staircase that leads to my parent's offices. They're directly across from each other, doors always open so they can see one another at all times. It makes me wonder why they didn't just decide to share an office.

Both of their doors are wide open, their voices carrying softly into the hallway. I drop my backpack with a thud in the doorway of Knox's office, resisting the urge to climb into his lap like I used to when I was a kid and had a shit day at school.

Time to grow up, Gideon.

"Hey, bud." Knox pulls his eyes from Beck who's made a home for himself on the edge of his desk. "What are you doing here? You don't have class tonight."

"High school fucking sucks." I throw myself on top of the faded, old loveseat he has in here.

Beck flies off the desk and walks towards me like I just told him the whole school went up in flames. "What happened? I'll call the school."

"Dad, no. You don't need to call the school. What are you going to do? Bark at Principal Donahue for not monitoring the lies people tell my boyfriend?"

He sits on the edge of the loveseat, swatting at my curls so he can find my face. "Something happened with Elliott?"

"We got into a fight." My stomach lurches the moment I say his name. "Today in school Jamie told him I wouldn't date him because he didn't have sex with me."

Knox chokes on air, swiveling in his chair. "What?"

"Yep. Apparently, that's also the reason why I dumped Sadie. Because I'm a horndog."

Knox runs his hands through his hair, staring at me with sad eyes. "That's... fucked up, bud. I'm sorry. *God*. I hate that people won't leave you alone."

"Did Elliott believe him?" Beck asks, running his hand through my hair like he used to. "Is that why you fought?"

"Yeah, dad. Elliott did believe him. Or at least he was considering it. He stomped up to me in the parking lot, shouting at me and wanting an explanation I don't have. Jamie and I kissed twice for shit's sake."

"Well, if it helps, dad and I believe you."

I let out a dry laugh. "I guess it does help that at least my parents don't think I'm a sleazeball."

"I have a hard time believing Elliott thinks you're a sleazeball." Knox stands from his chair, crossing his office and squatting down to my eye level. "Maybe he was just confused, projected his feelings in a bad way."

"I guess so." I considered that in the moment. Maybe I just got too caught up in spending time with someone who ignores the rumors, I let the moment he started to believe them crush me a little too much. "Still sucks though. I mean, he's my boyfriend. He should know by my virginity I'm not just in this for sex. I really care about him."

"Give him some time, bud." Beck whispers. "Let him simmer down and sort his thoughts. Then you guys can talk."

"What happens if he does believe it? I lose my boyfriend because Jamie is a dick?"

"Let's not go there yet, yeah?" Knox squeezes my shoulder. "Give him time to process what he heard and how cray it is."

My dad's use of the word cray is the only thing that can make me smile when I'm this upset. "He didn't give himself time, dad. He just barged right up to me, making accusations."

"Did you explain to him the truth? And how you felt?"

"Yeah. Of course. I told him it wasn't true and that I've never given him a reason not to trust me."

"Then what happened, kid?" Beck asks, his hand stilling. "He still didn't believe you?"

"I left."

"You left?"

"Yeah. I got pissed off and hurt so I left and drove around for a while. Now I'm on this couch."

"So, what you're saying is..." Beck starts, his lips pursing. "You fled before he could apologize?"

"Ah, man." Knox shakes his head. "Dude, you fled the scene of a fight with your man? Never do that."

"What?!" I fly up to a seated position, gawking at the

men who have preached words and words of knowing when to walk away. "You guys tell me all the time to walk away from a fight."

"True." Beck nods. "But we were talking more of a fist fight. Or one that isn't worth the victory."

"Great. So now I suck for walking away?"

"No." Knox says fiercely. "You don't suck. Neither of you do. He got scared and lashed out and you ditched before you two could resolve anything."

"So we're both fucking this up? Awesome." I flop back down, dragging my hands down my face. Elli and I are supposed to be good at managing chaos together. But I left. So... I guess we aren't managing anything together.

I created a problem on top of a problem.

And now I have to fix it.

I jump to my feet. "I'm going to go find him."

"Listen, bud." Knox walks across the room and lifts my backpack, holding it out to me. "You and Elliott are young. You're supposed to mess things up, have doubts, and be insecure. Those aren't new relationship problems. People have been solving them for years. You and Elliott just need to talk. Sort things out."

I slide my backpack over my shoulders, giving my parents a quick hug before I pound back downstairs to find my boyfriend and hope he's not throwing darts at my face.

———

THE GOOD NEWS is that Elliott isn't in his room throwing darts or sharp knives at my face. The bad news is I can't find him. He's not at home with Spanky. Not at the shop. Not at the track. And he's not answering his phone.

I even went to the diner and thought he might be hanging out in the booth we always sit in when we go for pizza. He wasn't there either. Our booth was occupied by a middle-aged couple, harping at their kids to stop throwing cheese on the floor.

I can't stop thinking about how badly I screwed this up long enough to think of where he might be. I didn't give him any kind of time to apologize or absorb what I was saying—I just bailed.

As I drive towards my house, getting his voicemail again, I find myself wishing I would've listened to Nate and downloaded Find My Friends.

I try to sift through my messy thoughts while rolling into my driveway. My headlights hit the front of the house, projecting a spotlight on the porch. I slam on the brakes, my body lurching forward when my mind registers a figure sitting in the center of the spotlight.

Elli.

I ease off the brake and roll into the spot next to his truck. I make no attempt to move. I stare at his silhouette, scanning his slumped shoulders and dipped chin. I haven't come up with a way to approach this conversation when I kill the engine and push open my door. He's by my side in an instant.

"I'm sorry. Gideon... I..."

"So am I."

He blinks and steps back so roughly, it's obvious he wasn't expecting those words to come from my mouth. "I shouldn't have bailed like that. I got pissed and I ditched. I'm sorry. It just... it sucked... ya know? Hearing that you believed him. Even if it was just for a minute, it sucked."

He shakes his head violently, wringing his hands together. "I was so out of line earlier, Gideon. I shouldn't have bitched you out in a parking lot. I should've just come to you." His chest deflates. "I'm so sorry."

"Elli." I make my voice soft, hoping to ease the tension

in his shoulders. Seeing him so distraught at my expense isn't rewarding. I'm not even a little bit happy he's kicking himself for hurting me. "Do you trust me?"

"Yes." He answers quickly. "I do. I've never had a reason not to. I just heard them talking and panicked."

"Panicked? Why?"

"Because he said you'd ditch me and break my heart." He drops his head and kicks at the gravel. "And I really don't want you to break my heart."

"Elli..." My body turns to goo against my leather seats. Determination erupts inside my bloodstream. I mentally make it one of my life's missions to prove to him I will never break his heart.

He lets out a choppy, labored breath. "I just... are we done?"

"What?"

"Are you breaking up with me? Back there you told me to go make Appleweed my boyfriend and I really, really don't want to." He makes a choked sound. "I'm so sorry for fucking this up but please give me a chance to do right by you. I have reasons. I just have trouble sharing them."

"Elli..." I throw myself out of my car and into his arms. He hesitates for a split second before throwing his arms around me and hugging me tight to his chest. "Babe, I don't want to break up with you. I just want you to trust me."

"I do. I swear I do. I just... I had a moment. It's hard for me to explain."

The mist in his eyes confuses me. It jerks my system and forces me to wonder what else is happening inside his heart that's causing him to tremble in his worn boots. "That's okay, Elli. Take your time to explain. I'm not going anywhere."

"No?"

"No."

His body sags like a million pounds was just lifted off his shoulders.

I nudge my head towards the house. "You wanna come in? Talk for a bit?"

He nods.

Our hands link loosely as I lead him up the driveway and into the house. My parents got home from work sometime during my quest to find my boyfriend and are sprawled on the couch watching TV, Beck's head in Knox's lap.

"Hey." I slip my shoes off and wait for Elli to do the same. "Elliott and I are gonna go upstairs and talk."

"Okay." Beck sits up. "You staying for dinner, kiddo?"

Elliott seems to swallow his tongue.

It clicks in my brain he has no idea how to answer. He's stayed for dinner dozens and dozens of times. But that's when he was positive I wanted him here. Now, he's not so sure.

I hate that he's unsure.

"Yeah." I squeeze his hand. "He is. That cool?"

"Totes."

"Dad, people don't say totes anymore."

"I said totes and I'm a people." He looks at Knox. "I'm a people, right Knox?"

"Yeah, Stryker. You're a people."

Beck gives me a look that says "told ya so" and drops back down into Knox's lap. I chuckle softly and tug on Elli's hand, leading him upstairs.

The second the door clicks shut, I expect him to flop on my bed or my couch like he always does. Nope. He stands at the doorway, hands shoved deep in his pockets and his gaze focused on a stain in the carpet that came from Piper's attempt to teach me how to paint.

"Elli?"

He rolls his head upward. "Yeah?"

"You okay?"

He shakes his head. "Not really. I feel like such a dick."

I shrug off my jacket, letting it hit the floor. I grip his arm and tug him towards the couch. "Let's sit."

He slumps down into the cotton, his elbows on his knees, pulling at a frayed piece of his jeans.

"I'm sorry they were saying those things about me and our relationship."

He flinches so roughly, the whole couch moves. "No. Do not do that, Gideon. Don't apologize for their actions."

"I just... I should've considered how confusing and hurtful that was for you to hear." I tried to put myself in his shoes while I was driving around. I'd like to think I would've talked to him before I blew a gasket in the parking lot but I can't say for sure I wouldn't have done the same thing as him. "I don't like how you handled it. But I don't like how I handled it either."

"No, Gideon. You didn't do anything wrong. You're right, okay? At first, I told him it was total bullshit because I know the kind of person you are. But my mind decided to be a jackass when he told me to ask Sadie the reason you two broke up."

My fists clench. "What a fucker."

"Exactly. He's a total fucker and I'm sorry I believed him. I'm sorry I came at you. I spent the night sitting on your porch, going through the days since I met you and you've never given me a reason to believe you're in this for sex." He smiles sadly. "You're pretty great, Gideon. I'm so sorry I doubted that because Jamie is a jealous asshole. I let him get in my head and treated you like shit because of it." He slumps downward again. "I'm turning out to be just like him."

"Like who?" He stares vacantly at the wall. "Like who, Elli? Jamie?"

He shakes his head, seemingly snapping out of whatever daze he was in. "Nobody specifically. Just like everybody in my old school were a bunch of users and cheaters. Assholes not wanting me for anything but an experiment. Parents were getting divorced all the time because they got bored. There was literally this spot on an abandoned farm people used to go just to cheat and it tripped me out hearing him say that about you. I got insecure and pissed off. I judged you based on hearsay and my old school. That was such an asshole boyfriend move and I'm so sorry I acted like every other jerk in that school who judges you."

There is not a shred of doubt in my mind that he's sorry. It's obvious by the wringing of his hands, the slight tremor in his body, and the way he won't meet my eyes that he's beating himself up about this.

"Babe." I wrap my arm around him and drop my head to his shoulder. There's no doubt he's got curls in his face. He just doesn't care. "Will you do me a favor?"

"Anything." He says it like it'd be his greatest honor. And man does that do something to my mushy gushy heart.

"Don't jump in front of the bus."

"What?"

"When you told me about your mom, you said it'd felt like you'd been hit by a bus. After that, you were waiting for the bus to hit you." I kiss his shoulder. "Don't wait, Elli. Don't jump in front of it. Just trust I don't have bad intentions. Can you try that? Ask if you hear something and then hear me out? I promise I'll stay around and let you."

He shifts his body, brushing my curls back so he can find my eyes. "I try for you and you try for me?"

"We try for each other. I think that's how this is supposed to work."

"I think so too."

"So, yeah? You'll try?"

A slow smile starts on his lips. "I think you're the only one I'd try so hard for."

"It's because of my trophies, isn't it?"

"And some other things."

"My super hot bod?"

"And some other things."

"What other things?"

His finger finds a curl. "Your easy ability to forgive is a good reason."

"Oh, there's a condition to my forgiveness."

"Oh really?" His signature smirk unfolds, flashing a glimpse of his crooked tooth.

"Yes. My forgiveness requires a full night of kissing and an MCU marathon."

He chuckles softly, cupping the sides of my face. "Easily done."

EIGHTEEN

HAVE SOME BACON

ELLIOTT

I WAKE up to the sound of an alarm that isn't mine. There are curls in my mouth and a human is lying directly on top of me—a human that happens to be my boyfriend.

"Shit!"

I fly out of his bed, searching quickly for my phone and my boots.

Where the hell is my shirt?

A thud and a loud groan comes from my feet. "What the fuck, Elli?"

I reach down and grab him beneath the armpits, hauling him back on the bed. "Sorry, baby. I can't find my shirt."

"You look better without one." He mutters, burying his head under a pillow. "Come back to bed."

"Gideon, it's morning!" I shove my feet in my boots and pull on the jeans I was wearing last night before stuffing my phone in my back pocket.

He groans. "Yes, Elli. I heard the alarm."

"We fell asleep."

"That's what people do at nighttime."

"In your bed." I gesture to it with wild arms. "We fell asleep in your bed. Together! And now it's morning."

He pulls the pillow from his head and stares at me beneath wild hair. "We stayed the night together."

"Oh my shit! We stayed the night together. In your house! Oh my God, your dads are gonna kill me. Where the hell is my shirt?"

"Elli, my dads aren't gonna kill you for staying over. They probably already know."

"What?!"

"Babe, why are you freaking right now? We fell asleep watching a movie. No big deal."

"Are you nuts?" I fall to my stomach and look under the bed for my shirt. "It's a huge deal. Gramps is probably gonna kick my ass. We've only been dating a few months." I fly back to my feet. "Gideon. I can't find my shirt!"

"Then borrow one of mine."

"Yours will be too tight."

"Exactly." He grins, lifting up the comforter. "Come back in here."

Tempting. His bed is pillow soft and I like how warm it is when he lies across my chest.

No, Elliott.

I point my finger at him. "You're trouble. I need to go."

He sits up, rubbing his sleepy eyes. God. He looks so cute and confused in the morning. If only I could stay without the threat of getting chased down by his parents. "What, why? Don't leave."

"We have school and I can't find my shirt."

"Borrow one of mine. We can eat breakfast together."

"And let your dads see me? No, thanks."

He rolls his sleepy eyes. "They already know you're here, Elli. I promise you. Nothing gets past them."

"I need to go." I zip my jeans and yank open his bedroom door.

"You aren't wearing a shirt."

"I know. I need to go home and change before school. See you there."

I pull his door shut and start down the stairs as quietly as one can while wearing heavy boots. This little sleepover between my boyfriend and I wasn't planned. We fell asleep watching a movie.

I know—lamest excuse in the book. But it happened and it's not all that surprising. I spend a lot of time in his bed. Sometimes we're watching movies and playing video games. Other times, I'm taking his shirt off and running my tongue along the washboard abs that come from many years of acro jazz.

I'm obsessed with him. I won't try to sugarcoat it. Gideon has weaseled his way into all aspects of my life, and I am not mad about it. Sure, I'm a little vulnerable and a lot insecure but that isn't his fault.

The bullshit I pulled yesterday at school almost cost me my relationship. I equated him with assholes from my past. That wasn't fair of me but sometimes my mind is a jackass and mutes my voice of reason. Especially when the past is involved. I'm five states away from Iowa but every once in a while, it feels like I never left. I'm lucky I have a partner who listens and forgives.

I used to know some people whose partner would have never let them crawl into bed and pick the first movie after a fight like that. I'm so damn lucky because the last thing I remember from last night is his cheek on my chest and Thor finding The Hulk tearing shit up in Sakaar.

"Morning, Elliott."

I jump and let out a small shout. Sheepishly, I turn my head to find both of Gideon's dads staring at me with my hand on the knob of their front door. Knox has a plate of scrambled eggs in his hand. Beck's got a strip of bacon hanging from his mouth.

"Uh, hi, I was just..."

"Sneaking out of Gideon's room?" Knox lifts an eyebrow and shovels a bite of eggs in his mouth.

"Uh." I swallow tightly.

"Baby, you're scaring him." Beck swats Knox and stares at me. "Where's Gideon?"

"Gideon?" I look around the entryway like he's gonna appear out of thin air. "Uhm, I don't know. Why would I know where he is?"

"Because you just came from his room."

"Did I?"

"Where's your shirt?" Knox blurts, eyeing me.

"Gideon's room." I clamp my hand over my mouth and try to shove my confession back in.

Beck laughs. "Stop being so fidgety. We knew you were here."

"You did?"

"Told you they knew." Gideon comes around the corner, rubbing his eyes. My jaw hits the floor when I get a good look at him. He's shirtless, wearing nothing but a pair of boxer briefs. He's basically announcing to his dads we just spent the night half naked next to each other. They are gonna think I'm the one who took his clothes off. I mean, I was. But still—they don't need to know that!

"Gideon!" I whisper shout like his dads can't hear me.

"What?"

"You're naked!"

He looks down. "No, I'm not. I'm wearing underwear."

"Where are your clothes?"

"Pretty sure they are on the floor. Isn't that where you threw them?"

"Oh my fucking God." I pinch myself a few times to make sure this nightmare is real.

"You hungry, Elliott?" Knox asks casually. "Beck made bacon."

"I make good bacon."

"It's true. He does." Gideon yawns and reaches for me. "Come on, babe."

"I can't. I have to go."

I ignore the three stunned faces and take off down the driveway. Shirtless. Is it still called the walk of shame even if you didn't have sex? And if you're dating the person?

In retrospect, it probably wasn't necessary to freak out and run like hell. Knox and Beck are super supportive of Gid and I's relationship. Supportive enough that they gave up their Christmas for me.

They're whacky as all get out, and I shouldn't be surprised they were super chill about seeing their son's boyfriend sneaking out of the house at seven in the morning. Maybe that's why I freaked out—because they *weren't* pissed.

They didn't ground Gideon for life, and they didn't threaten to shoot me. They offered me bacon. If that was my father, he would've grounded my ass and given me a long lecture about respecting my mama under her roof. Lucky for me, my dad doesn't give a shit what I do anymore.

But gramps does.

Which is why when I make it to my room in the den with no trace of him, I breathe easily and start gathering some clothes so I can take a quick shower and still make it to school on time.

"Did Gideon steal your shirt?"

Goddamn it! What the hell is it with people scaring the shit out of me this morning? "Gramps. Hey. I, uh, just woke up."

"Boy, don't bullshit me. You just got home. Next time, call or do that thing with the keyboard and make the words pop on my phone so I don't have to worry."

"Texting?"

"Is that what it's called?"

"Gramps, come on. You aren't that old. You need to learn these things."

"Oh, pish posh." He looks me over. "You planning on wearing a shirt to school today? Or...?"

"Uh, yeah. I just need to... wait... did you say next time?"

"Well, I assume the two of you are gonna make this sleepover mumbo jumbo a regular occurrence. So call or something, ya little shit. I'm too old to worry."

"You're, uhm, not super pissed?"

"Why would I be super pissed?"

I swear to you I am in an alternate universe. "Because.... I spent the night at my boyfriend's house. In his bed. With him in it. Shirtless."

"Still can't impregnate each other?"

"Uhm, no. That's never gonna be possible."

He shrugs. "Then I ain't pissed. Do we need to have the disease talk?"

"Absolutely not."

"Alrighty then. Shower up. Also, tell Gideon he's coming over tonight. I found that model car I've been wanting to show him."

I roll my eyes and dig through a pile of hopefully clean jeans. Gideon comes to watch me train for the season all the time, but each time gramps steals his attention more and more with model cars.

No. I'm not jealous of my gramps.

"Chop chop, boy! Get your ass in gear before you're late."

Gramps ushers me down the hall and into the bathroom. I take the fastest shower of my life and book it to school so I can get there early and talk to Gideon.

When I pull up to school and don't see his car in his usual spot, I trudge across the parking lot and into school to wait at his locker.

ME: I'M WAITING AT YOUR LOCKER.

GIDEON TWO-TIME NATIONAL TITLE WINNER: I'M GONNA BE LATE.

ME: STILL WAITING

GIDEON TWO-TIME NATIONAL TITLE WINNER: YOU'LL BE LATE TOO

ME: DON'T CARE

GIDEON TWO-TIME NATIONAL TITLE WINNER: REBEL

I chuckle at his text, ignoring the warning bell and hoping no teachers come down the senior hallway and force me to English class. College composition is bullshit anyway. I'm not going to college. If I don't qualify to be a top fuel racer, I'll get certified to work on the important stuff at Speed.

I've never wanted to go to college. I entertained the idea for a while. Then I moved in with gramps who made it clear he'd support me no matter what. Besides, helping rebuild racecars at a world-renowned body shop sounds like a way better use for my time than college. I may be better at school than Gideon, and we aren't mortal enemies, but we sure as shit ain't friends.

It's been twenty minutes with no sign of a single teacher when Gideon turns the corner and starts towards me. I scan him with a smile.

I do a double take. My throat dries up and some strange feeling shocks my body when I get a good look at what he's wearing. I suddenly feel a need to stand on top of a mountain and pound on my chest.

Good God, what the hell is happening to me?

My T-shirt from last night is draped across his lean body. Speed is scrawled in big letters across his chest. Oakley written on the bottom of the short sleeve.

He's wearing my shirt. *My name.*

My boyfriend is not ashamed to say he's mine—not ashamed he may be broadcasting to the whole school I spent the night in his bed.

"Hi, Elli." He grins, stepping right in front of me. "I found your shirt."

"Looks better on you." It's looser on him than it is me, but he looks so damn good with it draped over his shoulders and half tucked into a pair of distressed jeans.

"Yeah? Maybe I should steal it then."

"You should definitely steal it."

His cheeks warm. "Okay."

I look around the hallway, finding the coast clear. Then I grip his reddening face and plant a hard kiss on his lips. I ran out of his house like a crazy person, refusing to share some breakfast meat with him, and he still shows up wearing my name.

Our lips part with a pop. His eyes are wide, his fingertips brushing his bottom lip in a daze. "What... what was that for?"

"That was because you're amazing. I'm sorry I bailed this morning."

"It's okay. Most people in your position would've. Just... my dads aren't gonna kick your ass. Okay? They said it's fine."

"Seriously?" In Iowa, I would've gotten chased down the street.

"Yeah." He shrugs. "They said you'd probably come over anyway and be sneaky. They don't want that. They'd rather us be honest. So, they said you can stay as long as Spanky is cool with it and we don't go behind their back."

"Gramps is fine with it because I can't impregnate you."

He gapes. "For real?"

"He said those exact words. Swear it."

He chuckles, shaking his head. "What an old kook."

"Right?" I step closer, kissing his forehead. "I really did like waking up next to you. Last night was special. I'm sorry if I made it seem like it wasn't."

"You didn't." He lifts his shoulder in a shrug. "I'm not mad. But maybe next time you could stay for bacon?"

"I'd like that a whole lot."

"Cool." He grins, his face reddening. "Last night was special for me too."

"Should we put it in the group chat?"

He cackles and swats my chest. "God, no. Nate would have so many awful jokes."

"He has awful jokes anyway."

"Eh, that's true." He turns and starts spinning the dial on his locker. "Maybe you could stay Saturday night after my competition?"

"You mean after I watch you win another trophy?"

Gideon's first dance competition of the season is this weekend, and it's only twenty-five minutes away. Nate, Preston, Piper, and I are all going. I'm buzzing with excitement about finally watching Gideon dance, but I'm more pumped I get to support him in what he loves like he supports me in what I love.

Things with Gideon are getting more serious every day. I've never been so happy to be terrified.

He flashes me a wink. "Are you gonna be jealous?"

"Of your trophy? Oh, definitely."

"I might let you hold it."

"If only I'm so lucky."

He smirks, gripping his textbook and slamming his locker door. "Come on. You can walk me to class."

"Man, he gets one more trophy than me and gets all bossy."

"Get on my level, Elli."

I lose it laughing, moving down the hall with him. *This guy.* Where was he years ago?

"See you at lunch, baby."

He moves to head inside his classroom, flashing me a wink over his shoulder. "I'll be the one in your T-shirt."

NINETEEN

TWENTY BUCKS

ELLIOTT

I THOUGHT when I'd stepped into the storm of sweaty bodies that was Fritz on a Friday night I'd hit my max of being entirely out of my element. There were no other aspects of North Carolina that could render me speechless.

And then I stepped inside a dance competition.

I really don't know why I was thinking it'd be some relaxed event where we all sit in movie theater chairs and eat popcorn while people dance across the stage and the judges hold up numbers.

I've never been to anything dance related, so I had no business holding any sort of expectations about what today would be like. That still didn't stop my jaw from scraping the ground when I waltzed inside of a giant performing arts center.

People. Were. Everywhere.

Guys and girls were barreling through hallways. Groups were practicing in whatever space they could find that was big enough. Clouds of hairspray suffocated me as I walked by.

And that was before I even stepped foot inside the auditorium. There was no popcorn and nothing about it was relaxing. Audience members were standing up in aisles, screaming loudly as dancers pounded across the stage, moving their limbs at speeds that would definitely give my dragster a run for its money.

My whole body was rocking with the force of the bass coming from speakers the size of my truck. I was just getting used to the adrenaline that comes with being inside an auditorium packed full of screaming people.

And then Gideon walked onstage.

Piper's laughter at my reaction could barely be heard over the screams erupting from the audience. My jaw smacked the ground as I flew out of my seat so I could ensure I didn't miss even a single moment of my boyfriend flying across the stage like some majestic bird. He told me he was good—and I knew he won two trophies but I guess it didn't dawn on me what it takes to get a trophy in the dance world.

Apparently, it takes spinning in a circle on one foot a million times in a row without falling over. Running across the stage, flipping into the air and landing in a position that I'd think broke his back if he didn't keep soaring across the stage in a loose blue shirt I'm positive matches his eyes impeccably.

Watching Gideon dance was like some sort of out of body experience. I was entirely captivated—completely bewitched by my boyfriend's dancing skills. If he messed up, I wouldn't have known or cared. He was still the best one to step on that stage.

And I didn't even clap for him.

"I can't believe I didn't clap for him."

"Dude, it's fine." Preston clicks through his camera, giving not a single shit he got yelled at three times for taking pictures inside. "It's like a thing here."

"It's a thing to stand there like a total noob and not clap for your boyfriend?"

"I'm not sure if the noob part is a thing." Piper says, rummaging through all the stuff for sale while we stand in a congested lobby area and wait for Gideon to come say hi before he has to dance again. "But Preston's right. Not clapping is a thing. It means he rendered you speechless with his awesome skills."

"You totally just made that up."

"I did not. Swear to God. It's a thing." She lifts a pair of funky pants, grimaces at the price, and sets them back down. "But you're still a noob just because."

"Here he comes." I spot him squeezing through the crowd of people. "Nobody say anything about me not clapping."

"Hey, guys." He grins, addressing everyone but only looking at me.

"Elliott didn't clap for you." Nate says.

I turn and hurl my fist in his gut.

"Dude." He groans. "It's. A. Thing."

"I'm gonna clap next time." I tell Gideon, who's trying to hold back laughter induced by Nate's dramatic wailing. "Next time gets double claps."

"You didn't clap for me?"

"No, but I swear I will next time."

"He was standing there like a noob." Preston thrusts his camera in Gideon's face. "I got a picture of him looking all starry-eyed. Check it out."

"Awwwww." Gideon croons. "He's totally obsessed with me."

I roll my eyes. "I am not. I barely even like you."

"Go tell that to the drool on the floor under your chair."

Nate gets another punch for that comment.

"Elli." Gideon chuckles. "It's okay. Not clapping is a thing."

"Told you." Piper smirks. "It's like a compliment."

I have no idea how that adds up but judging by the stars in my boyfriend's eyes, I'd say me not clapping for him while I supposedly drooled on the floor is the world's best compliment.

How strange.

He nudges my hip with his own. "So, does that mean you enjoyed it?"

"Are you kidding, babe? It was beautiful. I had no idea you could do that."

Piper rests her head on Gid's shoulder. "I believe he compared you to a majestic bird."

"A majestic bird?" He chuckles. "Why?"

"Because of the soaring and what not. And your shirt."

He peers down at the shirt. I'm able to confirm it does match his eyes impeccably.

"It's bright. And... pretty."

"Pretty?"

"Yes. For lack of a better word, you look pretty."

Damn. Can't a man admire his boyfriend by comparing him to exotic animals?

"Guys, did you hear that? Elli thinks I'm pretty."

"Oh for shit's sake." I mumble. "You just looked beautiful, okay? I've never seen anything like that before."

Nate throws his arm around my shoulder. "Elliott lost his dance competition virginity. I'd put it in the group chat, but we're all right here soooo." He takes a bite of a granola bar. "Anybody lose any other virginities recently?"

"Dude." Preston finally drops his camera. "Where'd you get that granola bar?"

"Snack table."

"What snack table?"

Nate drops his arm. "Come on, man. Stick with me."

"Ooo." Piper links her arm with Nate's. "Me too."

The three of them disappear into the crowd while Gideon continues to stare at me like he just won the jackpot at a casino.

"When do you dance again?"

"Like an hour."

"I'll clap."

"I like it better when you drool." He chuckles at my expression and nudges his head. "Come on. I left my water in the dressing room."

I follow him reluctantly. "Am I allowed to go in there?"

"It's the male's dressing room. Are you a male?"

"Last time I checked."

"Then we're golden."

I follow him down a long hallway, stepping over dancers stretching. We pass a ton of rooms that all appear to be dressing rooms for women. He turns a corner and quickly yanks me into a small room.

"Uhm..." I peer around, finding the lights dimmed. I'm almost certain we're in somebody's office. And I didn't spot a dressing room sign on the door like there was on a dozen others. "This is the dressing room?"

"Nope." He attacks me.

It takes me a second to comprehend his arms around my neck and his lips moving against mine. Once my brain registers what's happening, I wrap my arms around him and lift him off his feet, plopping him on top of the desk.

Holy shit.

"We aren't supposed to be in here, are we?" I whisper against his lips.

"Probably not." I feel his smile form against my own. "But I just wanted to kiss you."

"You won't be hearing any objections from me."

"I didn't think so." He kisses my cheek. "You're still coming to stay with me tonight?"

"Nothing could keep me away."

I cup his beaming face and kiss him softly, playing with his curls until loud footsteps turn our bodies to stone.

"I've got some extras in here."

"Elli." His eyes fall from his face, his voice hushed. "I think someone is coming in here."

"Shit." I yank him off the desk and peer around frantically, looking for a closet to hide in or a window to shove him out of. There are both options. I grab his wrist and go with the closet.

Probably the better option so I don't drop him on his head before he's supposed to dance.

The door clicks behind us, trapping us in total darkness.

"Here we go. Should be in here."

I clamp my hand over Gideon's mouth to mask his gasp and drop my face to his curls to mask mine.

We definitely don't need to get caught in a closet together at a public event where he's representing his parent's business.

Talk about a reckless teenager.

Silent laughter bubbles in my chest at the thought. It knocks against his as we fight to keep our shit together.

"Awesome. Thank you so much. You're a lifesaver."

"No problem. The show must go on."

As soon as the door closes with a thud, we give in to our laughter.

"Holy shit, babe. We almost got caught making out in here."

He rubs his face on my chest. "That would've been so funny yet so bad. My dads would've given me the longest lecture."

I push the closet door back open. "Let's go get your water, trouble."

"Me?" He gasps. "I was just gonna go for one kiss. You're the one who mauled me."

I pinch his side. "Liar."

He winks at me. "Come on."

I follow him back down the hall, trying not to look like I just spent ten minutes with my lips locked on his. I'm sure I'm failing epically. I always have a weird look on my face after I kiss him.

Gideon says it's just a smile. I say it's more. My eyes are brighter, my cheeks redder. I look more... alive, I guess. I haven't tried to analyze it. It doesn't matter what kind of look it is. I like it.

Gideon pulls open a different door. This one has a sign on the front and leads to a room where lights are actually turned on. There are only two other guys in here. One's dead asleep using a backpack as a pillow, and the other has headphones strapped over his head as he peers at his phone screen.

"Most everybody is in the audience watching or in the hallway practicing." Gideon explains, squatting down and unzipping his backpack. Art In Motion is embroidered on the front with Stryker sewn into one of the straps. He pulls his water bottle free and starts attempting to tug a sweatshirt free.

"Cold?"

"No. Starving. I have food here but my dad will kill me if I get something on my majestic bird shirt."

I shove his shoulder. "Don't tease me."

"Me? Tease you? Never!"

I chuckle at the innocent look he's attempting to keep on his face. It's a failed effort as he tugs on his sweatshirt.

"I need a bigger backpack." He yanks roughly. The

second the sweatshirt comes free, so does everything else he has inside. "Oh, shit."

I lung to grab the runaway items when something rolls past my feet and catches my eye. I jerk abruptly at the bottle of pills rolling across the carpet. I freeze as though ice water was poured directly into my veins. My brain short circuits and fails to create a reasonable explanation as to why he has a massive bottle of pills.

My jackass brain can't come up with anything other than the fact that he's dying.

Pills equal sickness. The last person I loved who was sick was my mama. And she died.

My chest burns as I try to comprehend the idea of him dying. It's completely incomprehensible. I can't even begin to handle the magnitude of—

"Elliott!" I snap back to reality with an aggressive jolt and find his palms on my face, wild eyes searching mine. "What's wrong?"

"Are you dying?"

He rocks backward. "What?"

"Pills." I manage to choke the word out. "In your backpack. Pills mean sickness. Sickness means dying. Like my mama."

His face morphs into something I can't read. "Elli... don't move."

As if I could right now.

I watch with hazy eyes as he digs in the backpack he must've repacked and forces the bottle in my hands.

"Elli, look."

I peer down and turn the bottle so I can see the label.

Fucking Christ.

Men's Multi-Vitamins.

He's not dying. He's taking multi-vitamins, and I'm a total lunatic.

"I'm sorry." I take a long breath. "I just…"

"It's okay." He tosses the bottle back at his bag. "I'm gonna hug you right now. Okay?"

"Okay." I mumble, dropping my face to his curls as his arms come around me. "You're not dying." I don't know why I say it. It's pretty obvious now but some part of me that isn't healed from her death forces the words out anyway.

His face finds home in my neck. "No, babe. I'm not. I promise."

I hug him tighter. The knot lodged in my chest starts to smooth out. The idea of losing another person I love is—*holy shit.*

My barely functioning brain works double time as I rethink that sentence and the one that came way before it.

The last person I loved…

I'll be damned.

My chest warms as I smile into a bundle of his curls.

I'm in love with Gideon Stryker—and I owe gramps twenty bucks.

TWENTY

HUG IT OUT

ELLIOTT

I'LL BE the first to admit my initial attitude when moving to North Carolina was that I'd finish my final year of high school a miserable, cynical jackass. But somehow, in a world of chaos and mayhem, I've managed to find some peace.

I started racing again, found some great friends, and fell in love with a guy who still has no idea. I thought the potential for strange things to happen had timed out. I thought I was used to the chaos.

Then gramps brought home a girl—and I. Am. Shook.

"Boy, close your damn mouth before a fly buzzes in and chokes ya to death."

I snap my mouth closed though I'm positive my eyeballs have fallen out and hit the floor. "There's a girl at the table."

"She's eighty years old, Elliott." Gramps grunts, pulling on his belt. "She ain't a girl."

"Thatcher." The woman in question chides. "I'm only seventy-three."

"She calls you Thatcher?"

The wrinkle in his forehead deepens. "What the hell you going on about? That's my name."

"Your name is Spanky. Everybody calls you Spanky."

"Well, Minnie calls me Thatcher. Take your damn boots off at the door."

Take my damn boots off.

He doesn't make any attempt to introduce me to the petite woman sitting at our small dining room table with snow white hair piled high on her head and long pink nails wrapped around a dainty looking mug I've never seen before.

Holy shit. He's buying her special dishes. Now that I scan the kitchen, I find some sort of sugar cookies stacked neatly on a plate and not a single model car in sight.

I wonder if he met her at the grocery store or bingo.

A smirk unfolds on my face as I stand there. "Is Minnie your girlfriend?"

Minnie's pink lips pull into a small smile. Gramps gawks at me like I lost my damn mind. "Boy, I'm pushing eighty. I don't have girlfriends. She's a friend."

"A friend you bought special dishes and cookies for."

"She's prettier than all my other friends."

"Well damn. A dude goes to work and comes home to find his gramps with a girlfriend. What a day."

I slip off my boots and slide into the kitchen, plopping into a chair across from Minnie. Maybe they are too old to call each other boyfriend and girlfriend, but there's definitely something twinkling in my gramps' eyes I haven't seen in a long, long time. He's also wearing some seriously overbearing old man cologne.

"So, where did you guys you meet? Frozen waffle aisle?"

Gramps grunts. "I'd smack your head if I could reach it."

"Thatcher." Minnie swats him. I like her already. "Elliott, dear, Thatcher and I met years ago. We decided to catch up when I was at Speed."

My ears perk up. "You were at Speed? When?"

"Yesterday afternoon. Just visiting some old friends."

Old friends? What elderly woman is friends with the sweaty jokers that fix up racecars? "Uh, cool. Do you know Dan?"

A raspy laugh rattles gramps' gut. "Kid's sitting in front of a racing legend and has no idea."

Racing legend?

Minnie's lips pull into a friendly smile behind the rim of her dainty cup. She clears her throat, setting her cup back on top of a paper towel torn in half because we don't actually have napkins. I reach for a cookie and shove the entire thing in my mouth, chewing slowly as I study gramps' non-girlfriend.

She's not dressed like a typical old lady. No floral prints, pearl necklaces, or fancy scarves. She's wearing a plain black t-shirt with a worn denim jacket slung over her shoulders. If I was a creeper, I'd look under the table and see if she's wearing jeans. I'm not a creeper. So, I'll take my best guess and say yes.

"Minnie, you want me to get ya some more tea?"

I grunt. Since when does gramps make tea? This is such a head trip. I can't wait to tell Gideon.

"Oh, I'm fine." She all but croons at him. "Elliott, your grandfather told me you're getting back into racing?"

"Yep. First race is at the end of April."

"How exciting. Then it's the top fuel races, huh?"

"That's the plan."

"Oh, I'm sure you'll be burning gallons of nitromethane in no time."

I narrow my eyes and snag another cookie. Gramps must've really filled her in on all the racing lingo. Minnie knows more than half the dudes at Speed know. They'll look at you dumbstruck if you mention nitromethane.

Morons.

Then, as she smirks at gramps and pats the top of his hand like they're a couple of old friends, the clouds open up and take pity on me by dropping a bunch of sense into my pea-sized brain.

"Minnie." Half a cookie falls out of my mouth as I blurt her name and fly out of my chair so quickly, the old piece of wood crashes to the floor. "Holy shit! You're Minnie. As in Margaret. As in Margaret Minnie St. Thomas, the first woman to ever win a Wally Trophy."

"Ah. The boy's gears are turning now." Gramps snorts. "'Bout time."

"I can't believe I didn't know it was you. You're like... better than gramps."

"Whoa, boy. She beat me one time."

"Once was enough, dear." She pats his shoulder. "And now I have one more trophy than you."

I double over in laughter at the scowl that appears on gramps' face. Old man has no trouble dishing it out but apparently, he can't take it when it's dished to him. This is the best day ever.

"I'm so happy you're here, Minnie. Gramps needs his ego bruised."

"I'm very good at that." She grins.

I don't have any idea why Minnie St. Thomas is suddenly sitting in my kitchen, flirting with an old man when she's supposed to be traveling around the country and mentoring young racers. But I ain't complaining.

"Maybe you could watch me take a few runs? Give me some pointers?"

I do my best to act nonchalant. By the way gramps' eyes roll back into his head, I'd say I'm failing epically.

"Sure, dear. I'd love to. I'll be sticking around for a while."

I flash a wink. "Is it because gramps bought you special dishes?"

A cookie crumbles against my face. "Get your ass out of here. Go do homework or stare at the wall."

"I'm gonna go call Gideon and tell him you have a girlfriend."

"She's not my girlfriend."

"Liar." I all but skip out of the house and plop down on the porch with my phone in my hand. I pull up his number before thinking better of it. He's in dance class. The likelihood that he'll answer is pretty low. So, I text him instead and hope he's on a break and can text back.

ME: I HAVE THE CRAZIEST NEWS EVER!!!! YOU'RE GONNA LOSE YOUR MIND!

GIDEON TWO-TIME NATIONAL TITLE WINNER: FOR REAL?!?! MY CLASS STARTS IN TWO MINUTES AND YOU LEAVE ME WITH THAT?!

ME: GRAMPS HAS A GIRLFRIEND AND SHE IS A LEGENDARY RACER.

GIDEON TWO-TIME NATIONAL TITLE WINNER: SHUT THE HELL UP

ME: DEAD ASS. SHE IS SITTING AT THE TABLE RIGHT NOW. EATING A SUGAR COOKIE.

GIDEON TWO-TIME NATIONAL TITLE WINNER: SINCE WHEN DO YOU GUYS HAVE SUGAR COOKIES?

ME: EXACTLY! THIS IS THE CRAZIEST THING TO HAPPEN SINCE SLICED BREAD!

GIDEON TWO-TIME NATIONAL TITLE WINNER: STAY OVER TONIGHT! I NEED EVERY DETAIL AND MY CLASS IS ABOUT TO START!!

ME: OKAY! I'M GONNA GO STEAL MORE COOKIES.

GIDEON TWO-TIME NATIONAL TITLE WINNER: OOOOO COOKIES. I'M STARVING.

GIDEON TWO-TIME NATIONAL TITLE WINNER: CLASS IS STARTING. GOTTA GO. <3

ME: SEE YOU TONIGHT <3

GIDEON

"Alright! Roll the mats up." My dad claps his hands together, pointing at the acro equipment and gesturing for my team and I to get it cleaned up.

I guzzle almost my entire bottle of water, shaking sweat from my curls before I pitch in and help put studio six back to the way it was before we tore it apart to practice flailing our bodies in the air and standing on our heads.

Practice was filled with sweat, sore muscles, and reassurance that we're gonna kick major ass at nationals. One more trophy for me.

Elli's gonna be so jealous.

"Hey, kid. Dad and I are still gonna be a while before we head home."

I sling my backpack over my shoulders, flipping the light switch and following Beck out of studio six. "Okay. I'll just meet you at home then."

"You're on your own for dinner."

"Alrighty then. Guess I'm going to be stopping by the cafe."

"Eat something other than a soft pretzel, Gideon. That cheese comes in a bag."

"So why do you keep ordering it?"

He smirks and says nothing. He keeps ordering it because it's my favorite. We both know it. "You better hurry before Jamie shuts the place down."

My feet stutter against the carpeting. "Wait... what? Jamie? Jamie Atcot?"

"That's the one."

"What's he doing here?"

"Working."

"He quit."

"He quit so he could play basketball. Basketball is over. So now he's working again."

Frustration bubbles in my chest. "Why the hell didn't anyone tell me?"

He jerks, stopping in the center of the hallway. "Why does it matter?"

"Uhm, maybe because he's the jerk that made up lies about me and spewed them to my boyfriend? What the hell, dad? This is so uncool."

"This is real life, Gideon. I was upset about what he said too but fact is, he needs a job and he knows the ins and outs of that place."

My fists clench. "Are you serious right now? My parents hired the dude who went around telling people I'm a sleazeball?"

"Dad and I talked to Jamie about it for a long time, kid. We considered your feelings. He apologized to us for what he said."

"Well, he sure as shit didn't apologize to me."

"Did you give him the chance to?" He sighs roughly when I do nothing but spear him with a glare. "At this point, it doesn't matter what was said or what was done. You and Jamie started off on parallel ground here. Life got in the way, feelings were hurt, and things got messy."

"So, you're saying it's my responsibly to go after my own apology? What the hell? I don't remember spreading any lies about anyone."

"Jamie is not infallible, Gideon. Feelings get hurt and people make mistakes. If you're closed off and cold towards him, how can he feel comfortable enough to approach you and be vulnerable enough to admit he was wrong? If you don't open yourself up to the chance for an apology, you aren't going to get one."

Sorry seems to be one of those things that's difficult to give out and accept. The second I heard what Jamie told Elliott, I didn't even glance in his direction. I went out of my way to avoid him in the halls and keep my curls in front of my face.

My natural instinct was to dish the asshole attitude right back at him. Tit for tat, I guess. I got so sick of lies being piled on top of lies, I didn't consider the people spreading them might actually feel remorseful for creating them. I have never gotten an apology before, so why now? Why is it up to me to seek out the people who bully me?

I guess maybe it's because forgiving someone's mistakes takes a lot of confidence—confidence in them that it won't happen again and confidence in yourself that you won't let it break you down if it does. Giving Jamie the chance to say he's sorry means letting go of the superiority feeling I seem to have that says I don't need his apology to make things better.

But I do.

Nobody wants to end high school not on speaking terms with someone they used to be friends with. Nobody wants to wonder why the rumor was started or if feelings they hurt were the catalyst. Nobody wants to leave high school and wonder if they should have apologized too.

I spin around, heading towards the cafe in the back of the studio. I tap my knuckles against the doorframe, announcing my presence. I find Jamie in an Art In Motion T-shirt and jeans, wiping down a table in the center of the room.

"Hey, Jamie."

"Gideon." He blinks. "Uh, hey. Did you want a pretzel?"

"No, thanks. I was actually hoping we could talk."

He tenses, nerves filtering across his face. "Yeah, okay." He sways back and forth on his feet, twisting the rag tightly in his hands. "I've been meaning to talk to you. I'm... I'm really sorry about what I told Elliott. I know it's not true. I'm sure it sucked hearing it."

"It did. It sucked a lot, Jamie. It really hurt. Not just because you lied but because you told Elliott. Were you trying to break us up or something?"

"No. Yes." He shakes his head, getting his thoughts in order. "No. I was just feeling bitter and insecure. I lashed out."

"But... why?" I start towards him, sitting on the edge of the table he just wiped down. "If I hurt your feelings when I suggested we just be friends, I didn't mean to."

He scoffs. "Ya know, just because you didn't mean to doesn't mean you didn't."

"I'm sorry, Jamie. Truly."

"I put a lot of thought into that date, and it felt like you wrote it off."

"That's not what I was trying to do, Jamie. I had fun. I just—"

"You weren't feeling it. That's fine and acceptable. I'm not trying to make you feel bad for not liking me that way. I just wanna explain my mindset. You were the first guy I'd dated after I got dumped by the guy I was with since freshmen year. Getting rejected twice in such a short time burned a bit too much. I basically spent the summer partying with my older sister and drowning in my self pity."

"I tried to reach out though. You never texted back. I didn't want to stop being friends."

"Gideon, you texted me like a day after. Sorry if I wasn't jumping at the chance to hang out as friends after you dodged my kiss."

I grimace. Maybe I didn't try hard enough to maintain our friendship. Summer lasted three months and not once did I seek him out. I guess it's easier to pretend someone hates us rather than believe we caused them to struggle. "I'm sorry, Jamie."

"It's okay, Gideon. I don't want to make you feel guilty over not liking me or not attempting to keep being my friend when I purposely ignored you. I just wanted you to know that I don't think of you as the person I made you out to be."

"I guess I just don't understand why you did it. What happened between us went down almost a year ago."

He sighs roughly, ditching his rag to run his hands through his hair. "I guess I got jealous when I heard you and Elliott spent Christmas together. Not because I had feelings for you still but because you two are so happy and comfortable in your relationship. That's huge for a couple of gay kids in high school. I was jealous and had the mindset that nobody can have it if I can't. I was a dick."

"I get that, Jamie. You have no idea how bitter I was when I walked into school on the first day. It's hard seeing others enjoying aspects of life that make you miserable."

"I'm sorry I vomited my teenage angst on your relationship."

"I accept your apology, Jamie. And this world is so much bigger than high school. You'll find someone."

His lips pull into a smile, and I think I have a friend again. "I actually just met this guy."

"Yeah? He cute?"

"Totally cute." He blushes. "I met him when we were both volunteering at a youth basketball camp."

"He go to Hillside?"

"No. Durham Tech, actually."

"A college guy? Damn, Jamie."

He chuckles. "He's a freshman. Less than six months

older than me but my mom still had a fit when she caught us making out in his car."

"Eh, parents are obligated to do that. I'm happy for you."

"Thanks. I'm gonna apologize to Elliott too."

"I think he'd really like that."

"Yeah? Cool. He kind of terrifies me."

"It's just his face."

He chuckles. "Thanks for being so cool, man. I feel like such a dick."

"You weren't the only one who screwed up. I shouldn't have been so standoffish. I'm sure I made it hard to apologize. I'm happy for you and your basketball player. Maybe we could double date sometime."

"Well, that'd be an odd turn of events." He goes quiet, peering around the room like he's ready to bolt but doesn't know if he should. "So, should we hug it out or something?"

I chuckle, standing from the table and holding open my arms. "Sure, Jamie. Let's hug it out."

TWENTY-ONE

OVERPRICED NOODLES & A MISUNDERSTANDING

ELLIOTT

I SWEAR I get dorkier and dorkier every minute I spend in this town and around adults who aren't total dickwads. After I went and stole half a dozen cookies from gramps and his non-girlfriend, I attempted to do some homework. I failed. When gramps told me he was taking Minnie for a quick dinner, I lost my shit like a complete noob and started cracking jokes about curfew and taking a dime for a phone call home.

God.

Who am I?

Apparently, I'm some dude who smiles a lot and ditches homework to drive across town and buy his boyfriend noodles. Gideon loves noodles. And because I love him, I'll stand in an outrageously long line for one bowl of carbohydrates and then stride into Art In Motion with a skip in my step I'll never admit is there.

"Hey, kiddo."

"Hi, Beck." I slow my non-existent skip. "Do you know what studio Gideon is in? And can I bring this to him?"

Beck's lips turn up. "You brought him noodles?"

"He loves noodles."

"Yeah, he does. Kid's been obsessed with them since he was a toddler." He nudges his head towards a hallway. "I think he's back in the cafe. Better hurry up before he stuffs himself full of soft pretzels."

"Got it." I nod swiftly and start down the hall to the cafe that's big enough to be a cafeteria. When first walking into the lobby, you'd have no idea how big this place truly is. It has fifteen studio rooms, its own store, and a second story. It's basically a miniature mall. Except, it's filled with dance rooms instead of overpriced hipster stores.

I step through the entryway, the smell of nacho cheese stirring memories. The first time I visited the studio, Gideon showed me how to work the pretzel machine and we went nuts. I scarfed down so many pretzels, I swore I'd never be able to even look at one again. My traitorous stomach growls at the smell. I picture myself dipping the fluffy goodness into Alfredo sauce.

I stride into the room, the makings of a greeting forming on my tongue. I brush the tips of my hair out of my eyes and scan the large room for him. My stomach bottoms out when I spot him.

You hear that? That sudden hellish rumble that sounds like the earth is splitting in two? That's the sound of my heart cracking. I know because it's the same sound it made when my mama died.

My chest *aches* as I get a good look at James Appleweed smiling at my boyfriend, his arms locked tightly around him. I slam my eyes shut to stop the sudden moisture.

"Elli?"

They spring back open, trying to find Gideon's wide eyes behind a sheen of tears. Sweat pools at my temples, and I think I'm gonna hurl.

I was gonna tell him I love him.

"Elliott." His body flails from Appleweed's tight grip. "Oh my God. No! It wasn't—"

"You're an asshole." I grind, my stone body trembling.

Out of all the people he could be getting cozy with, it's the guy who's already tried to drive a wedge between us.

"No. It wasn't like that! He was just apologizing and we hugged it out." He rushes me, arms outstretched.

I stumble backward, the bag of food slipping from my grip. "I should've known."

Loyal partners are pretty few and far between for people in the Oakley family. I witnessed that shit show first-hand and still didn't learn my lesson. I fell hard for the curly-haired dancer boy who sucks at chemistry and was supposed to have a heart too big for his chest.

"Elliott. Oh God." Blood drains from his face. "I'm so sorry. This is all a misunderstanding."

"Yeah. It is." I wipe a tear that escaped. Fucking traitor. "You and me. A misunderstanding."

"What? No! Not us." He shakes his violently, his hands waving quickly like he's trying to rewind time.

He can't. The vision of him wrapped around someone who isn't me is burned into my brain forever.

"We're great, Elli! That hug? That was the misunderstanding."

"Elliott." Red tinges my vision when James takes a step forward. This fucker has the audacity to attempt to speak to me? "I'm sorry for being a dick. Gideon and I are just friends, man. Swear to God."

"I don't give a fuck who you swear to." I flip him the bird and decide to pretend he evaporated into thin air. "We're done, Gideon."

"No, we're not. Just listen. Please. I—"

"Don't tell me we're not, Gideon!" Hear that? That

high-pitched hissing that sounds like a volcano is about to explode? That's me losing the last of my mind.

"You're scum." My vision blurs with fury and pain, my foot making contact with the bag of food. Noodles go flying and I can't bring myself to give even a single shit. "I just stood in line at some hipster noodle place buying you over-priced Alfredo so I could show up here and surprise you. Turns out, I'm the one who's surprised. Joke's on me! While I'm rolling in here with a smile on my face like some loser, my boyfriend's in here getting all cozy with the asshole who tried to break us up. *Surprise!*"

I'm hysterical—I know. I'm making a huge scene and a major fool of myself. I just don't care.

"Elli—"

"Don't ever call me that again." I spit, my finger shaking as I hurl it into his face. "You're a cheater. You know what kind of people cheaters are, Gideon?"

I do. I know all too well, and I can't fucking breathe when memories start to blur my vision. Moisture threatens to stain my cheeks. My body trembles violently in the boots he bought me for Christmas.

"Cheaters are life ruiners. Heartless sickos who don't care about who they destroy in their path so they can get their rocks off."

I spin on my heels, wiping my face and body checking the people blocking the doorway who must think I'm psychotic for crumbling.

Fuck this town. Fuck cancer. Fuck love. Fuck Gideon Stryker, and fuck my heart for caring so much that's he running after me, yelling my name with a shaky voice. I sniff roughly and lift both my middle fingers over my head, projecting all the anger because I can't project the pain.

I'll never be vulnerable to him ever again. I should've

stuck to my original plan. I should have never given him permission to mess me up in that pizza place.

As I'm peeling out of the parking lot, wiping my face fiercely, I feel an extreme amount of relief under all the sudden suffering.

I'm so relieved he doesn't know how much I love him.

GIDEON

Spanky pulls open the door a crack and stares at me with eyes full of confusion. "Gideon, hey. Look, I don't think Elliott—"

"Yeah, he's pissed at me. I know. That's why I need to come in."

"I don't think that's a good idea."

"Yeah, well, it probably isn't but I'm doing it anyway." I push open the door and stomp inside the small living room, unsurprised when he doesn't try to stop me.

My boyfriend isn't the only one who's pissed off. After the scene he made and the way he just so casually chalked me up to being a cheater, after he promised to trust me and hear me out, has my fucking blood boiling so fucking hot, my fucking head is about to blow off my fucking neck.

Spanky sighs and rubs his bald head. "Elliott! Gideon's here."

"Tell him to go fuck himself!"

"Uh, Gideon... he said to go fuck yourself."

"Yep. I heard him." I push my way past Spanky and stomp down the hall to the den he lives in. I throw open the french doors, ready and willing to fight with him. Fight *for* him.

He sits up in his bed and glares at me. "I thought I told you to go fuck yourself."

"Shut up, Elliott. You had your chance to speak. You

told me what an asshole and a liar I was. I gave you your chance and I listened. Now, I want my chance."

"You think it's gonna make a difference? I told you I don't do cheaters."

"I'm not a fucking cheater, Elliott. Deep down, you know that."

"I know what I saw, Gideon." His anger starts to slip away, and I'm given a glimpse into how bad he's actually hurting. His hands are wringing together, his face is stricken, and his breathing is choppy. He's trying really hard to hold in the hurt, but he's failing miserably.

"Yeah, babe, I know what you saw. I know it doesn't make sense to you which is why I'm here to explain it. So shut up and listen." He opens his mouth to shoot off another pissed off reply. I talk over him. "If I would've known Jamie started working at the cafe again, I would've told you. But I didn't, okay? My dad just told me tonight. I had every intention of telling you. I confronted him about what he said to you and—"

"And what? You made amends? You decided you needed to wrap your arms around him one last time? Rub your chests together? Ever heard of a handshake? I TRUSTED YOU!"

"NO, YOU DIDN'T! You aren't trusting me right now, Elli."

"His hands were practically on your ass. Did you do it just to hurt me, or did you decide I wasn't enough for you anymore? I wasn't giving you what you needed so you went to the one you originally wanted?"

I know he's in pain. I know he's trying to mask that with anger but that was a low blow. And it fucking *hurt*. "You're an asshole for saying that. You're an asshole for even thinking that but hey, everybody else does, right?"

His anger starts to slip. "Gideon..."

"Ya know what, Elliott? Maybe you were right. Maybe we shouldn't have started this. If your first instinct is to run from me and use insults to mask your anger when you should trust me and respect me enough to let me explain, then something's wrong."

"Yeah, I agree, which is why I told you to go fuck yourself."

"That's actually what you want? You want me to leave?"

"I didn't even want you to show up in the first place."

"So, we're done then? Just like that? You aren't going to hear me out?"

"Nope."

Un-fucking-believable. "Kay, Elliott." I pull my shit together long enough to turn around and throw the doors back open.

A voice comes at my back. "Did you kiss him?"

"No, Elliott. I didn't kiss him."

"Were you about to?"

"Are you kidding me right now?"

"You didn't even notice me walk in, Gideon. You were too wrapped up in whatever you were saying to him that was making him all dopey eyed."

"I was talking about you, Elliott."

"What? Going over the best ways to cut me loose?"

"No, you asshole. I was telling him I'm in love with you."

TWENTY-TWO

CHAOS IN IT'S FINEST FORM

ELLIOTT

IN LOVE WITH YOU...

In love...

***love**...*

My mind barely registers the sound of the front door slamming. His words are throbbing in my head, the painful look on his face stuck in my brain like a broken DVD that refuses play.

What the hell have I done?

He just declared his love for me and I let him walk away filled with a mixture of rage and pain. Gideon asked me to try for him and I didn't. I didn't try at all. I saw Appleweed's arms around him and lost my shit. I didn't ask questions, didn't wait for an explanation or an apology. I couldn't. Not when my heart was cracking and my brain was filling with memories so painful, I lost my breath.

At that moment, Gideon wasn't Gideon. My brain replaced his face with someone else's. Someone who inflicted enough pain on me, I had to move five states away in order to escape it. Even now, I can't escape it. I took my pain and pushed it on the man I love.

Despite how terribly my heart is burning with the need to chase after Gideon and confess I love him just as desperately as he loves me, I don't. Because I hurt him. With the way my brain works, I'll probably do it again.

"Ya just gonna sit here wiping them tears or are ya gonna go get your lover back?" My foggy gaze finds gramps in the doorway, scowling at me with his arms crossed over his chest. "That boy just confessed to being in love with you. Now, you can bullshit me all you want but I know you're in love with him too. So get your ass off that shitty sofa bed and go get him."

"Gramps... I can't." I wipe my tears the second they leak from my eyes. "I can't do this with him."

"Elliott, you didn't even listen to what he has to say."

"I don't need to listen to what he has to say." I shout, finally allowing myself to feel something other than anger. "I know him. I know his intentions were good."

"Then what's the issue?"

"The issue is that my brain went there anyway." I fly up from the bed and start pacing. "For a moment, I thought the worst of him. I thought he was capable of breaking me. I screamed at him and probably embarrassed the hell out of him and ya know what? It could happen again. I had no business getting into a relationship with him—no business falling in love with him because it could happen again. Only next time, it could be for real. Relationships are fucked up. I've seen it firsthand. Gideon just has a way of making me not care."

"Because you're in love with him."

"Sometimes love isn't enough."

"Elliott... sit down. Now."

I stop pacing immediately and sit down on the sofa bed next to the place my gramps just claimed. His hand falls on my back and he starts rubbing. "Take a breath, kid."

I take a deep breath and try to get my thoughts in order. "Just because I love him doesn't mean he won't hurt me. Maybe today he didn't mean it. But maybe next time he will."

"Elliott... Gideon isn't your daddy..."

"Don't talk about him." The floodgates open, sending tears flowing down my face. All it takes is a mention and I'm thrust back into the awful place I was months ago.

"Elliott... what your daddy did... that isn't normal."

"He killed her!" A choked noise rips out of my chest. Monster tears pour down my face faster than what I can wipe away. "He killed my mama!"

"Oh, Elliott." His arms are around me in half a second. "Your daddy is an asshole. He's a sick son of a bitch and I hate him for what he did. But he didn't kill your mama. The cancer did."

"She was doing better. She was gonna get better and then he destroyed it."

"No, Elliott."

"Yes. I was there. He killed her and I hate him." I cry. "I hate him for taking my mama away."

"Kiddo, I know that's what you want to believe... Hell, that's what I want to believe. It's easier that way but it isn't true. You know it was the cancer. You're using your daddy as an excuse to push away someone you love because you think that boy is gonna be like him. You think that boy is gonna break you the same way your daddy broke your mama."

"I thought they loved each other. I thought he loved her but he didn't. He was lying."

"Just because your daddy is a liar doesn't mean Gideon is."

"I can't take the chance." I choke, pushing away and wiping my tears. I haven't cried since my mama died right next to me all those months ago. I've been holding it in and thought that maybe I'd feel better if I let it out. I don't. "I had a plan gramps. I was supposed to lay low, graduate, figure out what I want to do with my life and then get a job. That was it. There wasn't supposed to be a Gideon. He ruined everything."

"Kiddo, that's what happens. This is life. You can try to plan it the way you want it but something always comes in and wrecks that plan. Sometimes it's bad. Sometimes it's really good. Sometimes you get lucky and it's really, really wonderful."

"Well, what's Gideon?"

"You tell me."

"Wonderful. Gideon's wonderful." I wipe my tears. "He's the only person who could make me want to trade my comfortable plan for a life of absolute chaos. But every time something happens, something I can't make sense of, I picture the look on mama's face and I freak out."

"You're scared he's gonna hurt you? Because the relationship that was supposed to be perfect turned out to be a lie?"

I nod. "I'm terrified. He's different, gramps. The other guys, the ones from Iowa, they didn't want me for me. They just used me and tossed me aside. I hated it at first but then I thought maybe I could live with that because it means I'll never have to deal with anything serious. What 17-year-old needs to be serious anyway? But Gideon would never do that to me. He would *never* toss me aside."

"Kind of like what you just did to him?"

"What?"

"You tossed him aside. I get why you did it. I even understand the reason behind it but I don't think it's right. Gideon isn't your father, Elliott. That boy is kind, and I know you said the people in that school can't appreciate him but one day somebody will. For a while it was you. Now that he's gone, maybe it's someone else."

I scoff and clench my fists. "The fuck it is someone else."

"So, it's you then?"

"Gideon's mine."

"Really? Because I'm pretty sure you just threw him away."

"I don't know what to do." I pull at my hair and drop my head to his shoulder.

"Oh quit bullshitting yourself, boy. You know what to do. You declared Gideon was yours the second you kissed him. Now you're just gonna let him walk away? Because you're scared? Newsflash, kiddo. You've been scared this whole time. This is just the first moment you've been able to admit it." His lips press to the side of my head. "We've all got something we are afraid of, son. You're afraid of getting hurt. It's good you know that. You put a face on it and now you know how to kick its ass to the curb. Now, go get Gideon and work this out."

"I don't think there are enough sorrys in the world that will ever make this better. You should've seen his face, gramps. I trashed his parent's business with overpriced noodles."

"I don't think you give that boy enough credit."

"Yeah, well, what happens when I call and he doesn't answer? Or when I show up at his house and his dads kick me out? What happens when he refuses to see me?"

"Don't think you have to worry about that, kiddo."

"How do you know?"

"Because he's standing in the doorway."

My head snaps off gramps' neck. My eyes find Gideon with his hands shoved in the pockets of his joggers, his head resting on the doorframe. There's a tear racing down his cheek. He wipes it away quickly.

"Gideon..."

"Hey."

"You didn't leave...."

He smiles softly. "If you think I was just gonna give you up that easily, then I need to tell you how much I love you a couple more thousand times."

Never in my life will I ever understand why I was given such a beautiful person to fall in love with. "You should definitely do that."

He smiles and starts over to me, replacing gramps' spot next to me. The door clicks behind gramps, leaving me alone with my baby and an apology forming on the tip of my tongue.

"Gideon, I..."

He presses his finger against my lips, silencing me. "I don't know what your dad did, or why you think he killed your mama. I'm hoping one day you'll tell me. If today isn't that day, I'll wait. You know why? Because I love you, Elli. I love you so much, and these past few months you've become everything to me. You're my best friend. My partner. If soulmates are real, then you're that too. You have a piece of my heart and if you're struggling, going through something, I'm gonna be there for you. Whatever went down in your head today, whatever the reason is that you lost your cool, it can be worked out. We can work it out."

"I love you." I blurt. I know he just heard me say it to gramps, but now I need him to hear it directly from me. "I love you so fucking much."

"I know." He wipes his face again. "I've known for weeks."

"What? How?" I sure as shit would remember telling him I loved him.

"You talk in your sleep, Elli. I've been lying on your chest listening to you mumble about being in love with me for a while. I said it back the first time you mumbled it. Your sleepy brain just didn't comprehend what was being said."

"What the...?" My jaw hits the sofa bed. "We've been exchanging declarations of love for weeks and I haven't been conscious?" He laughs softly, nodding. "Why didn't you say anything?"

"I figured there was a reason your conscious brain wasn't saying it yet." His arms link around my neck, his fingers diving into my hair. "Now, I'm thinking it has something to do with your dad."

"Gideon..." His name comes out on a choke.

"Babe, it's okay. You don't have to talk about it right now."

"No. I want to. It's just... hard."

"Take your time, baby. I'm not going anywhere. I promise."

I press a quick kiss to his lips, take a huge breath, close my eyes, and fall into the past. "The day before my mom died, she decided she wanted to sit outside. I couldn't find the home nurse we hired, so I strapped a medical mask over my mama's face, lifted her into my arms, and carried her onto the porch. We sat out there for a long time. Listening to cars drive by, dogs bark, and the clicks of sprinklers. When she started to get sleepy, I lifted her into my arms again."

My body shudders, tears pouring out from beneath my eyelids. "I wish we would've stayed out there longer. I wish we wouldn't have walked in when we did because we weren't supposed to see it. We weren't supposed to find my dad having his way with the woman we hired to help my mama. We weren't supposed to find him cheating on his dying wife. But we did. And you know what makes it so much worse? He didn't even care he was caught. He didn't say a word or spare the tears his wife was shedding a second glance."

"So, I did the only thing I could do. I took my mama to her room and wiped her tears away until she fell asleep. She didn't wake up after that. The doctors said her heart gave out, couldn't handle the strain anymore. The rational part of me knows she was sick and she wasn't gonna make it. But the little boy in me says he broke her heart. He killed what will she had to keep fighting. I held her hand as she died while my father was tonguing the woman who was supposed to help save her." Palms that aren't mine press against my face, removing my tears.

"Mama knew she wasn't gonna make it. She spent part of the time she was bedridden planning her own funeral because she didn't want us to fuss over it. She wanted us to have our time to grieve. I didn't use my time grieving, Gideon. I spent it resenting my father. I hate him for what he did to our family. I hate him for ignoring me during the time between her death and her funeral. I hate him for bringing his young, arm candy girlfriend to my mama's funeral. I hate him for not calling after I moved thousands of miles away. I hate that every time I think of my mama, I can't be sad because I'm filled with so much fucking rage. And I *hate*, God, I *hate* that I'm hopelessly in love with the most beautiful man on the planet and I struggle with trusting him. Even though every ounce of my soul knows he isn't my father."

"Elli." He throws his body at me, crawling on my lap and wrapping his limbs around me as if he's desperate to comfort me. "I wish I could say something or do something to remove all the pain you've been harboring."

I squeeze him harshly, dropping my face to his soft curls. "This helps so much."

"Then I'll never move."

"Ya know, he never reached out. Not once. Didn't call on Thanksgiving or send me a gift on Christmas. He hasn't even sent me a text message asking if I'm alive. He doesn't care at all. I'm so fucking mad about it." More tears drip into his curls. "Goddamn it. Why won't I stop crying?"

"Elli." He tilts his head, cupping my face with one hand, removing my tears with his thumb. "You lost both your parents in one day. That type of loss is unmeasurable. I'm breaking imagining the type of pain you've been living with. It's okay to cry."

"I don't want to cry over him." I sniff violently. "I hate him for what he did. I hate him for destroying our family and leaving me alone while my mama was dying. He doesn't care where I am or what I'm doing. I just don't get it."

"Don't get what, baby?"

"Why he doesn't love me." My chest heaves aggressively as I choke on a mouthful of tears. "I don't know what I did wrong. He's never told me he loves me. He forced me out of racing when he knew how much I loved it. He never allowed me to go do things with friends. He made me work on the farm even after a local body shop offered me a job. He used to make all these backhanded remarks about me being gay. Like I'm somehow not tough. Like how I'd probably rather see a chick flick than an action movie. Rather paint my toenails than be outside and hang with the guys. He made some asshole remark about how I shouldn't be sad about losing racing because it was too tough for someone like me anyway."

"Oh, Elli." He wipes a stray tear from his cheek, wrapping his hand around my neck and finding that soft and rough spot he loves so much.

I drop my forehead to his and breathe roughly. "I'm so

angry, Gideon. I'm angry that parents are conditioned to love their kids and my father only tolerated me. I'm even angrier that I care so much. I shouldn't care. He wasn't even nice to me."

"Of course you care, Elli. He was your father."

"A shitty one."

"Still your father and the fact that he doesn't love you says so much more about him than it does you. Understand me? Every piece that made you who you are is beautiful. Every damn piece. You are talented in a unique way and a secret chemistry genius. You're witty. You have a kind heart. You stand up to bullies and are brave enough to walk away from your whole life and start a new one. I'm sorry if all this sounds like some cliché bullshit I read from a script, but loving you is so easy, Elli Oakley. It literally takes no effort at all. None."

"You're really laying it on me here thick, babe." I sniff, smiling softly. "I'm okay. You don't have to do this."

"That's the thing, Elli. I do have to do this. Because... *God.*" He breathes roughly, kissing my cheek softly. "I don't think anybody ever has."

I kiss his lips, not knowing whether I'm tasting his tears or mine.

"I just... I love you, Elli. I want you to know you're worthy of love. I grew up with parents who pounded it into my head that I'm worthy no matter who I choose to be, what I choose to do, or who I choose to love. Any version of yourself you want to be is worthy of love. Your dad can go straight to hell for making you feel otherwise."

"Amen, boy."

We both flinch, turning our heads to gramps' rough voice. He's standing in the doorway, arms crossed over his chest.

"I know it won't take away the knot in your chest that

comes from your daddy but you know I love you, kid. Yeah?"

I nod. There was never any doubt in mind about that. But sometimes, when you spend so long surrounded by one who doesn't care for you, you forget about the ones who do. "Yeah, gramps."

"Good." He waves his hands. "Proceed with your young love."

I let out a watery chuckle. "What a kook."

"A kook who loves you."

"Yeah..."

Gideon snuggles deeper into my lap, pushing his face into my chest. "When I was a kid, and something bad would happen, my parents used to preach to me about accepting the things life gave us even though we didn't ask for them. Because one day, life will give us something we didn't ask for and it will be everything we need. I can't help but think that life gave you this. Hillside High, Spanky, racing—"

"You."

"Me." I don't have to look to know he's smiling. "I know it won't remove your pain, but I hope knowing life had a plan in store for you after your mama makes it a little bit lighter."

Damn.

I blow out a long breath.

If my mama's diagnosis taught me anything, it's that when people tell you there's no way to predict the future, they mean it. They aren't telling you to preach some carpe diem bullshit. They're warning you—trying to tell you to bulk up and get ready because something is about to come along and knock you right off your damn feet.

Lucky for me, I had my gramps to pull me back up and Gideon to keep me standing upright. I have not a single clue what will happen in the future, and I won't kid myself by trying to predict it.

What I do know is this, I'm thankful for my mama and her easy ability to love. I'm thankful she taught me how to recognize it when it comes. Nobody will ever replace her, but I'm thankful I have a new family made of an old man, two dads, a curly-haired weird-o, and a bunch of non-cousins.

It's not traditional—chaos in its finest form. And for that, dad or no dad, my new family is as wonderful as they come.

TWENTY-THREE

RUNAWAY

GIDEON

I'VE ALWAYS FOUND it strange I'm terrible at school. I suck at taking tests, struggle with remembering the concepts, and grow frustrated when I have no damn clue what the hell Shakespeare was trying to say.

I may not have been able to remember mathematical equations or the square root of pi, but I had no issues remembering the things I felt passionate about.

Remembering French ballet terms and their meanings? Piece of cake.

Memorizing facts about firetrucks and fire engines? Easy peasy.

Every dopey life lesson my parents pounded into my head about loving myself? Forever burned into my brain.

I could remember just about anything—except the boring school stuff that would get me a good grade.

I have always considered myself proof that people hear only what they want to hear. They see only what they want to see, and do only what they want to do.

After what happened to Elli, I'm not so sure it's that simple anymore.

Actually, I think it's really damn complicated. We may be able to block out the things we don't want to see or hear—focus only on the chaos we wish to create and find peace in that. But I think that only works in a world where we're all alone.

I forgot to consider that the people around us create chaos too. It's not something we can control but it's often something we get sucked into anyway. Elli's father unleashed more chaos than anybody was ready for. Elli wasn't looking for it but he was affected regardless.

"Gramps, check me out. I'm so fancy."

"Well, I'll be damned, boy. Look at you." Spanky gawks at the newspaper, scanning a picture of Elli and I and the rest of our class in our caps and gowns, posing in the gym to announce our upcoming graduation the same as every other high school in the state.

"Look at my cords, gramps." Elli pokes at the newspaper. "You know what those mean? Honors!"

"What are you getting honored for?"

"My good grades, gramps."

"Really? Well, damn. Good for you. Half the time I think I need to take you for a brain scan."

Crumbles go flying at the sudden laughter erupting from my mouth. "Did you just say he needs a brain scan?"

"Damn straight." Spanky grunts, folding the newspaper nicely.

"Are brain scans even a thing?"

"Nope." Knox says, snagging a chip from the plate resting on top of the old picnic table that's practically a part of Spanky's front yard. It's been here so long, I'm pretty sure the grass has grown around the legs. "If they were, I would've taken Beck for one a long time ago."

"Well." Beck stands, gathering his empty plate and dirty napkins. "Perhaps you can take your next husband." He lifts his middle fingers and stomps into the house, likely to take care of his trash.

I chuckle at the way Knox grumbles in exasperation, jogging after Beck and ready to grovel. I doubt he'll have to grovel much. I give them three minutes before they're making out against a wall in Spanky's kitchen.

I rid my mind of that disturbing picture and take a big bite of a burger Spanky grilled for me, Elli, and my parents. A celebration barbecue is what he's calling it. Personally, I think Elli bringing home his cap and gown and a newspaper with his name inside gave him *all* sorts of feelings. Watching Elli hurdle a milestone without his mom here to witness it is another reminder of just how much Elli's had to endure and how far he's come. The bright smile on Elli's face is just a bonus.

I slide closer to him, wrapping my arm around his waist. He takes a sip of his water, flashing me a look. "Slide any closer and you'll be in my lap."

"Shut up, Elliott."

"Not complaining, baby. Just saying you might be obsessed with me."

"You might be obsessed with yourself."

He punches his chest and lets out a burp loud enough to rattle the table.

"Ten." I hold out my fist.

He bumps it with a smirk. "We should have a secret handshake."

"Fantastic idea."

"It can end with us posing next to our trophies."

I bark a laugh. "I like the way you think, Elli."

"Alright." Spanky grunts and heaves himself from the table. "I'm going in."

"You gonna call Minnie?" Elli croons, batting his eyelashes.

"Boy, I'm gonna swat you."

"Admit it, gramps. You miss her."

"She's been gone for four days, Elliott. And she's coming back."

"Well she should. She's your girlfriend."

"Damn, kids. Worry about your own relationship." He snatches his dirty plate off the table and scowls at us over his shoulder, waddling inside.

"You are gonna get kicked out." I joke. "You'll have to live with Nate."

He shovels a handful of potato chips in his mouth. "I'd rather live in my truck."

I bark a laugh. "I'll let you live with me if I can have one of your trophies."

"Still would rather live in my truck."

"Ug, fine. I guess you can live with me."

"Love you, babe." He winks at me.

I beam at the words.

Elliott Oakley doesn't mess around when it comes to love.

When he loves, he loves *hard*. He often blurts those words at random moments, filling comfortable silence with declarations of love. I never have to wait too long to hear those three words. Because even though he hasn't said it, I know his greatest fear is that I'll forget.

"Love you too, Elli."

I get a salty kiss on the cheek. "I hope you know me bragging to gramps about my cords isn't me trying to rub it in your face."

"I've known since kindergarten I wasn't gonna graduate with honors. I'm just relieved to be graduating at all. I'm proud of you, Elli. Really proud."

"Yeah?" His head drops to my shoulder. "I think my mama would be too."

"I don't know how she couldn't be proud of you, Elli."

"I don't know. I just wasn't ever the best at school. Average, I guess."

"Those cords in your room say you're above average."

"Well, you don't have cords and you're way above average, Gideon Stryker."

"I know." I tease. "It's because I can memorize ballet terms and useless firetruck facts."

"Exactly. Where are your cords for that?"

"Right? I should make my own."

He lifts his head, cupping my cheek and staring at me with eyes so intense, I think he's about to hypnotize me. "You're incredible in so many ways, baby. So uniquely talented and full of life. Cords or no cords, I'm damn proud to be your boyfriend."

I kiss him softly, throwing my arms around his neck. Weeks ago, for a split moment, I thought I'd lost him. I thought a misunderstanding had the strength to pull me from the person who's taken over every beat of my heart. Now I'm thinking there's not a force in the world strong enough to pull us apart.

After he confided in me about his father, and I detailed every second of my conversation with Jamie, there was no other direction for our relationship to go but up. And we were already so close to the clouds before we bared our hearts and shared our love for one another.

We're floating so high now, everybody around us looks so small—minuscule to these profound feelings we have for one another. The rest of the world is teeny tiny compared to what's happening between Elli and I. I'm not sure if either one of us really knows for sure what's happening, how much more intense our love will get, or how much deeper our connection runs. I do know we've barely scratched the surface.

"I love kissing you." His breath against my lips sends a shiver down my spine.

"I'll keep doing it."

"For how long?"

"As long as you'll let me."

"What if I say forever?" He runs the tip of his nose along my cheek, lips connecting with my ear. "What would you say then?"

Perfect.

"I'd say that sounds perfect, Elli." I don't know when forever starts, or how long it lasts. But I'll give it to him easily.

I'll give him everything.

"You make all my struggles worthwhile, Gideon Stryker."

Before I have a moment to come up with a reply worthy of that sentence, the sound of tires rolling against the gravel driveway intrude on whatever soul altering kiss he was about to give me.

The hairs on my arms rise when I tilt my head and find the intruding tires are attached to a police car.

"Elliott!" Spanky barrels from the house, eyes frantic. "What did you do?"

Elliott's jaw hits the table.

"Quick, boy. Tell me before he gets out of the car. Were you driving that dragster on the road?"

"I didn't do anything, old man. What did you do?"

Spanky stills and tilts his head like he's mulling over the last week and trying to decide if anything was worthy of a visit from the police.

He grunts, hobbling down the porch steps and hiking up the front of his pants. My parents barrel through the screen door and follow suit, heading towards the police cruiser. I peer at Elli, finding him peering at me. We stand up.

It seems like the thing to do when a cop makes a surprise visit. Maybe it's a respect thing? Protect and serve and all that.

A car door slams, heavy feet dragging across the gravel.

"Sheriff Landon. Hello." Knox steps forward, shaking his hand.

I blink, studying the officer.

I know him.

Well, kind of.

He's been friends with my parents for as long as I can remember. This guy has known me since I was born. Years ago, he was one of the officers who caught a guy that hurt my dads. He sends us updates as much as he can.

"Hello, Knox. Beckett." I watch with a stiff body as Sheriff Landon slides his sunglasses on the top of his head. "How are you?"

"Great, thanks. Everything okay?"

"Not really, boys." Landon rubs the back of his neck, stepping right up to Spanky. "Are you Thatcher Scott?"

"Yes, sir. Something I can help you with?"

"Hey, Sheriff." Beck steps towards Elli and I, pushing us backward like Landon's about to unleash the dogs. "What's the problem?"

"Do you know Thatcher well?"

"Knox and I do. Yeah. Wonderful man. Gideon's dating his grandson."

Landon nods at me like he's just now noticing I'm standing here. His dark eyes spot the hand that's now attached to Elli's. "Hey, kiddo. How are you?"

"Uhm." What an odd question to ask after he shows up out of nowhere and starts asking questions about my boyfriend. "I'm okay. I guess."

He nods, inching towards us. "Elliott Oakley?"

"Why ya asking?" Spanky's body rocks as he steps forward, looking ready to throw down with a man who's half his age and armed.

Landon's answer is swallowed by the now familiar sound of gravel getting pounded into the ground from tires.

An all-black Cadillac Escalade pulls right behind the police cruiser, rolling to a stop. The driver side door creaks open and I swear to God a bunch of men in suits from the FBI are about to step out and tell us some crazy person is running around pretending to be Elliott Oakley.

That's not what happens.

One man drops down from the Escalade, slamming the door and walking around the front. I'm not one to judge based on appearance, but this man's torn jeans and dirt covered flannel tell me he is not part of the FBI.

I watch in confusion as he rests his back against the vehicle and crosses his arms over his chest, spitting a wad of brown saliva into the dirt.

"Who the hell are you?" Knox barks, stalking towards him.

"Jackson Oakley." Elli breathes, his body tensing as if he's bracing himself for the biggest hit of his life. "My father."

The urge to barrel forward and throw my fist into that man's gut repeatedly rolls over me in waves. The death grip Elli has on my hand is the only thing that stops me from going ape-shit.

My flesh burns from the inside out as I stare at him, taking in the ways my boyfriend resembles his father. Same strawberry colored hair, high cheekbones, and same wide shoulders. Physical looks are where their similarities end. After that, Elli is nothing like this awful man who has yet to speak and hurl vomit all over his son.

I squeeze Elli's hand tighter, risking blood loss because I want him to know I stand with him.

"I don't know what the hell you're doing on my property, but you can place your scrubby ass back into that monstrosity vehicle and go home." Spanky spits. "You ain't welcome here."

Jackson's reply is to whip his head to the side, hacking spit into the grass.

"You best not be using my yard as your tobacco spit cup!"

He chuckles, pushing himself off the SUV and starting forward. Elli stumbles backward quickly, tripping over his own feet. I throw my arms around his waist, steadying him. My chest burns at the rough shudder that rolls through his body. I can only imagine the awful memories he can't make go away right now.

"How ya been, Thatcher?" Elli's father spits again. Now that he's closer, I can see a big bulge protruding from his bottom lip.

How disgusting.

"Alright." Knox raises his hands in the air. "What's going on? Sheriff Landon?"

"Mr. Oakley is here to collect his son."

Oh hell no.

Elliott's knees buckle so quickly, I'm afraid he's about to hit the ground.

"Oh no, he ain't about to collect his son." Spanky's round body turns red, eyes sending sharp daggers into Elli's father. "I don't know what you're smoking but you can take yourself and your crazy drugs back to corn country. Elliott's staying with me."

"He's not. He's gonna walk in that house, pack his shit, and get his ass in the car before I have you arrested."

"Arrested?" He scoffs. "What the hell for?"

"Harboring a runaway under the age of eighteen." Officer Landon clears his throat, stepping forward. "Elliott Oakley is registered as a runaway from the state of Iowa."

TWENTY-FOUR

AN UNEDUCATED SWINE

ELLIOTT

GOOD CHAOS AND BAD CHAOS—THERE'S a big difference.

Gideon is the good. The kind of chaos that makes sense and is easy to navigate. Jackson Oakley is everything that's revolting about the entire premise of chaos. He is the reason the word itself has a bad rep. He is why most people equate chaos with their upheaving. Because that's what Jackson Oakley does. He destroys life with the chaos he lets loose.

Most specifically, he destroys mine.

Repeatedly, he storms in with a bulldozer and destroys everything good I manage to build for myself. He plows down everything in life that makes me happy.

And I. Am. Sick of it.

When he stood there, tossing his spit around and barking at me to get in his fancy new car, I wanted nothing more than for him to go up in flames right then and there.

I did the only reasonable thing I could think of—I ran.

I dropped Gideon's hand and took off running like a bat out of hell. I was wearing my clunky ass boots and jeans that were a bit too loose, but I've never in my life ran faster.

Apparently, that's what I do. I run away. Can one be recognized as a runaway in two states? Hell if I know. I took off running anyway—straight into the patch of woods surrounding Spanky's house. I ignored Gideon's calls for me until they stopped. My brain needed a hot second to process what was happening and why.

My father registered me as a runaway.

What the actual fuck?

Never mind that he never attempted to reach out. It's not like I changed my phone number. Hell, he's still paying my phone bill. We're on the same plan for shit's sake and he's gonna register me as some delinquent kid who just disappeared? Then he has the audacity to threaten the man who gave me a place to sleep and food to eat with jail time?

There has to be some sort of loophole. I've been gone for *months*. Almost a year. Don't they have to declare runaways dead after a long period of time? Can't I just be recognized as dead or missing indefinitely? Bye, Iowa. Hello, North Carolina.

There ain't a damn thing waiting for me in Iowa—not since my mama is resting nicely in an urn on Spanky's fireplace. If my father thinks I'm just gonna pack my shit and go play house with him, I'll have to suggest he get drug tested. Ain't no judge is gonna side with him when he didn't pay no attention to me for this long.

I don't even know why he's doing it, and I don't actually care. The only reason, and I mean, *only* reason I heave my ass off the forest floor and stomp my way back to the house is to make sure they haven't hauled my gramps to jail.

Considering I've been sitting out here long enough for the sun to set, the chances my gramps is already slumped in a cell is high. I push through the trees, mentally calculating how much money I have saved up and how much bail would cost.

I don't have enough. I know that for sure.

"Elli!" I blink, finding Gideon racing through the yard. He crashes into me, throwing his arms around me.

I squeeze him back, peering around the yard and finding two more cars parked randomly in the driveway.

"Did they take gramps away?"

"No, Elli. He's in there. But listen, they're gonna take you back to Iowa."

"The fuck they are." I scoff, breaking away from his hold long enough to take one step before he throws himself at me again.

"Elli! Listen to me." He grabs my face. "You're under the age of eighteen. Spanky isn't your legal guardian. You aren't even a resident of this state. You didn't think to get registered?"

"No, I didn't think to get registered, Gideon! I had other shit on my mind. My dad can shove it up his ass and go back to Iowa. He's good at pretending I don't exist."

"Elliott!" The unfamiliar bark in his voice forces my struggle against his hold to lighten. His hands slip down my face. The light from the moon reflects the wetness forming in his eyes. "This is real, okay? There are cops and lawyers in there. The whole damn cavalry is trying to take you away."

Maybe it's the intensity in his face, the tremble in his voice, or the death grip he has on my arms that cause goosebumps to rise on my skin. "He has a lawyer?"

"Yes. My grandpa Hank is here on your behalf but it's not looking good, Elli."

I've met his grandpa Hank once. Over Christmas. I know he's a lawyer but I don't know what kind. I'm not even sure if it matters. "What do you mean?"

"They are saying you don't live in this state or some shit.

You technically ran away from home without parental consent."

"Without parental consent? He watched me drive away with a giant ass duffel bag. What did he think I was doing? Getting a hotel room?"

"It doesn't matter, Elli. Even if you fight it, you still have to go back to Iowa. How did you even get enrolled in school?"

"What do you mean? I called them and told them I moved to my grandfather's because my mom died."

"And that was that?" He releases me, tearing at his curls. "They didn't ask for any documents?"

"Sure. I gave them gramps' ID, proof of his residence, and my mama's death certificate."

"They didn't think to ask about your father?"

"I don't fucking know, Gideon. I called my old school for transcripts and gave gramps' a bunch of shit to sign."

"What kind of shit to sign?"

"I don't know! A packet or something."

"And neither of you thought to read it? Elliott, if Spanky signed something stating he's your legal guardian when he's not, then he's gonna be in so much more trouble than just harboring a runaway."

"He wasn't harboring me! He was taking care of me."

"You aren't the law, Elli." He thrusts a shaky finger at the house. "The law is inside saying you have to go back to Iowa."

Not. Happening.

I eye the woods again, my feet buzzing with the need to take off. "I can't go back there, Gideon."

"Okay. So let's run."

"What?"

"Run." He reaches for me, fingernails digging into my forearms. The fear etched on his face mirrors mine. "You and me. Let's go. We have money. We only have to make it work until you're eighteen. That's what? Five weeks away? We can do it, Elli. Let's go. Right now."

"I..." The temptation to grab his hand and take off somewhere is so real. To just get in my truck and drive around for the next five weeks. Worrying about nothing but loving him is an escape I'd cut my arm off for—but I can't bring my feet to move.

He'd miss the last bit of high school, risk failing classes, leave his dads, miss nationals for dance, give up dance recital.

We'd be a real runaway, reckless teen couple cliché. And goddamn I've never wanted to be a cliché so bad.

But it can't happen. Not when he loses so much.

"Gideon... we can't."

"Yes, we can. As long as we don't spend money on crazy things we don't need then we can."

"We can't. It's only a temporary solution."

"We only need temporary, Elli! Just until you turn eighteen."

"Gideon, no. This isn't..." I press my forehead to his, my eyes burning. "I like it here. I wanna stay with you. Help me find another way. *Please*."

"I don't... I don't know all the legal jargon, Elli. It sounds like they can take you away because Spanky isn't legally seen as your guardian. Once they find out about the school records, shit is gonna hit the fan."

"That's bullshit, G. I can give proof my dad hasn't tried to contact me at all. Why now? Why does he show up all the sudden, stomping around and demanding me go back? After all this time he suddenly cares? No. *Fuck no.* He's doing this for his benefit somehow."

"Okay." Gideon nods quickly, backing away from my hold. The sudden pacing and the way his eyes squint tell me he's thinking. "Maybe we can prove that your father is unstable. Get Spanky granted emergency custody or something?"

I sigh roughly, running my hand down my face. "I can try. Yeah. I mean, what judge wouldn't grant custody to gramps after everything he's done for me?"

"A dumbass one."

A humorless chuckle escapes me. "I love you, you know that?"

"Yeah, I do. And I love you too. I'm on your side, Elli."

Taking his hand in mine, we start towards the house. I know he's on my side. There's never been any doubt Gideon is my partner through all forms of chaos. Good or bad. Maybe we didn't create this chaos, but I'm positive he will go to hell and back helping me fight my way out of it.

"Elli, wait." He grips my wrist, prying my hand off the door handle. "Before we go in there, I need to warn you of something." I wait, dread spreading through my veins. This just keeps getting worse and worse. "She's in there, Elli. Your father's—"

"He brought his fucking mistress?!" Are you kidding me? He brought the whore to help convince me to come back and live with him?

How fast can we get a drug test?

"Elli, they..." His face pales. "They're married. He married her."

The world goes blurry, and the next few moments seem to happen in slow motion as my blood boils to the point of pain. I kick open the door, flames growing hotter as I search the overcrowded room for him. When I spot him, I hurl him a look so venomous, it's some kind of miracle he doesn't drop dead right here and now. Not a soul in the room tries to stop me as I throw both hands at his chest, forcing him to stumble.

"You fucking bastard." My nostrils flare as anger burns in the pit of my stomach. "Less than a year. She's been gone less a year. You heartless, son of a bitch!"

"Elliott. Come on, son. Take a step back, okay?" The sole reason I let Knox drag me away from my father is because he isn't worth whatever repercussions I'd get for laying him out on this tile floor.

"He ain't your son. He's mine."

My jaw clenches. "You are not my father. You're a sicko who married a whore."

"Boy." Jackson thrusts a finger at my chest. "You best watch your goddamn mouth talking about your stepmother."

My stepmother.

Who the fuck is he kidding? She isn't my mother. She's the nurse who was too busy screwing my father to be any sort of help to my mama.

"How about you stop staring at me?" Gideon clips. "Kay, thanks."

My eyes land on the mistress, also known as Norah the slutty nurse. She's sitting at Spanky's old table, gawking at my boyfriend like he's made of glitter or some shit.

My heavy feet pound against the floor. "He said stop fucking staring at him."

"I'm... I'm so sorry, Gideon." She squeaks, making no attempt to drop her gaze. "I don't mean to make you uncomfortable. You've just... *wow*. You've really grown into a wonderful young man."

What in the ever-loving fuck?

"Get 'em tested." I blurt. "Both of them. They're on drugs."

"Listen, lady." Beck snarls, eyeing Norah intensely. "Quit gawking at my son."

"Your son. Right." She nods, dropping her eyes. "I'm so sorry."

"It's okay, darling."

I grit my jaw so hard, it aches. Did he just call her darling? And is he rubbing her shoulders? The only thing I ever heard him call my mama was woman.

"Woman, what's for dinner?"

"You iron my pants, woman?"

"My car won't start, woman! I gotta take yours."

"I'm sick of pussyfooting around, boy." Jackson snaps. "Norah isn't feeling well. Get your shit and let's go."

"Now, hold on a damn minute." Spanky's fist pounds the table, his eyes finding the Sheriff. "This man is no more than the horse shit on the bottom of his boot. Elliott left months ago and he's made no attempt to speak to him. He hasn't sought him out at all. Elliott has been dependent on *me*. *I've* been caring for him."

"And look where the hell that got him!" My father's angry roar is not an unfamiliar sound to my ears. I flinch anyway.

"Jackson, getting angry won't help anything." The whore rests her hand on his bicep, gripping it and using it as leverage to pull herself out of the chair. Her struggle to stand from a kitchen chair confuses me until I see it—the giant bump protruding from her middle.

"Oh my God." He got her pregnant. Judging by the size of that bump, it could've easily happened before my mama died.

Bile rises up my throat. I barely make it to the flimsy trash can at the end of the counter before I'm hurling.

"Elliott—"

"No!" Gideon's voice cracks under the weight of his bark. "Don't you dare come near him, you heartless, heartless man." His hand hits my back as I stand there, my throat burning and my head in the trash just in case my body decides to reject the idea of going back to Iowa again. "Are you people blind? Grandpa, do something. He's so upset he's throwing up."

When my stomach stops rolling, I stand upright and wipe my mouth with the back of my hand, pushing my wet face into my boyfriend's neck. "He's had a family this whole time, Gideon. He just didn't want me to be a part of it. He didn't even tell me he got married."

"Alright, let's break things down. Elliott, son, can you sit down? I'll get you some water." I practically drag Gideon over to the chair his grandfather pulls out for me, dropping into it and pulling Gideon on my lap. A glass of water drops to the table in front of me. I don't drink it. I just stare into the face that looks exactly like Knox's. Just a bit wrinklier.

"Okay." Hank crosses his arms over his chest, staring deep at my father and the man in a suit who has saddled up next to him. My high school education tells me he's his lawyer. "Let's go down the list here. Elliott's father watched him leave the driveway, made no attempt to contact him, no attempt to come see him, and no attempt to call any friends or existing family members to search for him. Your documents state you didn't report Elliott as a runaway until five days ago. Elliott has been living happily with Thatcher since late-August. It's now mid-April. You do the math, but I can assure you that is a lot more time than five days. As you can see, Elliott doesn't wish to leave with Mr. Oakley, and Thatcher is more than willing to keep providing for Elliott. We can take this to court, but you will save a lot of money and time if we didn't. You haven't cared for him in months, and we can make that very evident to a judge with phone records and the lack of visits."

"This is an absolute waste of time." My father rolls his eyes. "Whether you want to admit it or not, Thatcher has spent the good part of a year harboring *my* underage kid without my consent. If Elliott wants to stay, I'll press charges, Thatcher will be arrested, and Elliott will be sent back to me anyway."

"This is absolute bullshit." Gideon shouts, eyes reddening. "Grandpa, *do something.*"

Hank sighs roughly, dropping into the chair next to me. "Elliott." The stricken look on his face forces my stomach to roll again. "I'm afraid there's not much I can do."

"Are you kidding me, grandpa?" Gideon's hands start flailing. "His father is an asshole."

"I'm certainly not disagreeing, kiddo. But the fact is, Elliott is not a resident of this state. Any trial regarding custody would take place in Iowa. And unfortunately, the probability that Thatcher be arrested is high."

Sheriff Landon steps forward. "The only reason I haven't been forced to bring Thatcher into custody is because Mr. Oakley requested this be settled amicably. He made it very clear he doesn't believe Thatcher is a bad man. He just wishes for his son back.

"Yeah? Then why did he bring a damn lawyer? Amicable, my ass! My father is blowing smoke up your ass, Sheriff."

"Elliott, you can't talk to a Sheriff like that." Hank places a comforting hand on my shoulder. "He's simply doing his job."

"So, what are my choices here? Go home with Satan and the whore or stay and let my grandfather get arrested?"

"Those are exactly your choices, Elliott." The asshole father barks. "And I will not tell you again to quit referring to Norah as a whore."

"Your grandfather could fight it and file for emergency custody." Hank explains, talking over my father. "But you'd still have to go back to Iowa and wait for a court date there.

You legally can't be here without your father's permission until a judge has granted Thatcher custody."

"How long would a court date take?"

"It depends solely on the state of the emergency. But Elliott, you need to understand that adultery is not a crime. Your father hasn't broken the law."

"He neglected him." Gideon grinds. "Doesn't that count for something?"

"It does. It counts for a lot, but it takes time to gather proof and present it all in front of a judge. By that time, Elliott may already be eighteen and any custody fight would be pointless."

"So what you're saying is, I have to live with Satan until I turn eighteen? Is that even legal? Am I allowed to live with the man who's in a custody battle over me?"

"Yes, Elliott. You are. And a judge will often side with the parent unless abuse is involved."

"What if I go back but don't live with him? Can't I stay in a hotel or something?"

"No. You're a minor."

The other lawyer clears his throat. "Mr. Oakley is willing to allow Elliott to stay in a runaway assessment center."

"Are you kidding me?" Hank snarls. "A runaway assessment center is in a juvenile center. He'd be sleeping in a six-foot room with a roommate, going to therapy five times a week. He wasn't a homeless teen or into drugs. He was grieving his mother's death."

"Which is exactly why he needs some therapy!" My father throws his hands in the air, hurling a nasty glare at me. "Quit acting like a damn sissy. You're wasting this officer's time. You're coming back to Iowa in the morning. You'll be at the assessment center or in your room. You choose."

I peer around the room, panic welling up inside me and threatening to swallow me whole. I stare helplessly at Hank, praying he comes up with another option. I have not one choice that ends in my favor.

I wipe quickly at the moisture on my face.

"Buck up, Elliott. You have a warm room and a house full of food to go home to. You're acting like an ungrateful brat."

"I hate you." I state, sniffing roughly. "I hate you so much."

"Teens hate their parents. Nothing I can't handle."

"No, I actually, truly despise you. In less than a year, you have managed to take everything that brings me joy away from me."

"Elliott, I know how much you loved your mom. But it wasn't my fault she died."

"No, it was your fault I sat alone and watched her die. It was your fault I cried myself to sleep. It was your fault nobody hugged me, offered me condolences, or tried to make it any easier. It's your fault you spent her funeral showing off your younger girlfriend, and it's your lack of giving a damn about me that led me here." I slide Gideon off my lap and stand on shaky legs, letting tears flow freely. "It is your fault you're pulling me from a family I love so much. And for what reason? You suddenly care after all this time? It's not like I'm unsafe or being uncared for."

He scoffs, folding his arms over his chest. "You've gotten back into drag racing. A sport I made clear I felt was too dangerous for you."

"I got one concussion in seven years. Football players get like one concussion a season and you still hounded me about joining that."

"I was trying to man you up, Elliott. You lasted one year."

"Because I hated it! You don't get to decide what type of hobbies I have."

"Actually I do. It's called being a father. If I decide something is dangerous, that's it. You're done. Thatcher disrespected my wishes by encouraging you to get back into it."

"Do you not understand in your tiny, pea-sized brain that drag racing is what makes me happy? Can you even comprehend how devastated I am that I'll miss five races of the season before I turn eighteen and don't need your permission? I have a chance to qualify to be a top fuel racer. That is the dream I've had since I was five and you couldn't give a damn. That hurts me, dad."

"One day you'll thank me."

"I won't." Goddamn it. What is he not understanding? Tears flow down my face, soft sobs erupting from my chest. "The thought of leaving with you made me hurl. You're taking away my gramps, racing, my new friends, my boyfriend—"

"Do not even get me started with your boyfriend. That is ending the second you leave this town."

How much can a heart take before it stops functioning? "What?"

"You've been running around this town, staying out all night, sleeping at his house. I can't even begin with how inappropriate that is."

"If you have something to say about my son, we can go outside." Knox growls, stalking towards my father. "Those two are like any other teens who are head over heels for each other. Doesn't matter what damn town they are in."

"Well, in Mount Vernon, Gideon doesn't exist."

Norah gasps, swatting my father on the chest. "Jackson! Do not say that. Gideon exists."

"Yeah, Norah, he does. But not as my son's boyfriend. That's disgusting and wrong whether he knows it or not."

I'm surprised the smoke alarm doesn't go off from the steam that rolls off Knox's body. "You did not just call their relationship disgusting."

My dad rolls his eyes and risks getting decked in the face by four men who are nothing but proud to love someone the same sex as them. "I don't care about his sexuality. Not what I would've wanted for my boy, and I think he's going to change his mind one day, but I couldn't give a rat's ass he is dating a boy."

Change my mind someday. *God.* What an uneducated swine.

"So, it's just my son you have a problem with?"

"Frankly, yes and if you knew the situation at hand, I'm sure you'd have a problem with it as well."

"Yeah?" Knox crosses his arms over his chest, widening his stance. "Try me."

"My wife is your son's biological mother. Your son is dating his brother."

TWENTY-FIVE

G PLUS E

GIDEON

YEARS AGO, I sat next to Piper in freshman mathematics only half listening to Mrs. Reyes give us a brief rundown of Chaos Theory. From what I remember, and it isn't much, Chaos Theory is the mathematical study of unpredictability. In some strange way, Chaos Theory states that with the randomness that is an entirely chaotic arrangement, there's some underlying pattern that makes it easily predictable.

Say what?

Every day, people deal with complicated circumstances that feel like nothing but a series of random events that severely affect their lives.

Those types of events are truly random—few and far between.

Life, in general, is actually repetitive. We do the same thing every day. We wake up at the same time, eat dinner at the same time, use the same shampoo, and talk to the same people. Life is merely a series of patterns. If it weren't for those random, unlikely events that flip our world upside down, life wouldn't be considered unpredictable.

But it is.

Because it is.

Nothing is guaranteed, and that's why people spend so much time in constant terror of not knowing how an event, situation, or relationship will play out. They live in fear. That doesn't help the quality of anyone's life. So why do it?

That is my parent's outlook on life—an outlook I inherited. Why worry about the things we can't change or predict? Why dwell?

I *never* dwelled. I never thought much about my mother or how remarkably different my life would be if my parents hadn't adopted me. I stuck to the pattern that was my life and ignored Chaos Theory when it told me my life pattern was hiding something massively chaotic.

I have to think Elli ignored it too. But even if we hadn't, there was no way to prepare for the shitty part of chaos. Even though those random, chaotic events brought us together, it also made us somewhat stepbrothers. I truly believe Mrs. Reyes wasn't considering the damage Chaos Theory can do when life lets it loose.

And sure, Norah could just be lying, finding ways to upset Elli, but just looking at her tells me she's the one. I have her bright blue eyes and petite frame—her nose and the same strange earlobes. Maybe it's my fault for never asking her name or wondering what she was doing or where she lived. Maybe I could've prevented the moment that stopped the war happening in Spanky's kitchen. But I stuck to the pattern and didn't ask. Now we're drowning in so much chaos, it's getting hard to breathe.

"Gideon."

Blood pounds in my ears, my limbs feeling like jello as my eyes take on a sudden case of tunnel vision and are only capable of seeing her.

My mother.

How strange. I don't have a mother. I mean, I do. I have

a woman who carried me and birthed me. A woman I share DNA with.

But she is not my mother.

She wasn't there on my first Christmas or first birthday. She doesn't know my favorite color is red or that I despise celery. She didn't take me to the pet store to pick out my first pet or spend hours helping me with homework I never got right. She didn't hang my spelling tests on the refrigerator or give me Band-Aids when I didn't really need them. She didn't teach me how to drive or ground me for backing into a tree. She wasn't the one I came out to when I was fourteen, and she didn't wipe away a single tear in all the years I've been getting bullied.

Though I don't even know her last name—or her favorite color and what she does for fun. And I can't stand what she did to Elli and his mama, I'm so grateful for her.

"Gideon?"

Suddenly, she's right in front of me, peering down at me with fresh tears in the eyes that look just like mine. I'm not sure if it's the blood throbbing in my ears or if it's actually just this quiet right now. When she lowers herself into the seat next to mine and reaches for my hand, I let her take it. I let her hold it tightly and study all my features. It's likely she's been waiting for this moment for eighteen years. If this is the last time she'll ever see me, I won't take that away.

She tilts her head, smiling as her eyes rake my face. "You are very handsome."

"Thank you."

"What do you do for fun?"

"I like to dance. I'm on a competition team. I listen to music a lot. I love to swim and travel with my parents."

"Your parents are pretty great, huh?"

"The best. You, uh, wanna meet them?" I don't figure she does, but it seems polite to ask.

"Oh. We've met. Eighteen years ago when I signed over my rights to you. They were wonderful then. I have no doubt they still are."

"You've met? But... they didn't recognize you." If they would've, they would've told me. I know that for a fact.

"I look much different as an adult than I did when I was a teenager. I was still a kid when I had you, Gideon. Barely sixteen. Besides, your parents only had eyes for their son that day."

My apprehension towards her loosens just a fraction. It dawns on me then her intention isn't to intrude on my parents or the life I've always known. She just wants to know I'm doing okay.

So, I shock the audience that's watching this personal moment and lean forward to hug her. She jerks, clearly surprised. It's a long moment before she hugs back.

It's kind of awkward—like hugging a stranger or someone you've just met. Her baby bump makes it hard to get close but I know how much she appreciates it. I tighten my grip and hold her for a long time.

In the midst of the worst chaos created, there's something magical happening for her. I won't take that away too fast.

"Thank you." I say once I pull away.

"Wh... what?"

"Thank you for keeping me safe and healthy for nine months. Thank you for recognizing you couldn't take care of me, and thank you for bringing me my parents. I have wonderful parents, Norah. Thank you for giving me to them."

She swipes at her tears with her palms. "You're welcome. I've always hoped you were happy. I've always wanted to reach out."

I tilt my head. "Is that why you're here?"

"I'm sorry?"

I stand from my chair, launching myself easily back into the war zone. I go to battle for my family, and Elliott is my family.

I seek Jackson's gaze. "Are you here because you care about Elliott or because you wanted to reunite your wife with her biological child?"

"I'm here because after I tracked down my kid and found him drag racing again, I made a trip here only to find out from a friend he's dating the son of Knox and Beckett Stryker. The world works in strange ways, Gideon. I've been waiting three days to collect him. Finding out he's dating his brother just makes it clearer he needs to come home."

"But I'm not his brother. *I'm his boyfriend.* You taking him away won't change that. Take his phone, his computer, erase all forms of contact because it won't change anything. I'll wait for him. This family that he's created will wait for him. And I hope you understand your demands for him to leave his family with no time for a goodbye are cruel and they're breaking his heart. Fortunately, he has me and a little family to put it back together again. Because what you failed to do as a parent, and are still failing to do, is recognize when your child has had enough. Elliott has had enough, Mr. Oakley. And you've never made him feel safe enough to tell you that. I can see very clearly you hold two eyes inside your head that are working very well. Take a long look at your son. If you care at all that you've managed to rip his life out from under him two times in less than a year, you'll reconsider trying to take him away from the people who put him back together again."

The room grows quiet again as we all stare at Jackson. A room full of lawyers, policemen, parents, grandparents, a boyfriend, and the woman who somehow managed to give me everything I need yet take it all away from Elli.

An unlikely group at war.

You know what they always say? The good guy never wins.

By the darkness still swimming in Jackson Oakley's eyes, and the way he doesn't even glance at my broken boyfriend, I know we're about to lose.

"Here's what's gonna happen." Jackson clears his throat and steps to the center of the room, hands on his waist. I hate that everyone is staring at him like he's some sort of king when he's really the slimy creature that poisoned Elli's life.

"I'm taking Norah back to the hotel. Tomorrow morning at nine, I'll be pulling into this driveway. If Elliott isn't packed and ready to go, I will be calling this nice officer to make an arrest. When he turns eighteen and decides to leave, so be it. The law says I can't stop it."

Pieces of my heart fall to the pit of my stomach. I watch with glassy eyes as he takes Norah's hand and leads her from the kitchen, shaking Sheriff Landon's hand. His lawyer leads him out, and the Sheriff follows after having some words with Spanky I don't bother to listen to.

I'm looking only at Elliott—who looks like he's in so much pain, I want to scream at life for doing this to him.

"I gotta go back." He chokes roughly, tears flowing out of him like a broken faucet. "Gideon, I gotta go back."

"Hold up!" Knox stumbles forward, looking just as distraught as Spanky. Of course he is. Knox loves Elli. Despite how Jackson Oakley makes Elli feel, he's easy to love. "We have less than twelve hours to figure this out."

"Knox." My grandpa shakes his head. "He has to go back whether he fights it or not."

"No fighting." Elli sniffs, staring at the tile. "No. I won't let my gramps face jail time for me. And I'll be back. This is my home now. I'm coming home." He peers upward, his wet eyes hitting mine so fiercely and with so much love, tears drip down my face and I swear my lip quivers.

"Promise me you'll wait for me."

"I promise, Elli."

ELLIOTT

A FEW WEEKS AGO, Gideon and I stayed over at Nate's house with Preston and Piper. We were all lying around, stuffing ourselves full of junk food and asking random, unimportant questions.

Nate asked me what my favorite texture to touch was. Without thinking, I blurted it was Gideon's skin. It was a rookie mistake, telling my friends my favorite thing to run my hand across was Gideon's warm body. They all laughed at me—turned it into some dirty joke and haven't let me live it down since.

It wasn't meant to be a dirty joke. It was simply a fact. Touching Gideon fuels the bond I crave with him. It fuses our connection. Whether it's my palm against his, or my fingertip on his big toe, or our chests pressed together, I feel it.

Less pain. Less stress. My worries drifted away, replaced with a feeling that can only be described as relief.

So, *yes*, my favorite thing to touch is my boyfriend's skin. But not because I'm some horny teenager—because touching him makes it easier to breathe.

Now, as I run my hand along his lower back, dipping my fingers into his back dimples, I'm barely even thinking about my impending departure back to Satan in less than an hour.

His lips pull into a lazy smile, his eyes closed and curls wild against my pillow as he revels in my touch.

I push my finger into his back dimple and very stupidly say, "this is my love button."

He doesn't laugh at how sugary I've become. He rewards me a megawatt smile. "Your love button, huh?"

"Yep." I splay my fingers against his lower back. "Your skin is soft."

"Ya know, studies say your brain tricks you into thinking your significant other's skin is softer than it actually is so you'll like touching them."

"Well, then I'm glad my brain is tricking me."

"What a sap I turned you into."

I flick his forehead. "Brat. I don't even know why I like you."

"It's my trophies."

"Ah, right. The trophies."

"And maybe some other reasons." He slides closer, tangling his naked body in my sheets.

I grip the nape of his neck and a handful of his curls, pressing our noses together. "What other reasons?"

"I think you probably love me."

"Oh, do I?"

"Yeah, you're probably pretty obsessed. I'm like a fairy-tale come true."

"You're like way too extra this early in the morning." I kiss his forehead. "I think you're probably right."

"I make all your dreams come true."

"Last night you did. Most beautiful dream I've ever had come true was making love to you."

"You know what they say, reality is better than dreams."

"I actually think it's the other way around."

"Not anymore."

I chuckle softly, holding him tight to me. What a cynic I

used to be—believing love doesn't exist for people this young. After falling in love with Gideon, I'm able only to believe that love is more powerful for people this young.

There's so much unknown with young love. There's so much to lose and so much life left to live, you don't know always know how the person you've fallen in love with will fit into that life. You try to pack as much life as you can into just a short time so you'll have loved with everything you've got when the time comes you'll have to drift apart.

But I'm not ready to leave Gideon. I'm not ready to drift from the guy that put me back together when I wouldn't even admit I was broken. I'm not ready to leave him in this old pullout bed alone and drive fourteen hours away. I'm not ready to kiss him goodbye, and I'm certainly not ready for the impending heartbreak that's a prerequisite for teen love. Gideon isn't just a teen love. He's *the* love, and I'm terrified of what happens when I walk away.

"Elli, no. Please don't cry."

"There's like dust in the air or something."

"Dust in the air, huh?"

"Yeah." I sniff violently, pushing my face in his curls, not giving a crap if I get some snot in them.

"Hey, ya know something?" His warm hands run up and down my back in the most comforting way.

"Hmm?"

"The first time your sleepy brain told me you loved me, I low-key freaked out. I mean, I knew I loved you too. Without a doubt. But I've never been in love before and giving you my heart was kind of terrifying. The more you kept saying it, the less scary it was. After a while, it just became a fact. Like the way of the universe. You love me. I love you. Gideon and Elliott are together. It sort of became this unbreakable thing for me. This part of life that was written in stone or carved into a tree for everyone to see and recognize. You have my heart, Elli. Wherever you are, it's yours."

My breath comes out in shallow shakes, my heart aching and bursting at the same time. "Carved in a tree, huh? Your sappy self has probably already done it."

"Oh, yeah. Totally. Getting a tattoo next. G plus E right across my forehead."

What a goon. "I love you, Gideon. I swear I'll take really good care of your heart."

"You do every day, Elli."

I tug on his curls so he'll tilt his head and meet my lips. We kiss for a long time, my tears slowly drying against my cheeks as we hold each other and say goodbye without really saying it at all.

"I'm gonna miss you, babe."

"I'll fly down to Iowa on your birthday and ride back with you."

"Yeah?" I squeeze him.

"Yeah. We can make it a road trip."

"Your brain works in wonderful ways."

"I'll buy my ticket tonight."

"Text me your arrival time. I'll be waiting."

He kisses my nose, brushing away my leftover tears. "So will I. I want you to remind yourself that I'll be waiting for you."

"I trust you, Gideon. I do. I know past events say otherwise but I trust you more than anyone. I'm still terrified you'll find someone else to create chaos with, someone who didn't drag you into more than I'm sure you anticipated. I hope so much I didn't make you hate it."

"No, Elli." He breathes, his grip on my face tightening as his intense eyes lure me into whatever he's about to say, desperate to have my attention. "I still love chaos because if it weren't for my mother giving me up, she would've never moved to Iowa for nursing school or met your father. You would've never moved to Durham. So no, Elli. I don't hate chaos because it brought me you. You are worth the creation of the worst forms of chaos imaginable. Because you're the good, Elli. You are the good."

Damn.

"Bad chaos is a thing, Elli. We can't stop the shitty things from happening, but the universe worked its magic and gave us each other to make some good together."

"I swear you write this stuff down in a little book titled *'sentences to wreck my boyfriend.'*"

"Damn it. How'd you know? I'll have to find something different now."

"No, don't. Keep it. Text me one every day."

He smiles softly. "I will, Elli. I promise."

We kiss softly again until my phone alarm sounds and tells me I have twenty minutes until Satan rolls in and I'll have to spend fourteen hours driving behind him and fighting the urge to take a wrong turn.

"I gotta get up, baby."

"I know."

"See you on my birthday?"

"Absolutely."

I slide from my bed, yanking on old jeans. I move to slide on a T-shirt when my eye catches his sweatshirt lying on the floor. I reach out and grab it, slipping it over my head. It's not as loose as mine usually are—but it smells like him. As dorky as it sounds, it's as close to a hug as I'll get for five weeks.

I packed a duffel bag with clothes and a backpack with my electronics quickly last night. Why pack everything when I'll be back in less than two months? Besides that, if I have my room mostly the same, I'll be able to convince myself that nothing will be different when I get back.

Throwing my backpack over my shoulder, I slip my feet into my boots. I bend down to kiss him one last time. "I'm keeping this sweatshirt."

"Okay. I'll steal something of yours."

I kiss him again. And then again. And then again.

"You go say bye to Spanky, babe. I'll get dressed and come give you a hug goodbye before you leave, okay?"

I nod yet everything inside me revolts.

"Elli, call me if you need me, okay? Whenever something gets to be too much, you call me. I'll answer. No matter when. Call me and we'll talk for hours."

I nod. "Love you."

"Love you too."

I kiss him one last time and use all I've got not to lose my shit when I hug gramps goodbye.

"You're strong, boy. You know that? Stronger than anyone I've ever met. You hold tight. Everybody will be waiting for ya when you come home."

"Love you, gramps. Thank you for everything."

"Boy, stop saying that like you ain't coming back." He hugs me fiercely. "Love you too."

I hug Knox and Beck because of course they came to hug me goodbye. When they tell me they love me, I swear I almost lose it. Because people didn't always say that to me. I didn't always feel love.

Now—I feel so much of it.

As I crawl into my truck and pull out of my driveway, I hold tight to all the love that doesn't go away with distance.

TWENTY-SIX

DRESSING UP FOR DINNER

ELLIOTT

MY MAMA USED to say everybody has a hidden talent. In this town, those talents are things like spitting long distances, opening a beer bottle with your teeth, and eating two dozen chicken wings in less than thirty minutes. They aren't exactly hidden since nobody in Mount Vernon ever stops bragging about themselves.

My mama was never a bragger. The only thing she ever bragged about was me, and I'm not all that sure I was worth it. She had better things to brag about.

My mama had a real talent. She jumped rope. Double Dutch to be more specific, and she was good at it. She went down to the rec center next to the church and jumped roped every Saturday she could. I guess it was something she did as a kid and didn't wanna give up. I don't blame her. She had *four* Double Dutch trophies—all of which are sitting in a box in my room at Spanky's house. I took everything of hers I could find when I left. Her trophies and the rope she used to jump were only a few things.

I used to go with her. I even tried to learn a few times. It wasn't really my thing but I took every chance I got to be around my mama. Besides that, it pissed my dad off. He accused mama of making me less manly every time she took me. The day he found me making out with Grant Gilbert when I was fifteen, he blamed it on the Double Dutch. As if failing at Double Dutch and spending time with my mama was what made me want to stick my tongue in Grant's mouth.

It was then I decided my hidden talent was pissing off my father. Because, really, I did it so damn often I didn't even have to try.

Now, as I sit at the new kitchen table my mama did not pick out, in a kitchen that looks nothing like the one she decorated, and stare at the wall she did not paint, I decide my greatest talent is staring off into an abyss of nothingness while my father speaks to me. Keeping a blank face while he attempts to have a conversation with me is my greatest talent.

Bonus: it pisses him off.

"Do your damn homework, Elliott."

I say nothing. I stare at the brand new stainless steel refrigerator that matches the new dishwasher and stove. The minute I walked back into this house, I had to go back outside and make sure I pulled into the right driveway. Everything was different—the furniture, the decorations, the unnecessary curtains, the colors of the walls. My childhood home went from being a warm, traditional house with faded white walls and pencil markings of my height, to some trendy bullshit that looks like it belongs in some dorky home magazine. Nothing is allowed out of place. It doesn't even look like anyone lives here. It looks like one of them demo houses people demolish for fun.

It certainly wasn't my father who upgraded this house. It was Norah. When she gave me a list of detailed instructions on where to place my things to allow for maximum room to move, I decided she was a control freak.

"Elliott, pick up your damn pencil and do your homework."

Again, I say nothing. I could probably sit here all day on autopilot. I could easily spend the afternoon thinking about Gideon and getting back to drag racing.

Three more weeks—that's all I have to endure. I have to survive three more weeks, and then I'm free to meet my boyfriend at the airport at 10 am on my birthday. Reuniting with him will be the best damn present imaginable. Who even cares I won't get a cake? Don't need to blow out candles and make a wish when he'll already be there.

It's hard not to smirk at that sentence. Gideon will be pleased to know I'm still disgusting nine hundred and eighty-two point four miles away.

"Fine!" I don't flinch when his hands smack the table. "Don't do it. Fail and don't graduate. I don't give a rat's ass."

The urge to roll my eyes is strong. I'm not ignoring my homework as some rebellion act against my father. I'm ignoring it because I already learned it all at Hillside months ago.

Okay, fine, maybe it's also a bit of a rebellion act but why waste my time and brain power for a school I won't be graduating from? I'll pass the unit tests, keep a steady grade to transfer back to Hillside, get home just in time for exams, ace all those, and then graduate with my friends.

Sounds like a solid plan to me. I don't believe doing homework I've already done was listed anywhere in that plan.

"Your stepmother is making dinner soon. Can you be useful and clear the table?"

Can't he just say Norah? He always refers to her as my

stepmother. Like some asshole attempt to remind me my mama is gone and this is what I get instead.

I tilt my head, staring at him blankly. "Nope."

I don't react when his face turns beet red. "You are testing my limits."

I scoff. Like I give a shit. He flew past all of mine and failed to even recognize what yanking me from my new home did to me. He probably enjoys I only ever smile when Gideon or my gramps calls.

"Jackson, why don't you give him a break? He's still adjusting."

I roll my eyes. It's the whore coming to my rescue. She does this all the time. She sides with me and tries to make my father see reason. As if it'll magically take away the vision in my head of my dad railing her on the living room couch while I hold my dying mama.

"He's had two weeks to adjust, Norah. He's acting like a brat who got her doll taken away."

"If you are going to continue being a grouch, Elliott and I will go out for dinner." She grins at me. "Won't we, honey?"

"Nope." I'd rather eat the stale chips I have hidden in my closet.

"Then fucking starve." My father explodes. He does this once a day. "You ungrateful brat. Get out of here and go do something productive."

"Jackson, you need to settle down."

"Norah, do not try to boss me."

"Why don't you go outside for a while? Get some fresh air?"

"How about you go outside?" He sneers. "He thinks he's just gonna be disrespectful to you in this home? Be an ass? That won't fly with me. You can take yourself to that assessment center. 'Cause I ain't dealing with it, son."

I throw more wood on the fire by lifting both my middle fingers. I'm so damn good at this bratty teenager thing.

He lets out a loud grunt. "Flash them fingers again. I will cut them off."

"Jackson Oakley!" Norah's jaw drops. "Knock it off right now. That is your son. He tells you all the time he hates you and you don't even care."

"I do care, Norah. But he doesn't actually hate me."

"Wrong." I stand up and gather my notebooks. "I do hate you. You're a monster. A heartless, slimy creature that gets off on destroying lives. I do not love you."

I make a scene, stomping heavily up the stairs and slamming my door so hard, I'm honestly surprised the wood doesn't split.

I ignore his loud shout about me disrespecting his home and flop on my bed, aggressively slamming my thumb over Gideon's name in my phone. I watch the screen until I hear the sound that signals he's connected and his face appears.

"Elli." The smile he gives me every time he sees me makes me feel like a king—like I'm made of gold or just won a million trophies.

If he doesn't cool it with these greetings, it's gonna go straight to my head.

"Hey, baby." My anger starts floating off my body in waves. "How was your day?"

"It wasn't too bad. Look what I went and picked up." The camera flips around and I'm staring at two garment bags hanging on his closet door. "Our prom tuxes. We are going to look so fly."

By some miracle, prom falls the day after my birthday. I'm going to have to drive like a bat out of hell and take minimal pee breaks in order to get us back in time to sleep and re-energize ourselves for a full night of dancing.

"Nice. Did you try yours on?"

"Yep." The camera flips back around and I'm met with his face, his cheek against a pillow. "I don't mean to brag, Elli, but I looked really good. If there's a trophy for the hottest tux, it's mine."

A laugh barrels out of me. "Try it on and send me a picture."

"Okay. I will later. How was your day?"

"It was shit, but whatever."

His face falls. "I'm sorry, Elli. Want to talk about it?"

"There's nothing to talk about, G. My dad yells at me, Norah sticks up for me like she thinks that'll actually make me not despise her, and then I lock myself in my bedroom. Same routine for the last two weeks."

"Maybe you could get out of the house? Go hang with some friends?"

"I don't have friends, Gideon. I'm an asshole."

"You are not, Elliott. You're closed off. That's all. And that's to be expected with all you've had to deal with."

"Yeah, well, I'm not keen on the idea of making friends. Almost nobody from my school has even spoken a word to me since I returned."

"Have you been scowling at everyone?"

My boyfriend knows me well. "No."

"Liar. Maybe just be nice? Get yourself invited to a party or whatever people in Iowa do."

"The people in Iowa have sex in an abandoned barn on Hartley Drive."

He frowns. "Don't do that."

"Like I would ever do anything to ruin us."

"I know you wouldn't. And it's not like anyone has asked, right?"

"Well... not really."

His eyes turn to slits. "Not really or no?"

"Grant tried moving in the day I came back but I shut that shit down."

"Grant as in first kiss Grant?"

"That's him."

"And he asked, what? If you wanted to go bone in a barn?"

I smirk. "No, babe. Not quite. He just asked if I wanted to hang."

"And what the hell is that code for?"

Seeing him get jealous and possessive is a real treat. Gideon is not a jealous person. Being a jealous asshole is normally my thing. Maybe it makes me a total dick finding pleasure in his jealousy. But to me it just means he hasn't lost any feelings for me.

"Calm down, killer. I shut it down. Told him I had a boyfriend waiting for me at home."

He snorts. "Damn right you do."

"You're cute when you're jealous." His middle finger fills the camera. "Ah, come on, baby. Don't gimme that."

"You're mean. I'm taking back your tux and getting you the ugly one with the ruffles."

"Fine. But that means your date is gonna roll in looking like a crappy, country version of Prince. And Prince is a legend. Don't disrespect him like that."

"Ug. You're right. Fine. I'll resort to cutting holes in all your shirts like the chick on Mean Girls."

"What the hell is Mean Girls?"

He sighs. "You're killing me, babe. It's the movie Piper and I forced you to watch."

"The one with the girl from Africa?"

"That's the one."

"I don't remember a part about shirts getting cut."

"That's because you fell asleep."

"Why would you drive across town to Spanky's just to cut holes in my shirt? Your threat is lame."

He rolls his eyes. "Elli, half your wardrobe is in my closet. Your flipping socks are scattered in my room."

There's no stopping the smile that creeps up my face. All of my things are surrounding him. *Good.* I want to suffocate him with memories of us together to get him through three more weeks.

"There's a smile." He hoots. "Keep that there, babe."

"This smile will fade the second we have to hang up."

"Elli, I'm sorry. I can only imagine how hard things are for you."

"He keeps making digs at me." I lower my voice to imitate him. "He says he doesn't love me, Norah. But he does." I scoff. "He's in denial."

Gideon's lips press into a tight line. Wisely, he says nothing. He knows the truth. Just like I do. Gideon just lets me pretend I actually hate my father and all his insults don't affect me.

I've gotten really good at lying through my teeth. I don't hate my dad. Not at all. I hate how disappointed he is with me and the hobbies I choose to love, the person I choose to date, and the future I want to have. I hate that I love him and he doesn't love me back. Or maybe he does. But I can't remember even one time I've heard the words come from his mouth. Not to mention, making a kid feel like shit isn't a great way to express love.

I've spent the better part of my life waiting for my dad to show some kind of interest in me. After I caught him betraying our family, I stopped caring. Every day, I love him less and less. He just becomes a stranger.

"Have you tried spending time with him?"

I snort. "Yeah, right. The dick keeps telling me the only reason I'm here is because he wanted his son back. And yet, he's made no attempt to spend any time with me. He hasn't even been a tolerable person. Just an asshole."

"Maybe try joining him for dinner once? Instead of skipping out?"

"Whose side are you on?"

"Yours, Elli. And you can pretend your dad's actions aren't hurting you but I know they are."

"It just... it doesn't make any kind of sense, Gideon. He dragged me here because he wanted his son back and then keeps talking about how I'll be free soon enough. I mean, what the hell? He's doing nothing and saying nothing to even *try* to get me to stay past my birthday."

He lets out a shallow breath. "He hasn't been nice at all?"

"No. He's been a prickly jackass. Doesn't at all seem like a parent who wants their kid back. I just... don't understand why I'm here. I'm like an unwanted house guest."

"Just try going down for dinner, Elli. Make an effort. If he says something, then get up and walk away."

"I've been dissed by my dad enough times in my life, Gideon. No, thanks."

"Okay." He huffs. "Your choice. I just don't want you to regret it, ya know? Could be your last three weeks seeing your dad and don't you want to say you tried?"

"He hasn't been trying."

"So? You aren't responsible for what he does. You're responsible for what you do."

"Have you been reading motivational books?"

"No, you damn cynic. I just want you to be able to walk away knowing you did everything you could."

"It's bullshit I have to make the effort. He destroyed everything. Not me."

"I agree, Elli. But sometimes, you gotta fight bad with the good. And you are the good."

I sigh, rolling to my side. "I'll think about it, okay?"

"Okay, Elli."

"Are you mad at me?" I could not handle it if he's mad at me too. Everybody else can despise me—but not him.

"Never."

"Good." I smile softly. "Tell me more about our tuxes."

———

MY MAMA TAUGHT me that dressing up for dinner was a sign of respect. So I swap out my old T-shirt for a button down flannel and my jeans for some that don't have holes in them. Unless someone is dying or getting married, this is about as fancy as it gets in Iowa.

I pad down the stairs, smoothing out the shirt I haven't actually worn in a long time. It's really soft but getting kind of short. I'll bring it home for Gideon. He'll go nuts over it. He goes nuts over everything I give him.

I stop outside the entryway to the kitchen and give myself a crappy version of a mental pep talk.

Don't be a dick, Elliott.

Make an effort.

At least you can say you tried.

"Are you going to leave a plate for Elliott?"

I still and back up two steps, hiding behind the wall and listening for my father's reply.

"I always leave a plate for him, darling."

Huh. Interesting. I thought it was Norah. He gets points for not starving me, I guess.

"You should make more of an effort, Jackson."

"He hasn't made one."

"He's not the parent. You are. You twisted his life twice in one year. You took him away from his new home with no explanation. Cut him some slack."

"You're gonna give me parenting advice? You gave your kid up. I kept mine."

Wow. I'm not a fan of Norah at all, but that was a low blow. Why any woman would want to be my father's wife is beyond me.

"I'm sorry, Norah. That wasn't fair."

"No, it wasn't." A dish rattles somewhere. "I gave up Gideon because I didn't want to subject him to a miserable life. You, Jackson, are making your kid more miserable by the day. Just let him go home."

"I can't do that, Norah. You know why."

"You've been nothing but rude to him since he got here. He won't give you an ounce of that social security check. He's leaving the morning of his birthday anyway."

My throat constricts. He wants the money I'm getting from my mama?

Hope is such a dumb concept. Why hope? Why hope when people pound you so deep into the ground, you can no longer breathe? Jackson Oakley has done nothing but pound me since I got here. Now, he's officially cracked me into tiny little pieces.

"He will if I tell him it's for his mama's medical bills."

"So, you'll lie to him? That's nice, Jackson."

"I don't have a choice, Norah. Lucille left me nothing but this house. She gave everything to him."

"He was her only kid, and you were the spouse having an affair."

"Yeah, well, I was counting on some of that money."

"For what?" Norah takes an unsteady breath. "To start a business? Jackson, you have a fine job."

"You were perfectly fine with the plan before. Now that he's dating the kid who doesn't want to know you, you're on his side? I was married to her for twenty-five years, Norah. I deserve some of that money. Especially after dealing with her cancer."

"Dealing with her cancer?" I spit, stepping into the doorway. My body burns with an immeasurable amount of rage. "DEALING WITH HER CANCER? You sick asshole. You think she wanted to get sick?"

"Elliott, I didn't mean it like that."

"No? So that money you want to con me out of, why exactly do you deserve it?"

Blood drains from his face. Obviously, he didn't consider I heard his whole confession.

"You took me away from the place I found peace to try to steal my money?" I squeeze my eyes shut. I will not give him any more tears. "You said you wanted your son back. You said you wanted to spend time with me. You're a fucking liar." I turn and throw my foot into the wall, a crack forming under the weight of all my pain. "You are wasting your time. I'm not giving you any of it. None! My mama obviously thought you weren't worthy, and neither do I."

"Elliott, calm down."

"Calm down?" How dare he. "You have ripped me apart time and time again. Over and over. And I still have fought for your affection. I came down here tonight to try to be civil. This is what I get?" The world opens up and the painful truth rains down on me. "You don't love me. You probably never did. You weren't concerned with spending time with me. You were using me to con me out of my dead mama's money."

"I need the money, Elliott."

"No, you don't. You have a great job. Your mistress is a nurse."

"She ain't a mistress. Watch your mouth."

"I'm not gonna watch my mouth." Is there even a brain in his head? A heart in his body? "I'm going back to North

Carolina. Try and stop me. Make me stay but you aren't taking the money my mama left for me. Fuck you and your slutty wife."

The metallic taste of blood fills my mouth before I even register I've hit the floor. There's a shift in the atmosphere as the world around me slows down. My hand feels heavy as I lift it to my mouth, blood staining the tips of my fingertips when I pull it back to inspect it. My ears start pounding as I register more wetness running down my cheeks.

The sound of Norah's shriek is barely heard over the sob that erupts from my swollen mouth. I stare at his shaking fist, bracing myself. I'm on the floor, and he's standing above me. Jackson Oakley has the advantage—again.

Instead of flying, his fist lowers as his feet stumble backward. Almost as though he's surprised. Maybe I'm surprised too. Not because he did it. But because he didn't do it years ago.

The second he's stumbled far enough away, I jump to my feet and run. I barrel out the front door, tears in my mouth and red staining my skin as I fumble with my phone. I put it to my ear, breathing harshly as it rings three times.

Pick up.

Pick up.

Pick up.

"Hello?"

Thank hell. Sobs of pain, betrayal, and relief roll out of my chest, making it impossible to utter a coherent word.

"Elliott, are you there? What's happening?"

I try to calm myself long enough to get a sentence out.

"Dads?" I choke violently on my tears. "I need your help."

TWENTY-SEVEN

THE ONE WITH THE BALCONY

GIDEON

I FELL in love with dance based on a lot of reasons. While my dad is one of them, he's not the only one. These days, my love for dance comes solely from the way it releases me from what's going on in my mind and gets me to focus on only what's happening with my body. I stop being something that's separate from everything surrounding me. Everything seems to just mesh together to create this feeling of wholeness.

It's almost as if I'm in a parallel universe, or in a different state of consciousness. Everything just blurs—swirls around me like I'm stuck in a dream where everything feels real while it's happening, but it's gone as soon as you realize it's over.

Dance is bittersweet that way. It's my favorite thing in the world because it takes me to a place so peaceful I'm able to escape everything that may be unpleasant about my life. But the escape doesn't last forever. As crazy as it seems, that's why I like it.

Dreams aren't supposed to last forever. They aren't something you get every night. They're exclusive for a reason. I'm only allowed to drift into that special state of consciousness when I'm on the dance floor. Otherwise, the walls around me come back into focus and my ears start to hear actual sound again.

For the first time in forever, I don't look forward to the dream ending. I don't find excitement in its exclusivity. I've spent all my free moments in the last two weeks on the dance floor chasing the dream. Because reality actually kind of totally sucks balls.

I forgot how much high school sucks—because *he* made me forget. The bullies were easier to ignore when I had him to lean on. Homework wasn't so bad when I had him to help me through the parts that made no sense. The boring assemblies all graduating seniors are required to attend seemed to drag on and on when he wasn't there to whisper jokes in my ear or hold my hand discreetly.

Everything just seemed to get harder when he left. Almost like I lost a limb or an organ. Life is still manageable and I can survive just fine without it, but I had to change the way I do things. I changed how I looked at things or dealt with certain situations.

Elli Oakley made life easier. Simple as that. He was my partner in all things. I think maybe I took him for granted. I didn't realize how much more bearable he made life until he was gone.

I try not to forget how lucky I am that I still talk to him daily. Our time difference is only an hour and I still get to see his face and that crooked tooth on the screen of my phone every night. He still sends me dorky texts and emojis I didn't even know he paid attention to. I still have an outlet to my partner. He isn't gone forever.

Except I haven't gotten a text or a call back in over twelve hours. He didn't text me to say good morning or complain about something Norah did. He didn't call me to whine about how his homework is stuff he's already done. He didn't return my call when I left him a voicemail asking if he's okay. If the nervous coil in my stomach is any indication, he is definitely not okay.

"Gid?"

"Hmm?" I blink away my haze. "What's up?"

"You gonna have some lunch?"

"Nah."

I toss my phone the air, catching it and checking the screen. It's the same motion I've been making since I sat up on this ledge at the beginning of the day and made the easy decision to ditch class and spend six hours in the art room. Piper's decided she's my human babysitter on the count of my parents leaving for a spontaneous work trip late last night and Elli being M.I.A.

"Gid, you have to eat."

"Pipes, you don't have to hang here with me. Go to class."

"I do." She argues, dipping the tip of her brush in some paint and slashing it across the canvas in front of her. "It's my moral duty as your best friend to comfort you when your boyfriend has ghosted you."

"What?" Did he ghost me? Is that what he's doing? Ghosting me? "Pipes, is he ghosting me?"

"What? No. Gid, I'm sorry. What a dumb joke to make. You're not some dude he randomly hooks up with and got sick of. He *loves* you."

"I know that, but I... I think I made a mistake." It's been consuming all my thoughts, stealing all my attention, and gnawing at me slowly. "Last night, I suggested he make more of an effort with his dad. I just thought it might help, ya know? So when he leaves he'll be able to say he tried everything."

She tilts her head, studying me while accidentally

swiping red paint down her cheek. "Why do you think that was a mistake?"

"Because, Pipes, what if it backfired? What if he made an effort and his dad was even more of a dick than he usually is? What if I just made everything worse and now Elliott's pissed at me or something?"

She says nothing. What can she say? She can't reassure me he's not mad—that my plan didn't backfire because she has no idea what the hell is going on in Iowa over nine hundred miles away. Neither of us has any idea, and all the unknown is eating me alive. Even if he is mad at me, I could, at the very least, find some way to fix my screw up.

"I think your intentions were good."

I scoff. "Serial killers who think they are ridding the world of sinners believe they have good intentions."

"Man, you're being a bit melodramatic right now."

"I know."

We stare at each other. She does her best to read my mind the same way she used to when we were kids and we'd tell secrets about things that weren't really secrets. Giggling over our plan to catch Santa, making yucky noises when watching our parents kiss, deciding we were going to dig a hole to China... simple stuff.

I guess I just didn't believe anyone when they said life got more complicated as we grew older. I tried to put it in the back of my mind. But now here we are, spending our day behind a bright green door while she paints a blob of nothing and I stare out the window because someone we both love was forced to be an adult long before he was ready. His sudden lack of communication is terrifying. I think we both know he isn't out digging a hole to China.

"God, Pipes, what if everything was just made worse? He was already suffering so much."

"He's okay, G." She ditches her painting and drops into the purple chair that's become Elli's.

I pinch the bridge of my nose. "I'll lose my shit if he's not."

"Me too. But he is."

"We had such a fun conversation last night after we got through all the tough stuff about his dad. We were talking about prom, making jokes about what cliché poses we were gonna do when my dad takes a million pictures. Now I'm probably flying solo."

"Stop thinking the worst case scenario."

"Can you blame me?"

"No." She blows out a rough breath, adjusting her glasses. "I can't. But it's not helping you right now."

My head clunks against the wall, the coil in my stomach tightening. "He asked me to move in with him."

"What? When?"

"After graduation. This summer. He asked me if I wanted to get a place together. I'll be at Durham Tech. for fire classes, he'll be here working at Speed during offseason and the days he isn't traveling for races." I flash her a wobbly smile. "He said he loves Spanky and North Carolina, but it was me who made him feel like he's at home."

"Wow. He turned into a total sap, huh?"

I choke out a laugh. "Right?" I let her take my hand and squeeze it tightly. "What if I ruined that chance, Pipes? Ruined his spirit? What if last night was so awful with his dad he just gave up?"

"Come on, Gid. You can't do this to yourself. We both know how strong Elliott is."

"I stayed up all night looking at apartments. I emailed him so many with jokes about where we could display our trophies in each one. He didn't reply to a single one."

Before last night, I hadn't thought too much about

where I'd go after graduation. I figured I'd just live with my parents until I completed my fire classes and then go wherever the job takes me. Then Elli suggested living together, and it made so much sense, I wondered why the hell I didn't think about it beforehand.

"There's this one that's like a mile from Speed that has a balcony. It's my favorite."

"Can you afford a balcony?"

"Barely." I laugh. "But I'd give up dinner every night for that damn balcony."

"You'll get your balcony, you hopeless romantic." She rolls her eyes at the adorable vision of Elli and I sitting out there together she knows is playing in my head. "He can call to you from below. Like Romeo and Juliet."

"Romeo and Juliet both die."

"Ug. I know. There's no reason they both had to die. Teen love is lethal."

"It's not though." I argue. "Teen love is powerful and really easy to navigate when it's just Elli and I. It's the way life goes against us that makes it lethal. All the obstacles we have to overcome, the unknown we have to face, the judgment and people who believe it's just sex. It gets hard sometimes and teens are too lazy to fight for it so they give up and make some emo Instagram post about it and move on. I'm not gonna do that with Elli, Pipes. I'll fight for him. He just has to let me."

"Gid, you ever consider that you've already fought all you can for Elliott?"

I gape at her, my body revolting at that question. "Are you suggesting I give up?"

"Not at all. I'm just wondering if maybe Elliott's fighting for himself this time? Like you got him where he needs to go and now he needs to get himself to the end before he comes back to you?"

I haven't considered that—haven't thought he might want to do this alone. Make his peace with his mama's death and say goodbye to his dad before coming back to essentially an all new life.

Suddenly, I feel selfish and like a stage five clinger for texting him so much.

"You think he's gonna come back, Pipes?"

"I do, yeah. Don't you?"

I do. I'm not sure what'll happen when I step off that plane in Iowa, but I'm positive he'll be there. Just a little confirmation to ease my nerves for three weeks would help.

I nod my head, clutching Piper's hand with one fist and my phone with the other, willing it to ring. It never does. It stays silent while Pipes and I sit there, doing our best to send good vibes to Elli. It still doesn't ring when she forces me to eat. It makes no sounds when the final bell of the day rings. It never lights up before I fold myself into my car and drive home.

———

THE FIRST THING I notice as I roll into my driveway is my parent's blacked out Dodge Charger tucked back into the garage. Normally, when they have to go away for business, they either take me or blow up my phone with text messages the whole time they are gone. I was so wrapped up in Elliott to realize they only texted me a handful of times and didn't even let me know they're home.

"Dads?" I kick the door shut behind me and pad through the house, searching for my parents. "Hello? Dads?"

"Right here, kid." I jump, clutching my chest and spinning around, finding them padding down the stairs in some sweats.

"You guys didn't text me and let me know you were home." It really isn't that big of a deal but it's something they've always done. After the day I've had, I don't want any more people I love shutting me out.

"Sorry, bud." Knox nudges his head towards the living room. "Let's sit for a minute."

I follow them to the living room and slump onto the couch, scanning their appearances. They look exhausted. Their eyes appear sunken in, they each have pale faces. Knox looks like he can barely keep his eyelids from drooping and Beck's face is puffy.

"Uhm, are you guys sick or something? When was the last time you slept?"

Knox drags his hand down his face. "Two nights ago."

"What the hell? Why? They didn't let you sleep in... wait, where were you guys?"

For the love of Christopher, I can't even remember where they said they were traveling to. I just remember them saying they didn't know when they'd be back and flying out the door. Bad son award goes to me.

"We were in Iowa, bud."

"Iowa?" I watch their sleepy faces and wait for them to tell me they're joking. "Hold on. Are you serious right now? You made a trip to Iowa for work and didn't bother to invite me in case I wanted to visit my boyfriend?"

"Gideon, listen—"

"No, you listen. He's been ghosting me all day. I haven't heard from him in almost twenty-four hours. I've been worried sick about him and now you're telling me I could've seen him? What the crap?"

I'm trying so hard not to blow a gasket but it's virtually impossible. This whole time I've been worrying about Elli, I could've been holding him and trying to make things better. Even if it was just for one day, it still would've helped.

Sometimes all anybody needs is a quick reminder to get them through the rest of their struggles.

"Since when do you guys go to Iowa for work anyway? This is like a random occurrence and you didn't think to invite me?"

"Gideon, stop yelling." Beck growls. "Just listen. Can you do that?"

"I'm seriously pissed right now."

"Well, if you shut your damn trap and listen to your dad, you won't be." Knox clips.

I press lips together and attempt to lighten my venomous glare.

"We didn't go to Iowa for work, Gideon." Beck starts. "We went for Elliott."

"Excuse you?" My hands clench into tight fists, my blood boiling to impossible temperatures and steam catapulting me off the couch. "You went to visit my boyfriend? Without me? What a load of bullshit. You two have spent almost no time apart in decades so maybe you don't understand how much this sucks but it does. This sucks so much. I keep trying to keep a straight face, tell him I love him and I'm doing great but I'm not. I'm not doing great and he's ignoring me. Now you're telling me I missed my chance to see him again?"

"Gideon, sit down." Knox pleads. "Please, listen."

"No!" My eyes grow suspiciously wet, my chest heaving as I peer down at them. "Is he okay? Did you see him?"

"We saw him, kid. Sit down."

I wipe my face quickly. My intention to sit back down is halted when a loud grunt comes from the staircase.

"Can't stand to see them tears, baby."

Oh my God.

"Elli?" I don't think. I fly over the couch and throw

myself at his figure, wrapping my limbs around him and patting him all over so I can convince myself he's real.

He pushes his face into my neck. "Saw your texts. I don't know what the hell ghosting is, but I wasn't ignoring you. I was sleeping."

"Don't care anymore. You're here." I squeeze him roughly. "How?"

I pull back to wait for an answer. All the air leaves my lungs as my eyes make contact with his face. His left cheekbone is marred with purple splotches, the left side of his lip is swollen and significantly larger than the right side. He winces when he attempts to flash me a smile.

"I'm okay, babe."

"The hell you are." I choke, my chest suddenly flaming. Bile rises in my throat at the sight of him hurt and physically in pain. Once again, I'm hit with how much I've come to love him. "What happened to you? It looks like—"

"Somebody hit me?"

"Did somebody hit you?" I'll kill them. "Who the hell would hit you?"

Pure sadness fills his eyes, and that's all it takes for my brain to register why my parents left, why he's here, and why his face looks like a bloody plum.

"Your father hit you, didn't he?" I whip my gaze towards my parent's solemn faces. "That's why you left? Because his father hit him?"

They nod. "Yeah."

I grind my teeth together, my bottom lip quivering as I work double time to hold back a rough sob.

"Gideon, I'm okay." He grips my chin and forces my gaze. "I swear to you, I'm okay."

"How can you say that?" I croak. "Oh my God, I'm sorry. I'm so sorry."

"Stop, come on. Don't cry. I'm okay." I'm pulled into his

arms and held tightly while I lose my shit and get swallowed by guilt. He's the one who was physically abused by his father and he's comforting me? There are so many things wrong with this moment but I have a hard time fighting it when we're holding each other so tightly.

"Please, Elli, tell me what happened."

"He wanted money."

"What?" I shake my head, stepping away from him. "I don't understand."

"I get social security and life insurance money from my mama on my birthday. He wanted it. I heard him and Norah talking about it. I lost my cool, screamed at him and said some hateful things he didn't like hearing."

"So he hit you?"

"Yeah, he did. He hit me and I took off running. I called your parents for help and asked them not to tell you. I just... I was struggling, Gideon. My dad went from prickly asshole to abusive father in less than a second and I couldn't get a handle on it. I wanted you nowhere near it."

As much as I would've loved to be there and hold him while he put himself back together after losing both his parents once and for all, I respect his choice.

"Your parents called and got me a hotel room. I went there and waited for them. They picked me up and put me on a plane. Your grandpa Hank did the rest."

"The rest? What do you mean?"

"Norah... she, uh, she called the cops on my father. I was already off the property and losing my shit in a hotel bathroom so I didn't realize it until hours later. She called the cops and he was arrested. Long story short, your grandpa looked into some things and discovered my mom changed her will a month before she died. She wanted everything but the house to go to me. My dad figured that out, and it pissed him off because he had some plans to open a business installing security systems in people's homes."

"That's why he forced you to come back? Because he wanted to convince you to give him your money?"

"Yeah. When I said no, shit got heated and he took it too far. The worst part is, it's not like the money gets dropped on my lap on my birthday. It takes a while to process. He didn't consider I would've been long gone before I was even in possession of it."

My brain is spinning a million miles a minute. I can't comprehend why a parent would try to con money from their child, especially money that came from their dead mother, and then assault them when they reacted to it. I've always done my best not to hate people. Hate is a strong emotion, and it's not something you can easily take back when you express that feeling.

But I hate him.

I *hate* Elli's father with every fiber in my body. I hate him for all he's done to break him down.

"You gotta quit with these tears, G. I'm okay now. I'm home."

"Where's Spanky?"

"Upstairs in the guest room snoring louder than the damn plane engine. Crazy old man stomped into the courthouse in Iowa and demanded emergency custody."

"It must've worked."

"Not quite." This time he doesn't wince when he smiles. "It was Norah's testimony, the pictures I took of my face right after, and your grandpa Hank working faster than lightning that got those papers signed and my ass on a plane for good."

"Who packed your things?"

"Norah shoved some shit in a backpack for me after

they arrested my father but I left most of it. Everything I need is already here anyway."

"What about your truck?"

He shrugs. "I think I'll buy a car with some of my mama's money. Gramps and I want to buy something old and fix it up together this summer."

"What about your father? What happens to him?"

"I, uh, I'm not sure."

"He's back at home." We both turn to face Knox. I completely forgot my parents were still in the room. "Grandpa is keeping in touch but for now that's where he is. His bail was posted and his brother bailed him out."

"What a sleaze." I blurt.

Elli chuckles. "Uncle Connor. He is a sleaze, actually. My mama hated him."

"Well, we can see why." Beck says. "Bailing his brother out of jail after hitting his son. Shame on him."

"Well, now that he's free, do we worry about him trying to get Elli's money?"

"Your grandpa said it's impossible for him to touch it." Elliott explains. "I didn't ask how. Your grandpa is a superhero."

"That he is." Knox stands off the couch and stretches his arms above his head. "Dad and I are going to finish our nap. Elliott, you need to do the same. You haven't slept in over a day. We will keep you updated about your dad but both of you need to be at school tomorrow."

"I don't get one day to decompress?" Elliott gawks. "Come on!"

"You can have all summer to decompress, kid." Beck rebuttals, standing off the couch. "School tomorrow or you both can spend the day washing mirrors in the studio."

"That actually sounds better than school." I quip. "Way better."

"You have four weeks left of school." Knox sighs. "Just go and get it done."

Elli chuckles and links our hands together, leading me up the stairs and into my room. The messy sheets and crooked pillows tell me he's already made himself comfortable.

He flops back into bed, burrowing his body into the mattress and patting my pillow. "Come cuddle me, babe."

I round the bed. "Do you need any ice for your face? Are you in pain?"

"I'm fine, Gideon. Just want you."

I smile and slide into his outstretched arms, dropping my head on his chest.

"I missed these curls going up my nose."

"Well, love them while you can. I gotta chop them off after summer."

"Noooooo." He bellows. "Why?"

"I had a small orientation at the fire academy last week, and the fire chief deemed them a fire hazard."

"What? You'll be wearing a helmet, I thought."

"Yeah but these curls are pretty wild. Besides, they'll grow back."

He shoves his hand in them. "Don't cut them all off."

"Should I put one in a baggie and save it for you?"

"Save it all for me. I'll make it into a bracelet."

"Elliott." I snort. "You are ridiculous."

"Just kidding." He kisses my forehead. It feels a bit awkward with his swollen lip but it warms my heart none the less.

"You should get some sleep." I kiss his chest and drag the sheets over us when he's caught by a long yawn.

"Okay." He wraps his arms around me. His chest pumps slowly. I trace the design on his T-shirt for a long time. I think he's asleep when I hear his soft voice.

"Hey, Gideon?"

"Hmmm?"

"I got your emails."

"You did?"

"Yeah." He mumbles, sleep threatening to pull him under. "I like the one with the balcony."

EPILOGUE

ELLIOTT

SOME PEOPLE LIKE to equate chaos with confusion...

Disorder.

Disorganization.

Complete mayhem.

Gideon and I like to equate chaos with life. If there's not even a little bit of chaos in your life, are you even living? Are you just lying on the ground, flat lining somewhere while those around you run in circles and learn to have fun with all the moments they were given? Even the ones that are filled with pain have to be part of the chaos.

Chaos gives us a chance to grow. To move on. To improve who we are, scream out all the bad, and start fresh with your hand connected to the one who taught you how.

Gideon Stryker is my chaos. He taught me how to find comfort in something that was supposed to cause mass destruction and pandemonium.

He taught me how to alter the chaos around me in order to turn something that wasn't supposed to make sense to several moments of absolute clarity.

Gideon showed me all the benefits of managing chaos.

Since falling in love with him, I've been desperate to create as much of it as possible.

"There's the birthday boy!"

I chuckle, tilting my head to give his lips better access to my cheek. He falls into my lap, draping his arms around me. "You don't have to keep calling me the birthday boy."

"Is it still your birthday?"

"Yes. I believe it is."

"Then you're still the birthday boy."

What a dork. He's been calling me birthday boy since the second I opened my eyes this morning. Literally.

My eyes fluttered open and there he was, face hidden behind a mass of curls and lips declaring me the birthday boy. I can admit it's pretty adorable when he does it. When anybody else who crammed inside my gramps' house to celebrate my birthday does it, it irritates me. Which is why Nate went out and bought a white T-shirt and wrote *I'm The Birthday Boy* with a permanent marker on the front of it.

The only reason I put the damn thing on over my T-shirt is because gramps said my mama bought one for me just like it on my first birthday. Except, it was in onesie form and not made of marker, but the wording was the same. So I'll keep this stupid shirt forever just because it makes me feel close to her.

"What are you doing sitting out here all alone on your birthday?"

"It got crowded. I just wanted to chill." I'm more than thankful for everyone in my new family who showed up to celebrate my first official day as an adult. But I got over-whelmed after spending hours not being able to walk anywhere without bumping into anyone. I escaped to the front porch and plopped into gramps' old wooden rocking chair. "Trying to get your whole family inside gramps' house is like trying to cram my foot into a shoe two sizes too small."

"Ain't that right." He snorts. "Can I chill too?"

"I guess I'll let ya since you're cute and all." I push my toes against the wooden boards of the porch, rocking us slowly.

"Oh, whatever. You're like so obsessed with me. You should put *that* on your T-shirt."

"Man, you're so lucky I love you or your ass would be on the ground."

"I ain't scared."

I pinch his side, howling in laughter at his attempt to flash me a glare.

"You're so lucky it's your birthday, Elli Oakley or I would body slam you into the ground."

"Psh." I grunt. "Try me, baby. I'll take you down with one hand."

"Don't underestimate me, Elli. I'm an acro champion. I could be the next Karate Kid for all you know."

"Yeah, well, maybe tomorrow after breakfast we can test that theory."

"You're on."

"Bring it on, baby." I chuckle, dropping my face to his neck. "Bring it on."

"Elli, look."

He pushes my chin upward, forcing my gaze to the sunset that's morphed the sky into a swirl of colors, creating rainbow clouds upon rainbow clouds. "Well, what do ya know? My mama made it to my birthday after all."

"Hi, Elli's mama." Gideon blurts, waving to the sky. "Nice to finally meet you. I'm Gideon Mason Stryker, born and raised in this lovely town. I have two trophies and I'm flipped over backward for your son. I promise to love him even when he gets more trophies than me and makes fun of my fire engine facts. I also promise to watch his cholesterol levels considering he eats cheeseburgers every day."

"You are such a goober." I throw my head back, losing it to an explosion of laughter.

"I wish I could've met you for real, and I'm sorry you're not here. I promise I'll take really good care of him and make sure he feels loved."

"Baby." An unfamiliar croak comes from my throat, my chest aching for my mama and craving him all the same. "You're pretty special, you know that?"

"Hear that, Ms. Lucy? He thinks I'm special."

I hold him tight and close my eyes, letting him talk to my mama. I've spent hours and hours talking to her over the last few weeks—venting to her about my dad being charged with assaulting a minor and getting over the idea that he won't be allowed on a school campus or any school affiliated events for five years. I still have the option of a restraining order if I want one, and I may never see him again. Even though he hit me, struck blood and broke my heart, it's hard to fully let go.

On top of all that, Norah sent me an early birthday card with a photo of my half-brother—a little boy who's gonna grow up without a dad. A little boy who also happens to be my boyfriend's half-brother from the opposite side of DNA.

What a world I live in.

"Bye, Elli's mama." His voice whispers, the sun getting lower. "See you soon."

"Bye, mama." I breathe.

We sit there together for a long time, rocking slowly until it's the moon giving us light.

"My birthday is almost over. You better hurry up and call me birthday boy a million more times. Otherwise, you'll have to wait another year.

"Almost over, huh?" His baby blues flash. "Then I guess I better give you this."

My toes still, the chair creaking as it comes to a stop and I study the little red box he pulls from his pocket. "What is that?"

"Your birthday present." He kisses me quickly. "I wanted to give it to you when we were alone but there's been people everywhere."

"But... you got me like five presents already."

"Elli, those were from my parents. Not me."

"I'm one thousand percent sure you helped pick out those clothes and that MCU box set."

"Well, I did. But this one is just from me. It's really special."

"Baby." He's beaming at me, holding the little red box in his palm with so much love in his eyes—like giving me this gift is the greatest, most important thing he'll ever do. Never mind that he and his parents already gave me more than I could've ever thought up. He thinks I'm worth more. He's *always* thought I'm worth more.

"Open it, Elli."

I keep one arm secured around his waist while I use my left hand to lift the box from his palm and place it on the arm of the rocking chair. Wiggling the lid off slowly, my heart trips when I find a trophy.

"It's, uhm, a pendant." He says softly, my eyes locked on the small piece of bronze that was flattened and molded into the shape of a trophy. "It came with a chain. You can wear it around your neck or hang it somewhere. Whatever you want. I just thought... you deserve this. You deserve some recognition for surviving the last year of your life and still remaining the strongest person I know. As much as it pains me to say, trophies aren't everything. But you, you're everything, Elli Oakley. You're everything to me and I hope this reminds you of that."

"Gideon." I close my eyes, my arm tugging him tighter to me. "Thank you. This is... this is the best. Thank you so much."

I never gave a damn about the trophies I won or didn't win. I wanted the title. The trophies were nothing but a hunk of metal my father would bitch about having to find shelf space for. It wasn't until Gideon came along that I learned a little bragging was okay. Because, really, who in North Carolina has won two junior racing titles?

But *this trophy*—this little trophy resting in a soft red cushion is not one to hide. This is not one to brush off or ignore. It's not for the shelves.

It's just for me.

I'll wear it around my neck and keep it close to my heart. This little piece of bronze will remind me I've won so much more than a title. I've won a family—and that's a win I'll never stop bragging about.

"Help me put it on, will you? I want it around my neck."

The smile that erupts on his face knocks my feet right out from under me. If I wasn't already sitting, I'd be flat on my back.

"Here. Let me see it."

He lifts the box, tugging gently on the trophy. It comes free, connected to a thin bronze chain he drapes around my neck. "There you go."

"Thank you, babe. This is the coolest present I've ever gotten." I inspect the way it falls down my chest, hitting just below my heart.

"Yeah? I think I can make it better."

I watch him with a tilted head, his lips pulling into a smirk as he flips the trophy around. My eyes inspect the wording. Even looking at it upside down, the words are clear as ever and the effect they have on me is profound.

There's comfort in chaos.

It's a little reminder. No matter how much chaos gets thrown at me, how twisted or painful my life becomes, there's comfort to be found in the midst of it all.

I blink away a thin sheen of moisture. "I love you, Gideon Stryker. Two-time national title winner."

His forehead hits mine, the tips of our noses brushing softly. "I love you too, Elli Oakley. Rookie of The Year. With *three* trophies."

ALSO BY LACEY DAILEY

Circuit Series

Specter

Mischief

Standalone

Alma Underwood Is Not A Kleptomaniac

Devil Side

ABOUT THE AUTHOR

The best place to find Lacey is with her nose in a book. She's a sucker for a good love story and a happy ending that has her swooning. When she's not obsessing over giving her own characters a happy ending, you can find her in the dance studio empowering young dancers and giving out tons of stickers. Thanks to her mother's pizzeria, Lacey can make a delicious pizza.

When she's not putting on her dance shoes or inhaling a slice of pizza, she's in front of her computer binge watching romantic comedies and penning stories with love so powerful, it'll last a lifetime. As a recent graduate of Central Michigan University, Lacey intends to keep inspiring people through dance and lots and lots of words. She currently lives in Central Michigan surrounded by her family and unpredictable weather.

Connect with Lacey:

www.laceydaileyauthor.com

ACKNOWLEDGMENTS

Nina, how many times can I thank you before you get sick of hearing it? Thank you for allowing me to talk nonstop and pretending to listen intently. You're my very best friend.

Elliana, thank you for drawing me the best mutated baby I've ever seen. You exceeded my expectations by a million. This book wouldn't be the same without Helga.

Monique, thank you for the numerous suggestions you provided, and all the time and work you put into this novel. You are an essential piece in my writing process.

Mom, thank you for always reading my books cover to cover.

Thank you to the bloggers and bookstagramers who have supported me nonstop. The love I feel from you all is profound.

Thank you to all the readers and bloggers who joined my reader group, Lacey's Lounge, on Facebook. I love learning about each and everyone of you, and I'm so grateful I have such a positive group of readers to share my journey with.

As always, thank you to all the readers who continue to read my novels and express their love and interest. It means more to me than you'll ever know. You chose to read my books over the millions of books available, and I'll never take that for granted. If you enjoyed it, please consider leaving a review. Reviews fuel indie authors.

Thank you from the bottom of my heart.

XO, Lacey